Inheriting Trouble

In Ashwood, Volume 1

Kinney Scott

Published by Mosquito Creek Publishing, 2017.

INHERITING TROUBLE

First edition. August 8, 2017.

ISBN: 978-1950800070

Written by Kinney Scott.

Also by Kinney Scott

In Ashwood
Inheriting Trouble
Trouble Brewing
Chasing Trouble
Addicted To Trouble
Trouble Undone

Watch for more at https://kinneyscott.com.

For readers who take a risk on a new author. Thank You.

ONE

Balanced on high heels, Natalie aimed her telephoto lens at the sailboats skimming Lake Washington. She had escaped her shabby studio apartment before dawn to catch the start of this rare, sunny, late March day.

Losing sleep paid off when an overwintering hummingbird paused in the cool morning air. The tiny iridescent bird hovered mid-flight and feathered her with the turbulence of its wings. Natalie crouched with her camera near shore and held her breath. Her Canon clicked, disturbing the early morning calm.

As it landed, a dry reed bent beneath the hummingbird's weight. Exhaling, Natalie prayed to the little thing, "Don't leave, just stay one more second." The shutter snapped again, capturing the bird before it lifted and zipped away.

A satisfied grin spread across Natalie's face as she anticipated this evening's darkroom session. She loved those solitary moments when chemicals combined with paper to initiate a magical reveal.

While swapping lenses, Natalie spotted the sun riding high against the horizon. Time had slipped her mind. Her fingers dug into her bag, fumbling to locate her phone.

"Fudge. Late, late, late!"

With the lens cover on and her camera stowed, she sprinted across the park in her three-inch heels, and the spikes sank into the damp green turf. Right foot, then left, she kicked off the impractical footwear and ran barefoot with her shoes dangling from her fingertips. Only a block away, her bus rounded the street corner.

"Yes!" She grinned as her day slid back into the lucky category. Hopping foot to foot, she slipped back into her shoes, climbed the steps, and swept her Orca bus card before eyeing a vacant seat. She stumbled over a splayed, long-limbed passenger, mumbled excuse

1

me, then her ample butt hit the plastic seat just as the bus pulled away.

Her hand held her chin as she watched Seattle slip by the grimy bus windows. Sleek buildings sheltered the homeless who huddled in doorways covered by blue tarps. She made fleeting eye contact with a woman who was close to her age. Natalie twitched, wanting to bolt from the bus to give that woman the ten in her wallet, but the bus rambled on. Two transfers later, she arrived nearly half-an-hour late to work.

A sticky sheen of perspiration dampened her face as she burst through the coffee shop's employee entrance. Natalie snuck a peek under each arm to check if she'd pitted her blouse. Parked in front of the oscillating fan, she fluttered the fabric away from her body, shooting cool air underneath.

"It's too hot out there today, isn't it?" Elsa said with a smile to her young friend.

Natalie stooped and tried to spot her reflection in the industrial steel refrigerator. "Do I look sweaty?" Elsa moved to tie the red apron strings around Natalie's waist, securing it with a bow.

"Of course not, you're lovely." With a smile, Elsa scooped ice and poured Natalie a tall glass of tea, handing it to her overheated friend.

"Thank you," she said gulping the ice-cold drink.

She loved Elsa—and was loved back. If she ever left this barista job, Natalie knew she'd be missed. Still, Elsa didn't need help running her small coffee shop. At seventy-two, the owner radiated energy and effervescence.

Natalie smoothed her palms over her apron and slipped behind the counter. "Sorry I'm late . . . again."

"Don't worry over a few minutes." Turning back to a recent order, Elsa slipped a snickerdoodle into a paper sleeve. The sweet treat was for a regular customer who had claimed an outdoor seat beneath the shade of a green umbrella.

Natalie's mouth watered and her stomach audibly rumbled. "Can I have a cookie?" she asked. "I didn't have time for breakfast." Elsa nodded, passed the open jar, and grabbed an apple for herself. She left to join her customer outside, taking a short break.

As Natalie restocked the refrigerated case with organic juices, she watched Elsa laugh with her friend. A sharp pang of envy cut, and Natalie looked away.

After university graduation, her world had shrunk. The third rejection letter from nursing school sent a clear message—she had to work full-time at the coffee shop or starve. Hiding from her future had built her bank account but eroded her confidence. Still, everyone here loved her, and Elsa paid well. Yet, this safe refuge in her grandfather's retirement community had cost her friends.

A group of silver-haired customers crowded the counter following a round of golf. Elsa followed the pack inside and went back to work.

"Where's your grandfather?" Elsa asked as the rush eased. "Pete didn't stop in for coffee this morning."

"He's probably still out on the boat with his Navy buddies. I don't expect him back until dark." Natalie's wrist swirled as she topped a tall iced coffee with whipped cream and caramel.

Elsa nodded. "I bet they'll take advantage of this stunning weather and stay out on the water all day."

"Grandpa usually does."

The café stayed busy until early afternoon. Natalie served dozens of cool drinks but couldn't keep her eyes off the clock.

"Why don't you scoot along? Your shift's nearly over," Elsa offered.

"Are you sure? We may get another rush . . ."

"Absolutely. We might not get another day like this for months. Please, take advantage of the sun."

3

"Okay. But only if you let me open tomorrow." Getting up early didn't bother her at all. Natalie didn't date much and rarely had a reason to stay up late.

A grin lit Elsa's face. "I'll take that offer. Maybe I'll join Pete for his morning walk."

Hanging her apron on the wall, Natalie gathered her camera bag. "See you tomorrow. I'll handle the morning shift, and this time, I won't be late. I promise."

Out the door, she didn't have sunshine on her mind. While she rushed along the path to her grandfather's condo, she obsessed about the hummingbird image trapped on the black and white film in her camera.

Natalie went to work immediately, in a hurry to set up her chemicals before Grandpa returned from fishing on Puget Sound. This darkroom, tucked into Grandpa's spare bathroom, was palatial compared to the dingy closet she seldom used at her studio apartment.

She closed the door and soaked in the silence. Immersed in total darkness, Natalie coiled the black and white film onto a metal reel. The spool slid into a canister and she bathed the negatives in chemicals, using touch as her only guide. Under a faint red light, she unfurled her film. Anticipation wiggled her toes on the cool tile as she exposed white paper to a fresh image.

Liquid sloshed in the shallow pan. She waited and watched while the reaction went to work. A black and white version of the sailboat she shot this morning gradually appeared. It was beautiful but the grayscale couldn't capture the radiance of the taut orange sail against the blue sky.

On to the next image, Natalie bit her fingernail and waited for the first hummingbird photo to appear. Her bare foot stomped the tile, and she deflated. "Crap, crap, crap. The wings are out of focus. It's garbage."

She tossed the blurred image, took a breath, and tried again. Her second shot, just as hazy as the first, followed its mate into the wastepaper basket.

As her last shot appeared, she danced and celebrated a victory in the red-lit room. In focus and framed perfectly, the delicate creature in front of her eyes seemed to take flight. Natalie clipped the stunning photo of the hummingbird to a cord strung across the tub and turned to her three final images.

The bathroom's bouncy acoustics rang with her happy version of a song she heard at the coffee shop three times today. Guessing half the words, she sang and wondered when Grandpa would return, but figured he'd probably stopped by a pub with his friends.

Her fingers attached another wet image on the line when the doorbell chimed. "Crud!" Natalie panicked and moved double-speed to cover her work before she was forced to open the makeshift darkroom door.

It chimed again. "Just a minute," she called but hoped whoever was outside would just give up and go away.

Insistent knocking followed. "One second!" she yelled and cringed, knowing half the retirement community must have heard her blaring shout. She opened the darkroom door and shut it with a slam—as if that would save her unprocessed work.

When the bright sunlight streaming in the living room blinded her, Natalie stumbled and whacked her shin on a coffee table. "Frick, that hurt," she grumbled, limped to the door, and flung it open.

Elsa's stunned pallor muted Natalie. "I tried to call, but you didn't answer," her friend mumbled.

"Call? Elsa, what's wrong?" Trails of mascara stained her carefully powdered face and her limbs trembled. Fearing her friend's collapse, Natalie gently led her to the couch, wrapped a soothing arm around her, and waited.

Elsa's frail shoulders rose as she inhaled. "I received a call from the hospital . . . your grandfather . . . I'm so sorry, sweetheart." Tears streamed down Elsa's face and tight pain seized Natalie's chest.

"What happened? Does he need my help?" Grandpa Pete never needed anything. Strong, independent, and steady, he was the man everyone depended on.

Elsa took Natalie's hand. "Your grandfather came back to the marina after fishing with his friends. He was on the dock when he had a heart attack. I'm so sorry dear . . . He's gone." The words yanked a cornerstone from Natalie's foundation, and everything tilted off-kilter.

Gone? It wasn't possible. The man who grounded her world couldn't be gone.

***

For two weeks, she thought about nothing but death announcements, casket choices, and head stones.

Frustrated by her inept mother, Natalie handled the frantic funeral arrangements with Elsa's help.

Nothing prepared her for the surreal meeting with her grandfather's lawyer, and the news that she was Peter Thorson's sole heir.

Unexpected wealth laced guilt with grief. When Grandpa left this world, he made sure to secure her future, but money couldn't fill her hollow loneliness.

Deep down, Natalie knew her brother, Ben, was there for her, even if he lived three-thousand miles away. She called him the moment his stunning flower arrangement arrived at the chapel on the morning of Grandpa Pete's funeral.

Her fingers trembled and she nearly dropped the small sympathy card tucked into the arrangement. "The flowers are gorgeous. Thank you, Ben."

"I'm so sorry I couldn't get away for Grandpa's funeral," he apologized. "We're in the middle of a crisis with an overseas client."

"That's okay. I just miss you," she said dodging another florist who sped past her carrying a massive bouquet.

"Miss you, too." Her brother's arrangement took up twice as much space as the others, sent for a grandparent that Ben rarely saw.

When their parents separated, they had moved the siblings to opposite coasts. Mom took Natalie and Dad took Ben. Her father lost interest in his nine-year-old daughter soon after the divorce. As time passed, Mom gave up fighting for the rare visits with her son, but Natalie still took strength from the connection with her big brother.

"Maybe you could visit me this summer after you settle Grandpa's estate," Ben asked with clear hope in his voice.

"I'd like that, I really would." She wanted to get away from Seattle. The city seemed hollow with Grandpa's large presence gone. "Ben, I'm sorry, but I have to go. I think the pastor has questions about the service." Natalie needed to end the call before she lost another battle with her ever-present tears.

"Love you, sis." Ben's voice tightened and trembled.

A hot tear dripped down her cheek. "Love you, too."

Music echoed from the chapel, sending a signal for everyone to find a seat. Natalie planted herself on the front pew beside her mom, stepfather, and her two half-brothers. Wearing shiny shoes, Ryan and Gabe's feet swung back and forth, not reaching the ground. Natalie focused on the paper program in her hand and the hard bench under her butt, at least the nagging discomfort kept her tears away.

Dressed in a brand-new suit, one of Grandpa's friends walked to the front and said a prayer. When his voice broke, Natalie swiped a single tear away with her thumb. Barely coping, she blinked hard as someone started playing the grand piano. *Oh, God, why did it have to be Amazing Grace?* Warm and salty, the tears that trailed over her lips tasted like grief.

Amazing Grace ended with a simple chord, and sniffles in the chapel broke the silence. Her little brothers squirmed, her mother wept, and her stepdad sat stoically as the pastor droned on. The odor of sweet flowers from the massive bouquets overwhelmed Natalie. Teeth clenched, she fought nausea and swallowed her thick saliva. She stared straight ahead and watched while a single white rose petal fell from Ben's stunning arrangement. It landed on the carpet just below an oversized black and white photo of Grandpa Pete. With eyes crinkled at the edges, he seemed to be smiling at her from the deck of his fishing boat.

***

With her shoulder propped against the doorway, Natalie scanned the meeting hall and wished perfect stillness could make her invisible. A smile tipped the corner of her mouth when a dozen Navy buddies lifted another Jack Daniel's to Pete's memory.

Three tables overflowed with Grandpa's hometown friends from Ashwood. Natalie recognized a few, and Elsa sat among them, smiling as she recalled Pete's days fishing Osprey Lake. Elsa lifted a hand and waved her over, urging Natalie to take the seat next to her. "How are you holding up? Have you eaten? You seem so tired, sweetie."

A hard blink erased the tears that threatened. "I'm okay. I just want today to be over." Now that the busy pace of planning the memorial had passed, exhaustion filled its place. "Will you sit with me while I talk to Mom?" Natalie asked Elsa. "I'm running out of safe topics."

"Of course, I'd be glad to. When are they flying back to Arizona?"

"Day after tomorrow, thank goodness. Mom's driving me absolutely crazy. She won't stop begging me to move back to Phoenix, but I know I'd only end up babysitting my little brothers. That seems like a step in the wrong direction."

"You need food and liquid courage before talking to your mother." Elsa pulled Natalie to the buffet table and forced food onto her plate. Before she knew it, Natalie found herself with a sandwich in her left hand and a glass of white wine in her right.

"Eat. Drink. Relax. This will all be over soon," Elsa encouraged.

Natalie listened while the conversation spun around her, took a bite, chewed her food, and tasted nothing.

***

Keeping to her usual routine, Natalie found comfort working at the coffee shop where Pete's friends shared her loss. The last customer left, and she joined Elsa at a table wrapping napkins around plastic forks. A sudden spring shower pelted the window with sheets of wind-driven rain, and she shivered. No matter how bright she dressed or how tall her shoes, Natalie felt drab and small. Something had to change.

"How are you, dear? Can I do anything to help?" Elsa asked.

"You've done so much already. Grandpa's lawyer sent a letter. I only have six months to sell the condo. I guess I'm too young to keep it . . . something about bylaws in this community. Too bad I can't move here and leave my studio apartment. That place is such a pit."

"It's for the best, dear. You're too young to spend every moment surrounded by people three times your age."

Natalie tore at a hangnail and it hurt, but she didn't care. "I guess you're right. Last week, I sold his boat to his fishing buddies. They gave me too much for it."

"I expected they would." Elsa listened to her as she dealt with a tangle of sadness and guilt. With her inheritance, she had considered

9

hundreds of options. Overwhelmed by her choices, she now had the freedom to run her own coffee shop or follow her photography obsession—anything that might bring her a sliver of happiness.

"What would you say if I took a break from Seattle? I'm just not ready to sort through Grandpa's things. It's too soon to pack it up, give it to charity, or worse, throw any of it away." Natalie took a sip of her tepid coffee hoping the caffeine would awaken her senses.

"That sounds like a great idea. You should try something new. Your grandpa took plenty of risks and never regretted it."

Risks. He had always told her that mistakes were the fastest path to growth. "Elsa, you're right, he'd want me to use my inheritance for something . . . amazing." An optimistic smile crossed Natalie's delicate features, the first smile she'd enjoyed in weeks.

***

Alone again on another Friday night, she sank into her worn thrift-store sofa with a bowl of popcorn nestled against her hip. Salty-buttery goodness crunched while she binged on the next episode of the Do-It-Yourself channel.

Tempted by unlimited options, she realized that her dream of escaping the city to a quiet refuge in her own tiny home was actually within reach.

A familiar location on the program caught her attention. It was filmed in Ashwood. Clicking the keyboard, she paused the program, backed it up, and watched the segment again.

The tiny-home builder that filled her computer screen lived in Grandpa Pete's remote hometown. She'd visited Ashwood a few times but never remembered meeting anyone this gorgeous. Not only did he specialize in tiny homes, but this man started out building food trucks. That fact sparked an idea.

"I wonder if he could combine a home *and* a coffee shop? That would be two kinds of awesome." Maybe this was fate.

After looking up the business, Natalie tapped into a hidden reserve of courage and typed a short email to Whitewater Homes:

I'm looking for info. I'm considering a combo tiny home & coffee shop for a mobile business. Would your company be interested? Funds are lined up. Let me know.

– Thanks, Natalie Journey.

After hitting send, she took a moment to scan Whitewater Homes' impressive webpage. The guy's work was stunning, nearly as gorgeous as the owner. A return email chimed, almost too quickly.

Her eyebrows shot up. "Wow. That was fast. The owner must not have much of a life." Natalie laughed at herself. "But I guess I'm not doing much on a Friday night, either."

That sounds like a challenge I'd like to take on. How many people plan to live in this house/coffee shop?

She answered rapidly—*I only need room for one, a commercial-style kitchen, and a service window.*

In moments, another message came through—*Look over options on our website. Then email any questions.*

"Yes!" A surge of adrenaline cleared a layer of fog from her mind—*Thanks! - I'll talk to you soon - Natalie*

Natalie studied the multi-page brochure he'd attached to the last message. The varied options turned into the exact distraction she craved. She obsessed over loft styles, floor finishes, bathrooms, and cabinets well into the evening as she sipped several glasses of wine.

Yet, even with the excitement, those details weren't as distracting as the owner. Rugged, but not too perfect, Seth Michaels stared back at her from his webpage with haunting blue eyes. Tall, with dark wavy hair that had grown too long, he wore a tool-belt slung low over nicely faded jeans. Natalie couldn't rip her gaze from the tempting man.

TWO

Seth re-read his email and took a moment to attach a PDF brochure before he hit send. He hoped to land this client. The build could be an interesting challenge. He had tackled both food trucks and homes before, but never a combo of the two.

From his master bedroom, Desiree's voice echoed again, "Seth, do you think I drove all the way up to your house to watch you work?"

He shut out the distraction. "Hold on, I'll be done in a sec." He didn't typically ignore a naked woman to handle business. But when his ex-wife turned up unannounced, she could wait.

The pile of home plans at his elbow tempted Seth as much as his ex. He nearly sent Des on her way. "You could have called first or stayed with your friends at Northside Grill," he said from his computer.

"I got bored when you didn't show at the bar. You should thank me. I knew you'd be home, *again*, working on a Friday night. Get your ass in here, Seth."

He could hear Desiree splash as she left the jetted tub. The thought of her, warm and wet, added girth. Their divorce wasn't ugly. If Seth could find a way to trust her, he might even consider Desiree a close friend.

Seth hadn't been too surprised when his ex showed up at his front door a few months after their divorce. He also didn't mind it when she decided to use him from time to time to take the edge off. Sex was never one of their many problems.

He switched off the monitor but left the computer on, knowing this distraction shouldn't take much more than an hour.

Sleek and bare, her toned body greeted him as he stepped into his master bedroom. Desiree lay face down, waiting for him.

12

Obsessed with working out at her gym, she'd lost the ample curves that Seth preferred.

Moving to the foot of the bed, already hard, his erection jutted against the tight confines of his jeans. After peeling off his shirt, he slid his belt from the loops and the leather rasped against the soft, faded fabric.

"Tie my hands this time," she begged. "I need to feel a little edge." Knowing exactly what she was asking for, he grabbed a couple of pillows to position her butt high in the air.

A sigh of pleasure escaped her lips as he tightened the leather belt around her overlapped wrists and secured her to the heavy wooden slats of his handcrafted headboard. His hands slid down her familiar body, gliding across her tanned shoulders, back, butt, and slim long legs. When he carefully secured each ankle with the restraints, she wriggled her ass.

"Patience, Desiree. Right now, I'm in charge." Starting at her manicured toes, Seth licked his way up her legs. Her writhing movements thickened his hard-as-steel shaft. Once he reached the tender spot on the back of her knees, her legs bucked in frustration.

"Stop fighting the ropes," he commanded before he administered a stinging slap against her ass.

"Yesss," she hissed in pleasure and relief. Another crack of his palm heated her muscular butt. A moan escaped her lips as each strike connected.

Seth was a little disappointed. The rounded mounds were too toned. He preferred a distinct jiggle when his palm landed on a more ample cheek.

"Oh God..." she cried out when his condom-sheathed cock connected with her wet heat.

Each surge forward pressed her against the firm pillow he used to keep her at this perfect angle, but it was not enough. Reaching around her slim hips, he slipped his fingers between her drenched folds.

Desiree's breathing became ragged. She struggled to speak. "Right . . . there . . . Seth."

That bite of pain she craved came as he pinched the tiny distended pearl between his finger and thumb. Desiree detonated. He pushed into her heat, buried to the hilt, claiming his own release. Seth growled as he surged into a mind-blowing orgasm. His legs quaked and he saw sparks behind his closed eyes.

He didn't linger but rose without speaking to get rid of the condom. Those playful soothing cuddles, after a long day in bed, had ceased months before their divorce.

By the time he came back from the bathroom, she was squirming, ready to escape her restraints. Once she was free, Desiree sighed and rolled over quickly on the bed.

He hadn't noticed the nipple clamps until now. His eyebrows rose. "Those are new."

After she released the jewels from their tight hold on her reddened nipples, Seth bent over her to sooth each tortured peak with licks and light sucks. His lips avoided her neck, and her mouth was off limits—they never kissed, not anymore.

Desiree savored a cat-like stretch as Seth toyed with the sleek hard plane of her stomach. He considered bringing up round two but didn't want to risk Desiree spending the night. He always avoided awkward mornings. Making breakfast had been one of his favorite things when they were married, but now that domestic scene conjured too many memories of everything they had lost.

While gathering her scattered clothes from his bedroom, she slipped on her thong and said, "As always, Seth, that was amazing, but I need to get going."

"No problem." He never assumed any different and watched as she shimmied her bedazzled jeans over her lean hips.

"I have to get back to Northside Grill. My sister sent a text. Paige needs a ride home after her shift."

Muscled and comfortably naked, Seth watched her from the still-warm sheets. Desiree tilted her head and said, "Damn. The closer you get to thirty, the better looking you get."

He shrugged, not quite sharing the same feelings for Desiree.

Her eyes narrowed when he didn't bother to return the compliment. "Hey. Why don't I stop by tomorrow before I go back to Portland?" she offered while hanging on to her frown.

"Text first, I might be working at Whitewater."

"We could mess around in your office. I had fun last time . . ."

Seth watched Desiree brush her hair in front of the mirror. The sleek, dark strands revealed no signs of their recent fuck, and her lipstick wasn't even smudged. He gritted his teeth. Her too-polished appearance, right after sex, set him on edge.

"No. Carlos will be around finishing a project. I don't want you running into my crew."

"Good thing I'm not some clingy girlfriend or I might think you were ashamed of me."

No, he wasn't ashamed of her . . . he claimed all the shame for himself.

***

Natalie came in an hour early to take advantage of the high-speed Wi-Fi before she opened the coffee shop. Hunched over her laptop, she lost herself, pouring through plans on tiny home websites and searching Pinterest for fresh ideas.

Ignoring a twinge of guilt, she also stalked Seth. How could anyone fault her? The man was gorgeous.

Natalie closed *his* image when keys jingled in the back door of the coffee shop. Elsa was early, perhaps she couldn't sleep. Losing Pete had been difficult for Elsa, too.

"Good morning, sweetie," she said as she stowed her purse beneath the counter and turned to take her jacket off.

"I'm glad you're early. I wanted to ask you to take a look at this website." Bringing up the home page, Natalie spun her laptop in Elsa's direction. "Do you know anything about this tiny house business? It's in Ashwood, your hometown."

"I don't recall a construction company called Whitewater. Why do you ask?"

"I've been thinking about an idea for a business."

"A business? Are you thinking of moving to Ashwood?"

"No, nothing like that. You know that tiny house show I'm obsessed with?" Elsa nodded and Natalie's voice bounced with excitement. "It got me thinking . . . If I combine a tiny home with a coffee shop, I can live and work from the same space. And I'd have plenty of time to shoot photos when I travel from place to place."

"I like it—adventure and travel. But how does Ashwood play into your plan?"

"This guy, Seth Michaels, builds tiny houses. I figured a Washington builder would give me better access to the process."

"Oh. The Michaels' family, of course I know them—they're great people."

"That's a relief because I already sent an email and he's interested in taking on my project."

***

Two weeks later, Natalie closed her computer and groaned. She'd exhausted her search for a place to stay in Ashwood. Hiking and whitewater rafting season had just started. Even the grubbiest seasonal cabins were already reserved.

Natalie unfolded the list Elsa wrote for her. The names almost glared from the fancy lavender stationary. Biting her lip, Natalie scanned the names and grabbed her phone.

She hesitated—humiliated that she had to beg for a room from a total stranger. Her fingers trembled as she punched in Kelsey Fisher's number. The phone rang—she waited and hoped this girl would answer. The call went to voicemail, and the inbox was full.

"Crappity-crap." She glared at the screen and typed. The text felt even more awkward—too long and too revealing. Yet, her words must have done the trick. Kelsey, Elsa's great-niece, sent an answer within seconds.

"Easy-peasy," she giggled, wondering why she'd worked herself into a quaking mess. Within minutes, her plans were set. Natalie had a room in Ashwood for the entire summer.

She cranked her music until the thin walls of her studio apartment shook. Natalie hopped onto her mattress and didn't care if her neighbors across the alley witnessed her joyful happy dance.

***

Seth sketched preliminary ideas with Natalie's requests in mind. He understood his new client's need to escape Seattle's urban chaos. With home prices skyrocketing, more and more city dwellers were choosing his compact, efficient homes.

Cities like Seattle and Portland might fit some, but Seth never wanted that life again. He and Desiree had both grown up in Ashwood and dated since their junior year in high school. Tying the knot after graduation seemed like a great idea at the time. His job at the lumber mill paid well, and Desiree worked as a cashier at The Stop-n-Shop. He was content with their uncomplicated life and had thought they were happy. One thing he always knew—the sex was hot.

A year after graduation, she started to take a few online classes. Her advisor at the local community college encouraged her to apply to University of Portland. When Desiree was accepted and landed a couple of scholarships, Seth supported her. He found a decent construction job in the larger city. Young, newly married, and too optimistic for their own good, they settled into a new routine.

They hadn't lived in Portland long before everything began to shift. Exhausted from working overtime, Seth rarely left their duplex. Desiree found new friends and they gradually drifted apart. Even the explosive sex wasn't enough to save the marriage.

After three years and, thank God, no kids, Seth filed for a divorce. Ashamed, he had crawled home to Ashwood to heal his wounds alone.

Seth put down his sketchbook and took a swig of beer to clear his mind—looking back on that failure still stung.

***

Kelsey Fisher hoped her new roommate would add a jolt of *something* to her crowd. She stared at the blurry image her Aunt Elsa had sent from the smartphone Kelsey taught her great aunt to use. Laughing, she grinned at the picture then passed her phone to Kent. "Here she is."

Her best friend snatched the phone from her hand. "Are you sure about this, Kels? A roommate could steal all your shit while you're guiding a float trip."

"For fuck's sake, Kent, you worry about the stupidest shit. I thought you'd be all over this new girl coming to town."

With his charisma and killer smile, Kent had that no-strings-attached thing locked down. Growing up together had created a shield of sorts, and Kelsey was immune.

Reclined on her couch, with his feet in the middle of her coffee table, Kent squinted at the picture on her phone and shrugged. "What's her name again?"

"Natalie Journey"

"Hmm, hard to tell. Isn't she sort of pale and mousy? I guess I'll check her out when she shows at Whitewater next week. We just started work on her tiny home."

Kelsey left her phone with Kent, shoved his feet to the floor, and gathered their empty beers before she headed to her kitchen.

"Any pizza left?" Kent asked. The guy was always starving.

"Nope. I had it for breakfast. Do you want to hit Northside Grill after our hike?"

"I don't want to wait that long. Let's eat before we hit the trail."

***

The early summer sun beat down on Natalie's shoulders while she loaded the last of her belongings into her inherited truck. Elsa tested the weight of the picnic basket she had stuffed to the brim and gave up. "Natalie, could you lift this for me? It's much too heavy."

"What's in here?" she asked, while hoisting the basket into the passenger seat of her F350.

"Oh, the basics—sandwiches, fruit, chips, and some of that organic juice you like. I made a batch of snickerdoodles, too. Kelsey loves them. I'm so happy you're staying with my great-niece. It will be easy to visit you both. Still, I wish you weren't leaving so soon . . ."

"I'll visit plenty this summer." Natalie had to come back. She couldn't avoid sorting through Grandpa's things forever. The condominium had to go on the market by August, and she was running out of time.

"At least I'll see you at the Fisher's place on the lake when I visit Ashwood. By then you'll be a local, just like me." Elsa's enthusiasm failed to reach beyond Natalie's frayed nerves, but she pasted on a smile and accepted the encouragement.

Lifting her final suitcase onto the tailgate, Natalie stumbled as she scrambled into the open bed of her lifted truck. With her last bag on board, she stood and straightened with a sense of pride. She was ready to leave Seattle and begin her new adventure.

Jumping to the ground again, Natalie folded Elsa into a hug and her friend teared up. Elsa always cried when family left, and Natalie *was* family.

"Call when you get to Kelsey's, so I don't worry. You've made a bold decision. I love you." Hanging on a little longer, Natalie absorbed enough love to last a while.

After climbing into the cab, she started the motor and cringed when the diesel engine belched smoke in Elsa's direction. After flapping away the black cloud, Elsa lifted both arms and waved with two hands for as long as Natalie could see her in the rearview mirror.

Miles passed and traffic eased the farther she drove from Seattle. Nearly three hours later, she left the freeway for the two-lane road that skirted the Columbia River. Panic threatened, but she fought it, determined to find joy instead of clinging to fear.

This risk was an unexplored path. She had never skipped class. Never ran a red light. Never drank 'til she got sick. She'd never even had a one-night stand.

A metallic female voice interrupted her thoughts and shouted from her phone, instructing her to turn left in a quarter mile. Natalie wondered why that woman couldn't do something useful and help her find a way to erase some of her *nevers*?

THREE

Natalie angled her truck toward Mount Adams and followed the path of the Little White River along a narrow switchback highway. She sang away the miles until the last Portland station faded to a hiss, then spun the dial and switched off the radio. Puffy clouds billowed ahead but didn't threaten to steal the sunshine that followed her into Ashwood.

South of town, a rustic *Whitewater Homes* sign caught her attention. Natalie tapped the brakes and pivoted her head for a longer look. She imagined the skeleton of her tiny home coming together inside the massive shop and slowed her truck.

Her dark side yelled *stop,* desperate to meet Seth Michaels. "Better not, Kelsey's waiting," she argued aloud with the voice in her head. As always, her sensible half won, and she drove on.

Ashwood was smaller than she remembered. She chuckled and wondered why childhood places always seemed to shrink. A stoplight hung over the road but flashed only yellow. Apparently, the trickle of traffic never needed red or green. On the west side of the road a bakery, a bank, and a thrift store stood out among buildings bearing faded *for rent* signs propped inside dusty windows. Each vacancy begged a daring individual to take a chance in Ashwood.

The east side of the street buzzed with small-town activity. Everyone waved as they came and went from the side-by-side grocery and hardware.

The Stop-n-Shop welcomed her with its familiar white stone façade. Before driving on, she swung in and parked while deciding at the last moment to pick up a few groceries. If Kelsey's refrigerator resembled hers, it probably contained pickles and soda, but not much else.

"Crud, I'm sore." She moaned and stretched, working out the kinks from the long drive before making her way inside. When the automatic doors swung open, Natalie inhaled the scent of fresh baked bread coming from a deli near the checkout.

From behind the sandwich counter, a tall girl with long brown hair waved and grinned as Natalie tried to pass. Strange, the girl seemed to expect her arrival.

Natalie slowed her steps, glanced at the deli menu, and decided that bringing something delicious to her new temporary home might help break the ice.

"What can I get for you?" the smiling girl asked. "If your favorite isn't on the board, I'd be happy to build a custom sandwich."

"Just a sec. I'm new in town and want to bring something over for my roommate," Natalie said, but felt foolish the minute the words passed her lips. It wasn't like this stranger cared about her next destination.

From across the counter, the girl tilted her head and smiled. "I'm guessing you must be Kelsey's new roomie. I'm Amanda. Welcome to Ashwood."

Natalie wrinkled her nose. "Yeah, that's me. How did you know?"

Amanda grinned and shrugged. "It's a small town and we know everyone's business. You'll get used to it, eventually. What would you like?"

"Hmm, the soup smells fantastic." Her mouth was already watering.

"It is, and the homemade bread is Kelsey's favorite. Food will definitely get you on her good side."

"Perfect. Thanks. Toss some in." Natalie spun her head toward the grocery store, and realized she'd done this out of order.

Amanda grinned. "Go. Finish your shopping. I'll watch for you on your way out and have everything waiting."

This bubbly girl seemed almost clairvoyant. Natalie liked her already.

The wheels wobbled as she pushed the cart up and down the aisles, tossing in essentials. When every person she passed tipped a head or smiled, Natalie wondered if Ashwood was part of some strange social experiment where people actually cared.

After bagging her groceries, she stopped by the deli counter to grab her order.

"I bet we'll become fast friends this summer," Amanda bubbled, lacking a social filter.

"How did you know I was staying?" Natalie asked as she paid.

"My brother, Seth, he mentioned you. He's building your tiny home. I'm Seth's little sister."

Learning this, Natalie flushed with instant heat, and the blush screamed, *I'm your brother's stalker*. With her head tipped to hide her face, she swept her debit card and tapped the code. Eager to escape, she turned toward the exit.

"Welcome to Ashwood," Amanda added as Natalie gave her wobbly cart a shove.

Natalie slowed her escape enough to answer, "Glad to be here!"

She sped her pace, tumbled out the automatic doors, and bumped her cart across the pothole-covered lot. Her dual wheeled truck towered ahead of her. Aiming the key fob, she pressed the button to unlock the doors.

To make room for her groceries, she decided to move Elsa's heavy picnic basket from the cab to the back. After stashing the bags in front, she stood with the cumbersome basket in her hand, wishing she had the power to levitate the bulky thing over the lip of the truck's bed.

"Need help with that?" a deep voice asked from behind her.

When Natalie spun, her eyes settled on two overwhelming men. The one wearing a baseball cap over his sandy-blond hair smiled and reached for the picnic basket.

"That looks heavy," he said as his hand wrapped around the handle.

"It is." His ropey arms rippled as he found a place for the basket between the boxes.

"Are you moving?" he asked on a slow head to toe perusal of her body that paused on his favorite places.

"I am," Natalie answered, held by the power of a hypnotic gaze. His lethal grin expanded as he chuckled, but the sound let her escape his spell long enough to notice the other man.

Blinking twice, her eyes locked on a face she recognized, and she nearly blurted *his* name aloud. *Seth.*

Sunglasses concealed his eyes, but she recalled from pictures on his website that beneath the shades his eyes were deep blue.

Natalie's attention shifted back when the guy in the baseball cap leaned against her truck's tailgate. "Hi. I'm Kent. Welcome to Ashwood. You wouldn't be the girl moving in with Kelsey, would you?"

"Y-Yes I am," she stammered as that grin intensified, and he leaned into her space.

"And your name . . . is?" he teased.

"Oh. I'm Natalie." She swallowed hard and glanced between both men, wishing a meteor would crash from the heavens and put her out of her misery.

The breeze picked up and tossed a length of wavy hair across her face. Her fingers tucked the unruly strand behind her ear. Seth's hand twitched when she smoothed her hair away from her eyes.

"I bet you could use help moving." Kent matched his grin with a leading nod of his head, urging her to agree.

She synchronized her nod with his without thinking. Damn, the things this guy could do with only a smile.

Kent stepped closer. "Just follow us to Kelsey's place. I wouldn't want you to get lost."

Once she found her voice, she stuttered, "O-okay."

Kent clapped his hands and rocked back on his heels. "Awesome. We're in that blue pickup, the one with the Whitewater logo on the tailgate. You won't lose us."

Her brain decided to start working a little too late. "You don't need to bother. I have the address in my phone."

"Not a problem. I planned to hang out with Kels later anyway." Kent rolled his shoulders, turned to the silent man next to him and said, "Seth, if you want to save the trip, I could ride with my new friend Natalie. That way you can get back to Whitewater."

Natalie worried her lip with her teeth and waited. When Seth lifted his chin, she realized he'd been studying her all this time.

"Kent. Get back in my truck." Seth's first words seismically rumbled all the way to Natalie's core. "I'm coming along to help with the move. And don't forget, you've got that roof to finish at the shop."

Kent deflated the moment Seth stepped forward and led her by the elbow toward her driver's side door. Dazed by the guiding touch, she waited while he pulled the handle.

"Climb on in," he said. A sizzle of awareness emanated when he moved his hand from her elbow to her spine.

Now at his height, she turned to face him as he removed his sunglasses. His website photos had not prepared her for his indigo gaze.

"Follow me," he said with a smile that held a secret promise.

"Okay," she agreed before Seth pushed her door shut and ambled away.

Kent spun, walked backward, and waved with that killer smile plastered across his face.

Reaching for the ignition, the engines heavy snarl grounded Natalie enough to clear her head. She had a roommate to meet and a day of unpacking ahead. Yet, she couldn't resist a lingering glance at the assets ambling away from her across the parking lot.

***

Seth joined Kent and headed across the parking lot. He resisted the urge to turn around when Natalie's truck's powerful engine turned over with a rumble behind him. "What the hell was that?" Seth growled over the deep engine.

"Just being friendly." Kent grinned and chuckled.

"How did you recognize her?" Seth asked.

"Kels had a picture, but that girl is way hotter in person. Damn. Summer just got interesting."

"Natalie is a client," Seth reminded Kent *and* himself.

"Why does that matter?"

"She plans to help with the build, and it's going to be a challenge. I don't want things to get awkward."

"Awkward? I just want to take her out for some beers."

Until he saw Natalie, Seth had only imagined the tiny home. Damn, now he pictured her in it. He clenched his fists and struggled to regain his original focus. "Keep your hands off and your mind on the project. God knows it'll be complicated—Natalie wants a coffee shop, a service window, and a darkroom. It's going to be a tight squeeze."

"Freudian slip, Seth?" Kent laughed as they settled in the cab.

Seth narrowed his eyes and sent a clear message to his employee. "Don't go there, not at Whitewater. I'm not putting up with that shit."

"Fine. I can keep work and fun separate. I'll see her plenty at Kelsey's anyway. I wouldn't want Natalie to get lonely once Kels leaves to guide on the river."

Glancing in his rearview mirror as she followed him to Kelsey's place, Seth wondered how that petite woman even managed to reach the pedals in those sexy heels.

His fingers still tingled from the electric connection. He'd felt the sensation right through her clothes. Natalie Journey intrigued him far more than she should.

Jaw clenched, he pushed the thoughts of his new client aside. He had particular tastes, and his rules were in place for a reason—he needed his privacy and intended to keep it that way. *Don't date local women. Don't bring women home. Keep relationships short and casual.* This new arrival to Ashwood wouldn't make him change.

His single exception, his ex-wife Desiree, came with her own set of guidelines. *No jealousy. No deep feelings. And no disclosure about what went on in bed or any other surface they decided to use.*

As his fingers tightened around the wheel, Seth wondered if Natalie might be worth *one* bent rule. Technically, she wasn't local. Anything that happened between them would leave with her when she drove away in her tiny home.

"Whoa!" Kent yelled and grabbed the wheel, bringing Seth's truck from the soft shoulder to the solid pavement. "Dude, do you want to roll this thing into the ditch?"

"Sorry. Thought I spotted an elk."

Kent's eyebrows lifted skyward. "An elk . . . yeah, right."

With his heart rate under control, Seth flicked the signal, and followed a one-lane drive that disappeared beneath dense evergreens. Dappled sunlight illuminated specks of airborne dust floating above the gravel road. After a final curve, he parked in front of a white one-story cottage with a red front door.

Natalie's rig rolled to a stop next to his. He automatically assessed its ability to pull her tiny home. The dual wheels surprised him. Few people needed that much truck, but with her home on his mind, he was happy to see the extra stability.

Natalie climbed out but hung back. Seth realized she'd never met Kelsey before. Because of her connection with Elsa, the town had already learned too much about this woman, yet she knew almost nothing about all of them. The granddaughter of Pete Thorsen already had an army of people ready to step in and help if she needed hometown support.

Kent jogged from Seth's truck and pushed through Kelsey's front door with a holler, not bothering to knock. With Natalie moving in, Seth hoped Kent wouldn't always make himself so at home.

Wanting undivided eye contact, Seth removed his sunglasses again. Natalie visibly relaxed and moved toward him. She smiled and shuffled her feet in those sexy heels.

Nervous and so damn cute, she said, "I'm sorry Kent tied you into this. I'm sure most of your clients don't rope you into helping them move."

Tied. Rope. Damn. Was she choosing those words just to tempt him? What he could do with rope and her petite lush body.

"No problem, glad to help." Seth watched her glance toward the house as Kelsey came out, but his attention dashed back to her light blue eyes. Pale, her skin glowed with a light dusting of freckles across her nose, and her hair shimmered with every shade of red and burnished gold.

"So, this truck . . . you must have done your homework when you bought it."

Natalie glanced at the rig then back to his face. Her expression had shifted from nervous to sad. "Well, no. I didn't do any research. I inherited the truck. Grandpa used it to pull his boat. I guess I'm lucky he always chose the best."

Damn, he'd hurt her and would have rewound those words if he could. How had he let himself forget about her grandpa's recent passing?

"I met him a few times," Seth said, thrilled when her face lit again.

"You did? When?"

"Two years ago, while fishing on Lake Osprey. Pete was visiting Ashwood with Elsa. They seemed close."

She nodded. "I think they were always friends. It became something more after Grandma died. I sometimes wondered why Elsa and Grandpa never married."

Seth understood. Once down the aisle was one time too many. That was a mistake he never intended to repeat.

They turned toward Kelsey as she jogged from her house. "Sorry I didn't come out right away. Elsa's called a couple of times."

Natalie had forgotten to call Elsa when she arrived. "I didn't think of your aunt when I stopped at the store. That reminds me—Amanda packed up some soup and bread. It's in the cab."

"You met Amanda?" Seth asked wondering if she was aware of the connection.

"I did. But I didn't know we'd have four to feed when I placed the order."

"If Amanda put your order together, there's sure to be more than enough," Kelsey said, circling to the passenger side.

After quickly introducing herself to her roommate, Kelsey reached in the truck to pass brown paper grocery sacks to the guys.

***

Natalie hung back, trying to ease in without causing a ripple. "Just let me grab my camera and then I'll call Elsa right away."

"No worries, I already told her you had arrived, and by the way, she says, *hello*." Finding a box marked *fragile*, Kelsey grabbed it to save a trip. Friendly and open, Kelsey grinned. "Nice to finally meet you face to face."

Natalie hung one messenger bag across her body and lifted an oversized duffle. "Thanks for all your help. Everyone here is so nice. I'll be honest, the city girl in me can't handle it. I'm kind of freaking out."

"Too nice? Oh, you must mean the guys. Yeah, it surprised me at first when Kent barged in, saying he came to help my new roomie unload her shit. But then I saw you."

Natalie's blush and raised eyebrows begged for an explanation.

Kelsey laughed. "Come on. You're gorgeous, curvy, and you have that damsel in distress thing going for you. Guys eat that up."

"Distressed? Absolutely—all day long," Natalie admitted with a chuckle, but she couldn't get her mind around the damsel idea. It bugged her a little.

"Let's get inside, feed the guys, and get their help with your things. You've surprised me—I thought a city girl would travel with a lot more stuff."

"I've already sold or donated most of it. I'm letting it go so I can fit everything in my tiny house." They crossed the threshold and found Kent making himself at home in Kelsey's kitchen.

"Are you and Kent a thing?" Natalie asked, apparently a little too loud. Both men turned her direction at once.

"Kent? Shit no." Kelsey laughed long and hard.

"Thanks, Kels," Kent yelled across the room. His eyes tried to glower but failed. "Kels and I, we sort of grew up together," he said over Kelsey's uncontrolled laughter.

Gasping for breath, Kelsey explained, "It would be too weird."

Kent's smile took on the melt-your-knees magnitude again. "Natalie, it looks like I'm all yours . . . if you want me."

She returned his grin. "Lucky me."

***

Later that night, exhausted from the long drive and move, Natalie settled her spine against a faded lawn chair and accepted a second beer from Kels. They sat side by side on a cracked concrete patio that overlooked the uneven grass.

The patchy lawn had tiny white flowers popping above a carpet of green. Unable to think of much to say, Natalie began picking the label from her bottle. "Do you know the guy who runs this brewery?" she asked. "The cold case at the Stop-n-Shop was bursting with this brand."

Spinning the bottle, Kels read the label. "Yeah. Mosquito Creek. Wade Michaels lives about an hour north of town. He owns it."

"Michaels. Another one? Older or younger brother to Amanda and Seth?"

"Not their brother. He's a cousin from the Yakima side of the family. Don't bother trying to keep track of the entire clan. If you meet a man who is tall, built, and has a streak of cave man running through him, you've probably met one of the Michaels men."

Natalie tipped her head back and laughed. "Seth does have that brooding thing down."

Kelsey shrugged. "Kind of sexy, but not my type."

Natalie didn't know if she had a type, but Seth was beyond tempting and completely out of reach. "Are you seeing someone? I could have sworn there was something between you and Kent."

Kelsey's laugh was honest and a little loud. Natalie relaxed as her second beer loosened the tight muscles in her shoulders.

"Nope. Not seeing anyone, but the summer is young. I usually hang out with a new guide at Venture. After rafting season ends, the summer fling ends with it."

"So, Kent's just a friend?"

"More than that, he's like a brother, just not biological." Kelsey's head tilted, and her expression softened. "I've got a sister, but I'm closer to Kent."

31

Natalie felt Kelsey's assessing gaze. She seemed to be looking for one of two things—a woman she could trust or a sign that Natalie was Kent-worthy. The close inspection made her nervous.

Quiet, Kelsey placed her hand in the path of a ladybug and let it crawl onto her finger. As it climbed, she opened up. "We were in the same grade. My mom taught our kindergarten class." Her lips narrowed and blew on the bug as if it were a candle. The wings stretched open and it flew away.

"I still remember that Monday when Kent didn't show up at school. The office had called his mom—you know, to verify the absence, and I guess Kent must have picked up the phone."

Natalie waited for Kelsey to press on, her voice not quite a whisper. "Kindergarten was half-day, so Mom and I went over to his house on our way home. He was alone."

Her jaw clenched for a moment, then Kelsey continued, "Kent's mom had taken off. He's never heard from her since. From what we can piece together, his mom thought his dad would be home on Friday night, but he didn't show. You see, his dad's a long-haul truck driver, and at the last minute he took an extra trip."

"Oh my God. How long was he alone?"

"Three or four days, tops. Even at that age, he was used to taking care of himself."

"What? Are you serious! Kindergarten kids are practically babies."

"His mom never had a shot at mother of the year. For a while, Kent's dad took jobs close to Ashwood, driving local routes, but money was tight. When he had to take longer hauls, Kent would spend the night at our place. By the time we were nine or ten, his dad was on the road again almost full-time."

"That's terrible." Natalie hurt for him, recalling her pain when her father left.

"Don't bring it up. He never talks about his mom," Kelsey warned, and Natalie nodded, giving a silent promise.

They were quiet for a while. The sun settled low on the horizon. Natalie stared at those tiny white flowers giving her mind room for a distant memory. She recalled stringing tiny white daisies in a chain to wear as a crown in her hair. Her brother had been there too, tossing stones into a crystal blue lake.

Kelsey jarred Natalie from the past to the present. "Another beer?" she asked while rising from the lawn chair.

"I'll pass. I have to unpack before I go to bed."

"Cool. Sometimes I'm a night owl. If I can't sleep, I go for a run. So, don't freak out if you hear the door rattle around two a.m."

"Good to know."

"Hey, if you don't have anything planned for tomorrow night, a bunch of us are going to Northside Grill. Kent will be there, along with half the town."

"I'd like that. Thanks for everything." Natalie said and followed Kelsey inside. Eager to settle, she disappeared into her room to unpack. In the closet, she found a sturdy shelf for her camera equipment. The sight had her missing the solitude of her darkroom. She'd have to shoot less film in Ashwood or get used to sending her work to a lab.

In the middle of the night, she woke, disoriented by the new space. Natalie recalled where she was when a door opened and closed. A few minutes later, the shower hissed and the pipes in the old house creaked. Kelsey must have just returned from that late-night run.

Flipping her pillow to the cool side, Natalie closed her eyes and drifted back into her dream. White flowers in her hair—she tossed stones into blue water and spread giant circles across a glassy lake.

FOUR

Wide plank floors, worn smooth by decades of customers, creaked underfoot as Natalie followed Kelsey into Northside Grill. A slightly burnt aroma surrounded her, the lingering scent of burgers, onion, and beer mixed with perfume and the faint smell of sweat.

Round tables surrounded a small dance floor, where a few couples clung to each other and shuffled to music from a jukebox.

At the bar, she noticed several beers on tap—the craft beer markets in Washington demanded it. Dominating these, Mosquito Creek Brewery outnumbered the others. The woman pouring drinks gave her a smile, and Kelsey leaned in. "I'll introduce you to Iris a little later—she's great and owns this place."

"Thanks, Kelsey." The mirror backing the long bar caught Natalie's reflection between bottles of whiskey, rum, tequila, and vodka. She tipped a grin and sighed, relieved that Kelsey had suggested her curve hugging black jeans and low-cut, pale green blouse. The skirt she'd originally slipped on would have been way too *nightclub* for Northside Grill.

Before they joined Kelsey's friends, Natalie peeked down to make sure the hint of lace that caressed her cleavage wasn't revealing too much—just enough to beg eyes to linger. When the uneven floor nearly caught one of her heels, she slowed and Kelsey pulled ahead, carried by boots with turquoise stitching.

Natalie envied Kelsey's mile long legs and athletic five-foot-nine body. Her new roommate looked perfect in a black top that dipped low in the back, accentuating her gorgeous lean lines.

As the pair walked through the dimly lit bar, a group seated near the pool tables yelled, "Hey, Kels, get your ass over here!" Kent waited among a knot of three guys and two brunette girls, clearly twins.

"Everybody, this is Natalie. She's staying at my place this summer. Natalie, this is the crowd." Kelsey swept her hand in the air over the bunch and Natalie sank into a chair next to Kent.

"Jasmine and Rose are obviously twins. You already know Kent. And Rick and Justin are hogging the pool table."

A chorus of friendly greetings barraged Natalie. Scooting his chair, Kent closed the space between them. His killer smile encouraged her to relax.

Justin left the pool table to pour another glass. He lifted a pitcher and asked, "Do you like IPA?"

Rick hung back, but offered, "There's also light beer. Or we can get you a soda." He was muscular, bordering on bulky, and obviously spent his free time in a gym.

"Light beer's perfect," Natalie said, feeling instantly welcomed.

"Chili fries and nachos are on the way but will take about twenty minutes." Justin passed Natalie a glass of light beer, while Jasmine poured a couple IPAs.

Kent slid an arm possessively across the back of her chair and said, "I'll get the next round." She gulped when he leaned in a little closer than she expected and asked, "How do you like Ashwood so far?"

"It's beautiful. I plan to explore it with my camera."

"Our cousin's a photographer," Jasmine said, attempting to find common ground.

"She's talented," Rose added, finishing her sister's thought, as twins often do.

"She works at the Stop-n-Shop."

"Her name is Amanda."

"Have you met her?" the twins volleyed.

Natalie's eyes flicked from sister to sister wondering who was Jasmine and who was Rose.

"Amanda's your cousin? I met her yesterday." The town shrank further when Natalie realized the twins were also related to Seth.

"Yeah, the youngest of four. She's just nineteen, and can't hang out with us at the bar," Jasmine spilled.

"Three older, way too protective brothers won't let her party too much." Rose finished.

Natalie nodded and listened while she built the framework of connections. Kent left to buy the next round before the food arrived. While he was gone, the twins peppered Natalie with questions about Seattle.

Jasmine and Rose planned to leave Ashwood for that city in September and would be heading off to finish their last two years of college. They mined her for information about dive bars, cheap restaurants, and places to dance on the weekends. Natalie came up with a few suggestions in the University district but worried they would find her meager information disappointing.

Returning with foaming pitchers, Kent pulled Natalie into a private conversation as the twins got up together for a quick bathroom break.

"That pickup you came into town with, will you be using it to pull your home?" he asked.

"I plan to, but I'm worried. I don't have a clue about pulling a trailer."

"I'll help. After a few lessons, you'll be a pro. The most challenging part is backing up. We'll practice 'til you have it down." Natalie thanked Kent, who moved in closer and draped his entire arm across her chair when the music got loud. She shivered when his fingers began to toy with a strand of her red hair.

Kent asked about her plans to travel in the tiny home, but Natalie couldn't shake the distinct feeling that someone was watching. When she trusted her instincts and scanned the bar, her eyes locked with Seth's.

He tipped his head up in that gesture that usually conveys a friendly hello, but in this case, the nod seemed to communicate intent.

Natalie blushed, broke from his gaze, and attempted to rejoin the group's conversation. Another pitcher landed on the table, and Jasmine pulled Rick to the dance floor. The music pounded. Loud chatter and laughter increased over the beat of country music.

After her second beer, Natalie relaxed and lost herself in the buzz of new friendships. She leaned into the group, shared another drink, and enjoyed the warmth radiating from Kent's hand at the small of her back. His touch began to feel natural. Maybe she'd spend time with this hot, small-town guy.

***

Seth's world shifted when she entered Northside Grill. After unloading Natalie's truck, he had decided to keep the tempting woman from Seattle at a professional distance. She'd be in Ashwood all summer and that might complicate his private life.

But ignoring her presence proved impossible. Natalie's name graced everyone's lips, popping up everywhere—from Kent at work and his sister Amanda. Even the guy at the minimart yammered on about that sweet little redhead who just blew into town.

From his perch at the bar, Seth watched Kent work his magic. That meaty arm drifted around her petite frame. His fingers looped through a stray curl of her red hair. Kent's hand caressed the small of her back and Natalie turned to give his employee a bright smile. He couldn't just sit on his ass and take it. He had to create distance between Natalie and Kent—arguably the biggest player in town.

Seth lied to himself as he stood. *Natalie needs my protection.* Yet, he knew this woman could make up her own mind.

She's new here and might get lonely. Clearly, she had plenty of potential new friends. He crossed the bar, telling himself to stop—to leave her alone. This girl was too young, too reserved, and too good for him.

***

A deep voice rumbled over the din, "Hey, Kent, how's it going?" Natalie froze as all eyes shifted to the presence that loomed behind her. She spun in her seat, staring skyward. Seth was so damn tall.

"Natalie. Join me for a dance?" He held out his hand, and without thinking, she slipped her fingers into his. The magnetic draw shocked her senses.

"Okaaay . . . sure, I-I'll be back in a bit," Natalie stammered while her new crowd of friends gaped. Seth grasped her hand and pulled her from the table to the pulse of the dance floor.

Natalie felt the heat of Kent's lingering touch on the small of her back until Seth covered the warm spot with his hand. His fingers induced a shiver with a potent touch.

Perched high on slim heels, she found herself encased in Seth's arms. Not only was he tall, his presence framed a protective space around her. She inhaled his woodsy scent—fresh cut lumber and something warm drew her in for more.

Responding to her physical invitation, Seth eased his thigh forward. She parted her stance slightly and sighed, giving him her weight. Natalie couldn't assemble a coherent sentence with Seth's hard body moving against hers.

Eyes locked, she struggled and found something to say. "I've enjoyed our emails these past few months."

His cobalt gaze held her eyes, then his glance dipped to her mouth. Natalie licked her lips and his smile tipped slightly at the corners.

She filled the dead space with a few more rattled words. "I recognized you right away at the grocery store parking lot." *Crap, now he knows I'm a stalker.* "You know, because your picture is on your website . . ." *Oh God, my hands are starting to sweat.*

She stared up at him, hoping he would say something, anything at all. The spread of his fingers expanded across her lower back, and she inhaled another dose of intoxicating man.

He finally said, "I recognized you, too. Your red hair stands out. It wasn't difficult to find you on social media." He didn't seem to care if she knew. His confidence put her at ease.

When Natalie felt a prickle caused by every scrutinizing stare in the room, she realized how snug his hand held her waist. But his touch felt so right she didn't move.

Natalie cleared her throat. "I really look forward to working with everyone at Whitewater, but I promise to stay out of the way." She heard herself prattling on but couldn't seem to stop. "Kent offered to teach me how to pull a trailer, he said he'd be happy to show me the ropes, with your guidance of course."

***

Seth swallowed a groan. *Ropes again. Fuck.* Her heat, her words, her vanilla scent induced all sorts of ideas. Absolutely none of those ideas included Kent. "Natalie, I want you working with me."

"That's perfect Seth. I feel like you know what I'm thinking . . . w-with the house I mean." She shook her head, blushing deeply. A settling breath lifted her breasts from her plunging top, and the delicate lace clung to her flushed skin. He simply couldn't peel his eyes away and wondered what that spot of pink skin would taste like.

The song finished too soon, and she stepped away. His arms missed the soft feel of Natalie when she wandered back toward her new friends. Determined to keep her close, he followed the sway of her gorgeous hips back to her table. As she approached, Kent attempted to coax Natalie back into her seat with his cocky smile.

One glance at that meaty paw draped possessively across the back of her vacant chair made Seth's decision easy. Locking eyes with Kent, Seth said, "Natalie, have you had anything to eat besides bar food tonight?"

On a turn, she tipped her eyes to his, and with a sweet smile lightly touched his arm. He felt the contact so much lower.

"I'm used to living on Top Ramen, so the chili fries actually seemed like a better than usual option," she said.

Seth eased her away from the group and spoke over Natalie's head, "Kels, I'll make sure Natalie gets home. We're going to grab something to eat."

Kelsey's eyebrows shot up, "Natalie, are you okay with that?"

Seth waited, hoping she would agree. Her voice sounded bright as she nodded and said, "Sure, I'll be fine. Seth and I need to talk about my house. We'll start on that over dinner." Apparently, the woman wanted to be alone with him just as much as he wanted her all to himself.

Natalie lifted her hand and gave the crowd a finger-wave. "So nice to meet all of you. See you later, Kels. I have my key," she called over her shoulder.

Seth almost regretted stealing her from this group when he spotted the stark jealousy shadowing Kent's pointed gaze.

FIVE

"Shit," Kent mumbled, pushed away from the table, and turned his back on the crowd. Kelsey watched in silence as he walked over to the bar and slid onto a worn stool.

"That was so weird," Jasmine muttered.

"I know. Seriously, Seth doesn't ever hang out with local girls," Rose finished her sister's thought.

Kelsey watched as Seth left The Northside with Natalie tucked close to his side. She leaned toward the twins and said, "Natalie isn't a local. Remember, she's leaving at the end of summer."

"Still, what's got into Seth?" Jasmine asked while staring at the vacant chairs around their table.

Rick huffed a knowing chuckle. "It's not what got into your cousin—it's *who* he wants to get into."

Rose kicked him under the table with her pointy boot. "Rick, you're disgusting."

"Damn, that hurt," he groaned, laughed, and bent to rub his shin. "Shit. Work's going to be a hazard zone with Kent and Seth going after the same girl."

Kelsey narrowed her gaze and whispered, "What about Desiree? I've heard rumors they still hookup."

Rick hunched a muscled shoulder. "Desiree comes around, but she's definitely not exclusive."

Her eyes travelled back toward Northsides entrance, the place where Kels last saw Natalie. "I don't know how I feel about this. Aunt Elsa asked me to watch out for her, and I won't be around much this summer."

Jasmine lifted her chin. "Seth won't hurt her. Well, not intentionally, anyway."

Kelsey sighed, if only Jasmine were more convincing. She had to find a way to coax Natalie into the group. "Do you guys mind if I invite her along with us for the festival on the river this weekend?"

"You should. It would be weird to leave her home alone." Kelsey relaxed a bit when Rose agreed, then let her gaze travel.

Kent sat on a stool with both elbows propped on the bar and rolled a shot glass between his finger and thumb. The one he'd already downed sat empty in front of him. When he swallowd the second shot of Jack, Kels worried.

***

As he led Natalie out of Northside Grill, Seth eased his hand lower on her back. Flexing his fingers at the base of her spine, he found that small strip of warm skin—the spot where her shirt stopped and the back of her snug jeans began.

He slowed their pace across the lot, steered her toward his truck, and held open the passenger door. The first step challenged her petite stature, and Seth helped her into the cab—finding another reason to sneak a touch.

Her eyes followed him as he circled the cab to take his place behind the wheel. When he turned the key, Natalie asked, "Where are you taking me, Seth? Ashwood doesn't strike me as a foodie hot-spot. Wasn't most of the town already inside Northside Grill?"

Seth hesitated for a moment then asked, "How does dinner over at my shop sound? That way you can check out some houses that are already in progress."

"Great idea. Do you live in one of your homes at the shop?" she asked.

"No. I have a place near the lake, but I keep a model home for my clients who'd like to give small-space living a try before they commit to a home. Sometimes I crash in the demo unit when I'm working late."

The lights from the dash illuminated Natalie's red hair, creating a radiance that surprised him. Her vanilla perfume warmed the interior, and Seth's mouth watered, eager to explore every warm place on her body with his tongue.

Tucking her leg under her, Natalie shifted in her seat to face him. The move broke Seth from his fantasy. "That's thoughtful, providing a home for a test run. I imagine people could make a mistake and give up their collection of stuff, only to discover their possessions define who they are."

Seth glanced to the side and noticed a wrinkle of worry around Natalie's eyes. "Are you ready for that kind of change?" he asked.

"I think so." He was relieved when she nodded and her posture eased.

"It should be easy. My apartment in Seattle was a postage stamp and a relic. The bathroom must have gone in a few minutes after the invention of indoor plumbing. Only one burner on my stove worked, and my entire musty apartment had a grand total of two electric outlets." He couldn't keep from grinning as her description progressed. "It wasn't all bad. It did have a peek-a-boo view of Puget Sound . . . if I stood on top of my bed."

"That sounds . . . terrible." Seth laughed while he pictured her cute pixie-body standing on her bed, stretching tall to see the water view.

Her musical laughter paused, "I spent a lot of time with Grandpa Pete and Elsa. His condo is fantastic, but I'll have to sell it soon."

Natalie went silent and leaned forward as he pulled into Whitewater's huge gravel lot. He rolled to a stop by the tall evergreens near the back of the shop. Sodium lights illuminated a tiny home twist on a rustic cabin. The home was complete with a deck, roomy enough for a couple of chairs and a compact barbeque.

Before Natalie climbed out, Seth circled the vehicle to open her door. With his hands spanning the circumference of her waist, he eased her forward and slid her body across his solid chest to lower her feet to the gravel.

Natalie pulled in a breath then glanced down. "I think I wore the wrong shoes for a construction site."

His response was immediate. Scooping her into his arms, he carried her onto the deck, then lowered his lips to hers. The kiss explored, savoring the feel of her cradled tight against his chest.

Sensing a small hesitation, he pulled back and opened the home with one hand. Natalie extended her legs, and he lowered her until her heels clicked on the floor. She shivered as if her body missed his warmth.

"Dinner. Let me get that started. Are steaks okay?" he said flicking on the lights.

"Can I help?" she asked while taking in the details of the home.

"There's salad makings and bread from the local bakery. Will that be enough to go with steak?"

"Steak, salad, and fresh bread? That sounds more than perfect."

Seth pulled out a table that disappeared into the wall when not in use. "Soda, wine, or beer?"

"Wine, please. This home is gorgeous, Seth. It's obvious—you love what you do." Climbing part way up the ladder, she peered into the loft to find an inviting bed flanked by two built-in nightstands.

Perched higher, her lush curves called to his primitive side, and Seth gave in to the pull. He moved behind her, unable to resist a taste now that she was equal to his height. Slow kisses nuzzled the soft spot where her neck sloped into her shoulder. "Natalie, you are mouthwatering."

She pressed her back against the firm plane of his body. Her smooth skin tempted further exploration.

The noise she made as he nibbled her neck piqued his curiosity. Could he get her to make that same sound again?

Taking a chance, he bit the base of her neck lightly, then soothed the sting with the tip of his tongue. Natalie hissed. Seth pulled away, fighting to regain control.

With a soft frustrated sound in her throat, Natalie spun toward him on the step and seized his mouth with a reckless kiss. Sliding her hands beneath his shirt, she caressed his back with light touches across the muscular plane. Just as he began to devour her mouth again, her stomach rumbled.

An involuntary giggle helped Seth set a slower pace. He stared into her eyes and Natalie brushed a thumb across his lip, "I could lie and say I'm not hungry, but it's obvious. I'm starving."

"I promised you dinner, and I keep my promises."

"You have no idea how sexy that sounds." That stopped him. She meant it. A promise meant everything to her. With a woman like Natalie, he knew he could keep a vow.

"Put me to work," she said, now consumed by more than one kind of hunger. In the compact kitchen, they prepped the meal together with simple ease, anticipating each other's movements like a couple that had been together for many years.

The salad was chopped and the bread warmed in the oven, filling the small space with a mouthwatering aroma. Seth moved to the grill with the steaks. Outside with him, her bare feet stepped silently onto the cool planked deck.

With their size-difference accentuated, she gazed up at him, and then gasped at the expanse of the starry sky. The vast Milky Way cut through the inky dark, covering the heavens with early summer constellations.

"Even on the clearest nights, I never saw anything like this in Seattle. Only on my grandpa's boat, far away from city lights, has anything ever come close. I can't wait to set up my tripod and capture this."

Seth wrapped her in his warmth. "I'd like to see your photos." he said tucking her head under his chin.

"Most of the black and whites are in Seattle. I have a small darkroom in Grandpa's condo, but I'm willing to give it up."

"I'm still working on the design to squeeze it into your home. Carlos has made it a personal mission."

"Carlos?"

"One of my builders. All of these Tetrised cabinets are his creation. He's a genius."

"I can't wait to meet him."

"You will, soon." Seth planned all the ways he could keep Natalie busy in his shop. Ordering, painting, taking pictures, he didn't care as long as she was near.

Steaks ready, he pulled them off the grill, and led her inside. While he watched her cut tiny bites, he answered her questions about her home. Building a perfect house for this woman became an essential promise he had to keep.

***

Natalie couldn't help herself—Seth's deep voice, the meal he'd prepared, and the cozy surroundings created a fantasy. Giving into the draw, she settled in and pretended they were planning their first home together.

Every detail about the man fascinated her—the curve of his fingers across her hand, the tilt of his head as he listened, and the smile in his eyes when he talked about his family. She simply didn't want the evening to end.

But after dinner was devoured, putting the house back in order passed too quickly. Still, heading home to Kelsey's seemed important. It was late, and she didn't want to worry her new roommate.

Seth hung the dishtowel through the handle on the refrigerator and asked, "Will you come to the shop tomorrow to meet up with Carlos? That darkroom has given him a worthy challenge."

Natalie smiled, thrilled that he wanted to see her again so soon. The passion she'd tasted on his lips left her hungry for more. "What time?"

"Is ten too early?"

"Not at all . . . I'm on barista hours. Ten is halfway through my day."

"I'll be here by eight," Seth lifted an eyebrow. "But I'm a bear before the caffeine soaks in."

"Thanks for the warning." Natalie let that image take hold—Seth at dawn, grumbly, brooding, and oh, so hot.

After she put on her shoes, Seth sly-grinned before scooping her into his arms again, earning a squeal from Natalie. "Don't ever wear anything but high heels. I plan to carry you everywhere."

She giggled and rested her head against his shoulder to enjoy the ride to his truck. Seth carried her to the passenger side, secured her in the seat, and took her face in his palms then eased in for a kiss. "So sweet. I can't get enough of your taste."

She melted into his claiming lips and sighed when he pulled away. Dazed by the intoxication, Natalie blinked as he circled the cab and climbed in to drive her home.

***

Kelsey whistled when Natalie pushed through the front door. "Damn. There was so much steam rolling off you two on my front porch. How did you manage to snare Seth Michaels in just a few short hours?"

Natalie blushed and shook her head. "He's not snagged. Tempted maybe, but not taken."

Kels pulled her new friend down onto the couch. "Ashwood women have been trying for years to do what you accomplished in just one night. Tell me he kisses like a god. And if he doesn't, lie. Just don't destroy my fantasy."

"No reason to lie. He's totally a god." Natalie sighed with relaxed satisfaction as she sank deeper into the sofa.

Kels nudged Natalie with her foot, "Come on. Give up the steamy details."

Before she could utter a word, Natalie yawned, incredibly tired now that the buzz of Seth and the wine was fading. "After we finished that dance at the bar, I would have followed him anywhere. Neither of us had eaten a real meal, so Seth cooked dinner."

"At his house? That's such a long drive out of town."

"No. He has a demo-tiny home at Whitewater. He cooked steaks while I put a salad together." Lost in thought, she let out a happy sigh.

"You played house? Very cozy. Besides the domestic bliss, what else?"

"We kissed, talked, hung out, and watched the stars." Natalie pulled her knees to her chest to hold the fresh memory in place. "I don't know if what started will go anywhere. With the entire summer ahead working on my house together, he may choose to keep things professional. It would be an epic mistake to obsess over Seth Michaels."

"Might be too late." Kelsey flung a supportive arm around her petite friend.

Natalie leaned in. "I'm exhausted."

"Anyone would be wiped out. You've had a lot to process—new home, new friends, and a new man. What are your plans for tomorrow? Are you sleeping in?"

"Seth asked me to come over to Whitewater and talk to Carlos about my darkroom."

"Darkroom? As in long strips of negatives and red lights?"

"Yeah, I have one in Seattle, but I won't for long. I need to move it or sell the equipment." A quick huff revealed her sense of loss.

"Don't sell. It seems important to you."

Her shoulders sagged. "Sometimes we have to let go of the things we love most." Natalie wriggled away from Kelsey's side. "I've got to get up early, I'm beat."

"I'll lock up." Kelsey put a dish in the sink to soak then found Natalie in the bathroom with creamy soap covering her face.

"Got to give you a fair warning, leaving with Seth tonight made you an instant celebrity. Half the town is probably buzzing, so be prepared."

Natalie's nose scrunched. "Really? I guess I have a lot to learn about Ashwood. How long does a newcomer have to live here before they're accepted?" She reached for her washcloth and shook her head. "Never mind . . . It doesn't matter. I'm moving in a few months, anyway."

After Natalie gave her face a final rinse, she found Kelsey's aqua-blue eyes studying her in the mirror. "Don't worry too much about fitting in with everyone in Ashwood. Pete's granddaughter is already *one of us*," Kelsey said in her best robotic voice. Natalie's right eyebrow lifted, and her roommate added, "Don't worry. We grow on you, like . . . moss."

Her laugh bubbled while she smoothed on moisturizer. "Perfect. I can't wait."

Finished with her nightly routine, Natalie shut her bedroom door and wondered what it felt like to *belong* to one place . . . to know all the street names, to recognize everyone at the checkout, to share a history.

Tucked in bed, she lay reading, a faint glow from her e-book illuminated her room. Natalie turned her head when Kelsey knocked. "Come in."

The door eased open a few inches. "One last thing . . . Kent's pride was wounded tonight. When you see him, try to let him down easy, especially if you think Seth's the real deal."

"Absolutely. I like Kent a lot, and this thing with Seth probably won't turn into anything."

Kelsey shook her head. "Yeah, right." Then pulled the door closed behind her.

Natalie shut her e-reader and lay in the dark. Her fingers drifted over her lips and neck, retracing every spot Seth had touched with his gentle, calloused hands.

SIX

Seth sat behind the solid desk that had belonged to his grandfather. The oak expanse grounded him. He'd come into work a couple of hours early with a plan to prioritize. That plan failed. He simply couldn't get anything done.

The shop was dark, and the window that separated his office from the workroom reflected his image. When he glanced up, the face staring back at him wasn't the man he'd ever intended to be.

Last night, he'd sunk into bed wearing a silly grin—eager to get Natalie in his arms again. Before dawn, he woke in a pool of cold sweat, remembering the gaping wound left by his failed marriage. He refused to make the same foolish mistake. Risking his heart for a woman who was destined to leave wasn't worth the pain.

The past few hours should have given him time to build his defenses. Yet, he'd spent those moments confused—staring at her home plans, torn between fast-tracking her project to get her out of Ashwood or slowing the pace to keep her around.

His crew—Carlos, Rick, and Kent—had already begun the home's outer shell. He still hadn't finalized the interior, because he couldn't find space for a dedicated dark room. Staring at her wish list, he compared it with his sketches—commercial kitchen, three-quarter bath, lofted bedroom, a spot for camera gear, and her one indulgence, a rooftop deck.

He didn't want to make promises he couldn't keep. The darkroom—and the relationship—had to go. The divide between wanting and having was too deep. They would both be happier if they faced that fact and split things now.

From his office, he heard and felt the massive saws at the opposite end of the old mill complex begin to hum. Soon everything he owned would start earning money.

He'd bought out the owners of the saw mill a few years ago. Renting the space for Whitewater Homes had kept the original owners solvent for a while, but they couldn't hang on. Jim Fraser eventually sold the unprofitable lumber mill to him. Seth made cuts, switched to specialty woods, and sweated out the downturn.

Fortunately, his food truck and tiny homes sales exploded, both products met the needs of people eager to survive with less. Three other massive buildings sat vacant on his property, waiting for someone to see potential in a huge industrial space.

Long after sunrise, the massive bay doors rumbled and flooded the shop with light. Temporarily blinded, Seth squinted at the outline of muscled bulk against the glare. Rick turned to chat with someone outside. When familiar curves appeared in silhouette, Seth's palms began to sweat and his heart rate sped. He resented the unchecked response his body had to Natalie.

Seeing her ignited a fresh need to possess someone he knew could not have, yet having this woman near also relaxed him. Maybe he could settle for keeping Natalie within sight but out of reach.

Rick spun toward the office and yelled, "Seth, come on out! Our *little latte* is here, and she brought coffee."

"Little latte?" Natalie's laugh traveled like music.

Rick took a step toward her. "Kent and I name all of the projects. I thought it was catchy." Standing in his office doorway, Seth grabbed the frame to hold himself in place.

"I like it!" she said to the muscular giant towering over her, then tilted her head to the side, considering the name permanently.

Natalie followed Rick inside and put two trays of drinks on a long counter near the door. She lifted her chin and smiled in Seth's direction. "I brought coffee . . . to do battle with the bear."

Seth didn't think she'd remember he wasn't a morning person. The fact that she did weakened his armor, and he stepped toward her. "I'll take one, and I promise to be nice."

Rick shadowed Natalie and asked, "Which one has the most sugar?"

"The white chocolate caramel latte." She pointed out the correct cup.

Rick tasted the sweet concoction. "Pretty damn good. Thanks, Nate."

"Nate?" she asked with a pleased grin.

"Kent and I discussed it—you're part of the crowd now and need a nick name. Nate. The owner of Little Latte."

Natalie giggled and her eyes shimmered. Seth fought the urge to claim those smiling lips and kiss her senseless. He needed a quick solution to keep her from burrowing deeper under his skin. Maybe he could find a cage to contain her magnetic draw.

"Let's set you up at my computer," Seth blurted, herding her into the smaller space. He was careful to keep his distance, no hand at the small of her back and no leaning over her at the keyboard.

He put her to work at the computer, compiling lists of favorites—flooring, countertops, and lighting—all the components she might like in her home.

After lunch, Seth finally relaxed. Natalie looked content and busy behind the sturdy walls of wood and glass. He could do this, no problem—he'd made it through half of the day without a taste of her lips.

Movement brought his eyes to his office where Natalie stood packing her things. Seth remained on task, and she left without saying goodbye. He'd met the challenge. Cool distance was far better than giving her the power to demolish his world.

"Got a minute?" Carlos asked before leaving for the day.

"Sure. Meet me in the office?" Seth led the way to the room where Natalie's perfume still lingered. A coffee cup sat on his desk with pink lipstick marks on the rim.

"How did your meeting go with our new client?" Seth asked. Carlos was the only man Seth had trusted with Natalie today.

"Good and bad I guess." Carlos leaned in, elbows to his knees. "I'd love to give her everything she wants in this home, but a darkroom won't fit, not with the commercial kitchen she has planned."

"Crap. Any creative ideas?"

"If we installed black-out shutters on every window the darkroom could share space with the kitchen."

"I don't know. What if someone knocks on her front door? I don't know anything about photo developing, but I think it has to be dark the entire time."

Carlos glanced at his notes. "Let me sleep on it. Damn, I wish I could see her darkroom. It's so much easier when I can visualize the space. If only there was a way to bring her darkroom here."

Seth grinned. "Not a bad idea." Without knowing it, Carlos had suggested the perfect solution to keep Natalie close and contained for the entire summer.

SEVEN

Kelsey held her front door open as Natalie rushed back inside to grab a jacket. "Are you sure I'm welcome at your family dinner? I feel like an intruder," she called from the living room.

"Of course, you're welcome. Mom's been dying to meet you. She'd kill me if I didn't bring you out to the lake. It's not a big deal. I always have dinner with Mom and Dad before my longer trips."

"You'll be gone for two weeks?" Natalie didn't know what to do with this unusual apprehension. Solitude had never bothered her before.

"Yeah. I leave after the beer festival. Are you still on for Saturday? Everyone is going."

Everyone except Seth. "Wouldn't miss it," Natalie answered past a tight smile. After this week's misery, she needed the distraction of cold beer and pounding music.

Each day at work, Seth had increased the distance. He kept her busy in his office, locked away from everyone except Carlos.

Watching Seth through the lens of his dusty office window was acute torture. If this lasted all summer, Whitewater would become an excruciating prison.

"Should we bring anything?" Natalie asked when her butt hit the seat of Kelsey's SUV.

"Mom asked me to stop at the farmers' market and pick up fresh strawberries."

"Perfect. I just love farmers' markets."

Kelsey chuckled. "Well, this is nothing like Pikes Place."

The parking lot was busier than Natalie expected. It took a while for Kels to find a spot. The moment Natalie escaped the SUV, delicious aromas of smoked meats, fresh bread, and coffee swirled together in the open air.

While Kelsey chose a flat of fresh-picked strawberries, the work of two local photographers pulled Natalie in for a closer inspection. She was surprised to find Amanda Michaels' name on a few of the stunning shots.

Kels ate a few berries while Nate chose a dozen cupcakes from the Goldfinch Bakery case.

"Another treat for work tomorrow?" Kels asked.

Natalie nodded. "Yeah, Kent and Rick love sweets." If Seth actually liked the treats, she'd never know it. That man buried all his emotions in a cave.

Nate spotted a table lined with bright flowers. "Wait a second. I want to buy something for your mom."

"Do you want me to pitch in?" Kels offered.

"No, I got it."

A blond girl with heavy eyeliner shifted their way. "Hi Kelsey." she said while completely ignoring Natalie.

"Hey, Annie. Have you met Natalie? She just moved here from Seattle. She's staying at my place all summer."

Annie's hazel eyes narrowed. "What do you think of Ashwood? I bet a city-girl like you must find our small-town terribly dull."

Natalie winced but decided to fight the nasty blonde with sugar-sweet kindness. "Ashwood is fab so far. Your flowers are simply gorgeous. Could you please ring up this beautiful planter for me?" Holding her grin in place, Natalie tilted her head and let the syrupy performance drip.

"No problem." Annie's pinched lips blanched white as she checked the price on the basket. "Thanks," she mumbled after snatching the cash from Natalie's hand.

Arms loaded with food and flowers, Natalie controlled her laughter until she and Kels were in the parking lot. "What was the deal with that girl's attitude?"

"Not attitude. Jealousy. Annie's had a crush on Seth forever."

"Seriously? She shouldn't be bothered—it was only one dance. And since that night he's been . . ." A long sigh revealed her disappointment to her roommate.

"He's been what? Hey, are you okay?"

"I'm fine. All week, Seth's been acting like nothing happened. I don't know what I did wrong."

"Shit, I'm sorry. I know it's not you. Seth has a wicked private streak and his divorce complicates things. Even Amanda complains about his distance from their family."

"Divorce?" Natalie stared off into the distance while Kels arranged everything in the rear of the SUV.

She looked back when Kelsey slammed the hatch with extra force. "He and Desiree married young. And his ex still comes around. I've heard rumors they still hit the sheets."

Natalie trembled. "Crap. I refuse to be the other woman. My mom put up with that from my dad, and I'm not going there."

Heading north out of town, Kels pressed the accelerator and let the miserable newsflash continue. "There's something else you should know."

"Why does there have to be more?" Natalie drew in a long slow breath and waited.

"Seth never dates locals. I know he's had girlfriends, but no one from Ashwood."

"It doesn't matter. I'm not local, but I'm also not a doormat. Seth can find someone else to torture."

"That's probably for the best." The playlist Kelsey flicked on left Natalie to focus on vistas she'd like to photograph instead of the man who haunted her dreams.

The pine trees thinned, revealing a deep blue mountain lake. When the gravel road split, Kels veered left and halted beneath a massive timber gate. Towering above, a heavy crossbeam held a metal forged trout wrapped around a large letter F.

Natalie's mouth dropped open as she took in the grandeur of the rustic *Fisher* family crest. "Wow, that's amazing. Are you famous or something?"

Kels laughed. "No. Not at all. Mom had a local craftsman design it for Dad's fiftieth birthday."

Pulling through, a field stretched from tree line to tree line where Natalie counted five horses grazing on lush spring grass. At the center of the velvet lawn, a two-story log house faced the glittering lake, encircled by a wide welcoming porch.

"Come on, let's give Mom her flowers and take the strawberries inside. Kent should be here soon." Natalie's mood brightened at the mention of his name. Kent was so easy to like.

The door swung open and Kelsey's mom rushed outside. The resemblance struck Natalie immediately. Mother and daughter both had the same white-blonde hair, though her mother's had a touch of silver at the temples.

Natalie hung back until Kels yelled, "Mom, look! Nate brought flowers."

"The flowers are beautiful Thank you."

"You're welcome, Mrs. Fisher."

"Please call me Mary. Dale, come and meet Kelsey's roommate."

Kelsey's dad jogged down the steps, gave his daughter a quick hug, then took the flowers. With her hands empty, Natalie found herself trapped in Mary's hug. "Welcome to our home. I hope you love it here in Ashwood."

"I already do." She followed the family into the kitchen and was admiring the home when Kent burst through the back door, completely at ease.

"Hey, Dale. Mary . . . thanks for the invite. Damn, I'm starved." He planted a kiss on Mary's cheek and she laughed.

"Follow me outside. I haven't seen enough of you," Dale said. "Did you catch the end of last night's game?"

Kent snagged two beers from the refrigerator and followed Dale—his arms laden with a platter of raw steaks. All Natalie heard before they closed the door was, "Twelve innings."

"That turd didn't even say hello," Kelsey growled and tried not to laugh.

"It's okay," Mary said as she rinsed cherry tomatoes to top the salad. "Dale's been talking about seeing Kent all day. Kelsey, why don't you show Natalie the place. And tell Dad to wait about fifteen minutes before putting on the steaks."

Kelsey grabbed a tomato and popped it in her mouth. "Are you sure you don't want some help?"

"Not until clean up," Mary added with a grin.

Kels groaned, grabbed a couple carrots from the refigerator, led Natalie out of the house and aimed for the field. A large black horse with a flash of white on his head wandered over to the fence. He snorted and waited for a treat.

"Do you want to feed him?" Kelsey asked.

"Not this time." Natalie giggled when searching lips snatched the carrot from Kelsey's fingers. A stamping hoof scared her a little, and Nate didn't mind when Kelsey turned toward Lake Osprey. Green, red, and gold, the rocky shore sparkled in the afternoon sun, where Natalie peeled off her shoes and tested the glacier-fed water.

Ankle deep in the lake, Natalie turned back and surveyed the barn, cabins, and boathouse. It wasn't showy, just spacious and inviting. "How could you ever move from this place?"

Kels chose a flat stone and skipped it across the surface of the lake. "Privacy. I'm the wild one in the family. Mom and Dad know, but I'm not going to throw it in their faces, either."

"You don't seem that wild to me. I like your independence."

"Give me time. Sometime soon, I'll do something stupid and piss you off. Dad says I was born without a filter. I haven't found a guy who can tolerate my attitude or the space I need, so I don't date much. Instead, I mess around." Natalie sensed a longing there, but Kelsey's dad cut off her next question with an ear-ringing whistle.

Over dinner, Natalie basked in the warmth of belonging and tolerated a pang of loneliness. This tight family had her missing Grandpa Pete.

After cleaning up, Kent pulled out a canoe while Kelsey stayed on the deck to visit with her parents.

"I'll steady the boat while you take the seat in front, just stay low and in the center," Kent instructed.

The canoe wobbled a bit, and she screamed. "Hey! Shouldn't you be in front? I don't know how to drive one of these things."

"Don't worry, it's cool." He chuckled. "I actually steer from back here, like a rudder on a boat."

"I'm such an idiot." Natalie giggled as he pushed away from shore and hopped fluidly into the canoe.

"You can't be an expert at something you've never tried. I don't know a damn thing about photography."

"I guess you're right—thanks, Kent, you always make me feel good."

"I have plenty of ways to make you *feel great* . . . if you'll let me." Kent had offered everything she thought she was looking for in a summer fling—until she met Seth.

Natalie stopped paddling, placed her oar on the bottom of the canoe, and spun slowly to face him in her seat, knowing this man deserved the truth. "I like you, a lot, but I don't want to take advantage . . . especially after how this week turned out."

"Because of Seth?" Kent dug the paddle into the water and the boat took on extra speed.

"Well, yes."

"But he's trapped you every day in his office and left you home alone every night. Do you have plans with him this weekend?"

"No. He's not really talked to me much . . . except about the tiny house. Anyway, I'm excited about going to the river with everyone."

"You see? That's exactly what I'm talking about. What Seth's putting you through isn't right. He's not into relationships. Don't commit yourself to him."

She couldn't think of anything to say that didn't sound pathetic, desperate, or lonely, so she shrugged and said nothing.

"Natalie, listen. If he keeps you dangling all weekend, just give me a chance. No pressure. No strings. Just fun." Kent turned up the wattage of his hypnotic smile and Natalie was drawn to the light.

She gave him a small nod. "A chance. I guess I can do that. If Seth hasn't talked to me by Monday, I'm yours."

When Kent's eyes flared and darkened, she giggled. Natalie hadn't meant her words to sound quite like *that*.

***

Kent lit the fire down by the lake. Kelsey couldn't sit still and ran into the house to grab marshmallows. With both arms wrapped snug around her legs, Natalie tried to stay warm. "Kels said you sort of grew up here, with the Fisher's."

Kent shifted closer, his arms twitched, almost reaching out to touch her, but he didn't act on the impulse. "It was just Dad and me. He had to be gone a lot, driving longhaul, so the Fishers took me in when Dad was on the road."

Natalie sighed and the flickering firelight illuminated her sympathy.

"Don't feel sorry for me," Kent warned with a hint of humor. "Growing up in Ashwood was awesome—hiking, fishing, and rafting as much as I wanted. I had freedom and managed not to kill myself, no matter how many stupid stunts I pulled. I've been lucky."

"I guess you're right. Kelsey's family and this place are amazing. Who wouldn't want all this?"

"I owe them everything," he mumbled. He didn't bother to mask the relief on his face when Kelsey walked up with metal skewers and a bag of marshmallows.

Natalie, flanked by Kels and Kent, warmed her legs by the fire while Kent twirled a marshmallow on a long stick, toasting it carefully.

"Damn," he muttered when it blazed. He brought it close to his face blowing it out. Kent pulled the blackened marshmallow off the stick ready to toss it into the fire. Before he could chuck it, Nate grabbed his hand.

"I like the burnt ones," she said stealing it from him. The sticky confection found a spot on her tongue. She closed her eyes savoring the toasty-sweet taste. "Yummy. Perfect."

Kent cleared his throat when Natalie licked the last of the gooey marshmallow from her fingers. He squirmed next to her, plunged his hand into the bag of marshmallows, and chose two, stabbing the white treats with the skewer. Natalie grinned, and tried to ignore the sizzling awareness bouncing from him.

As he balanced his stick higher over the fire, Kelsey's phone vibrated in her pocket. After answering, she passed it to Natalie.

"Who is it?" Nate asked, confused.

"Seth."

Her jaw clenched as she took the phone. "Don't you have my number?" Irritation punctuated her words, and he apologized, adding that he'd already tried her phone.

"Well, I'm at the Fisher's—I guess I don't have a signal on the lake."

Natalie wandered away from the fire and into the shadows to talk privately. She paced farther away, but the lake bounced Kelsey and Kent's conversation her direction. Natalie listened to Seth but couldn't completely block the words she would rather not hear.

"Are Nate and Seth the real deal?" Kent mumbled quietly as Nate meandered into the dark.

"I don't think so." Kels whispered. "She complained that he kept her at a distance all week."

"You know I'm better for her."

"Remember, at the end of summer, she moves on. No matter what happens, don't get too attached."

Sparks flew when a log shifted on the fire. "I won't. Seth's just stringing Nate along. It pisses me off. What if he hurts her?"

Kels glanced over her shoulder and Natalie spun away. Still, Kelsey's voice carried, "Can you really guarantee she'd be safer with you?"

"I'd be willing to try."

"Watch yourself. Seth's the one who cuts your checks."

"Fuck the job. Fuck Seth. I don't need him."

"Stop it. He's more to you than a boss—Seth's one of your closest friends.

Natalie turned as Kent flicked his uneaten marshmallow from the end of the skewer directly into the flames, sparking a sugary blaze.

When she sat down again, she slumped against Kelsey. "He only called to go over some things about my house. I told him I couldn't stop by Whitewater tomorrow. He asked where I was going, so I lied and told him I had plans with you."

Kelsey put her arm around Nate. "Good idea. You can come to Hood River with me tomorrow. I have to stop by work and take care of a few things at Venture."

"Do you think Hood River would have a place where I could shop for a bikini? I'd like something new for Saturday.

"Hell yes," Kelsey said with a grin.

63

EIGHT

Kent tossed a pink cardboard box on the counter next to the coffee maker. The impact popped the lid open. Seth's eyes cut from the box to Kent and then back. "You brought cupcakes?"

"Nate asked me to bring them in. She picked them up yesterday, but for some reason didn't feel like coming to Whitewater today."

Kent's pointed glare, Seth knew, was well deserved. "What? Were you at Kelsey's?" he asked while struggling to hide his jealousy.

"Yeah. I'm with Nate all the time. It's not like she has something better to do."

Seth spun away from the taunting. Was Kent challenging him to spend more time with Natalie? If anything, Kent should be happy she was available.

Her absence was as distracting as her presence. She could be anywhere—at home, behind her camera, in her truck—and not knowing drove him insane.

To add to his irritation, Seth noticed that Kent seemed restless today, like a kid waiting for Christmas. Fine. If Natalie moved on to the biggest player in town, that was her problem, not his.

Seth paced the shop floor, circling the footprint of her home. Only the metal skeleton was in place. He visualized the loft, the rooftop deck, and the commercial kitchen. But the issues surrounding her darkroom remained. Until Carlos found a solution, Seth refused to move on with the build.

In the dark of a nearly empty storage room, Seth stared at his phone, tempted to apologize for being such a dick last night. She'd been at the Fisher's place when he reached out to Kelsey, desperate to track Natalie down.

While they talked, he had stepped out onto his deck, and studied their distant campfire from his perch above the lake. That golden point of light in the distance was close to her, but she'd stepped away from its heat. He knew, because he heard the shiver in her voice.

Jealous, Seth had lashed out on the phone and warned Natalie to stay away from Kent. Trapping her pain in a quick inhale, she'd quietly whispered into the phone, "Why do you care? We're not anything more than a few stolen kisses."

Seth hated himself for hurting her. He only wanted to make promises to Natalie he knew he could keep.

***

"Turquoise?" Natalie asked while craning her neck to enhance her view. She smiled, loving the way these bikini bottoms clung to her butt.

"Please. You have to buy it," Kelsey insisted. "Even if you keep a T-shirt on all day, the outline will drive men mad."

"But it's so little," Natalie tried to tuck her breast under the tiny triangle of fabric, but her curves escaped, as the string bikini was designed to do.

Kelsey stood back for a better look and nodded. "It's only small where it should be."

"You're right, I'll do it."

While Natalie changed, she called through the dressing room door. "How about margaritas? My treat."

"Just one. I'm driving."

Before they went to the restaurant, Kelsey dragged her into Venture. The warehouse was part sports gear storage, part office, and part gym.

Foreign in every way, Natalie struggled to fit in with the athletic men and women who occupied so much of Kelsey's time. Natalie shrank as Kelsey transformed into a high-octane version of herself. Driven, louder, but chill, she joked with the guys and yanked Natalie into the chaotic office to meet Sig, her boss.

The owner of Venture offered Natalie a spot on Kelsey's next river rafting trip, free of charge. Nate's open-mouthed shock and shaking head coaxed an explosion of booming laughter from Sig.

"Don't you trust me? Kels asked.

"I do, but whitewater rafting's never been on my bucket list."

Laughing again, Kels vowed to get Natalie on the water as they left Sig's office.

***

Carlos ducked his head in Seth's office before he left Whitewater Friday night. "Hey—do you want me to shut off the lights on the work floor?"

"Yeah. That'd be great, thanks." In a dark mood, Seth turned back to his computer, ready to bury himself in design work.

"Seth?"

He tipped his head away from the screen and met his friend's wisdom-filled eyes. Carlos had three kids and a wife who had battled cancer and survived. A life filled with greater purpose.

"It's not too late," Carlos said, evenly.

Seth's brows furrowed in question.

"She's only waiting for you to make up your mind. You haven't lost Natalie. But she doesn't deserve this test you've designed"

"Test?" Confused, Seth tilted back in his chair.

"Natalie is nothing like Desiree."

Seth's lips tightened, refusing to answer. He never talked about his failed marriage. Carlos knew that, everyone did.

His friend straightened from the spot where he leaned against the door. "Natalie's just a woman, searching for something she hasn't found. What if she's searching for you?" Carlos waited for his words to hit home, until Seth gave him a quick nod.

On a huff, Carlos pulled the office door shut. Lights flicked off across the shop, an engine hummed, and his truck drove away.

Seth wondered if Carlos was right. If Natalie was willing to put up with his shit, then why was he keeping her at this frigid distance?

***

With shopping bags weighing down both arms, Natalie staggered into the house and tossed everything onto the center of her bed. "Thank you for the day of shopping therapy."

"My pleasure," Kels flopped across the end of Nate's bed. "I can't wait to see you strut around in those shorts and that bikini tomorrow."

"With my pale skin? This ginger is allergic to direct sunlight."

"I have the perfect solution. Sunscreen, lathered on thoroughly by Kent's expert hands."

Natalie waved her hand in front of her blushing face, dismissing Kelsey's suggestion. She wanted to give Seth two more days to figure out what he was missing. Something intriguing still sizzled between them, but Seth was scared.

"Are you ready for a day of bands, beer, and hot men in the sun?"

"I will be, but those margaritas wiped me out. Do you mind if I skip The Northside tonight? Nothing sounds better than a hot bath and going to bed early."

"Whatever you want. There's vanilla sugar bubble bath in the cabinet."

"My favorite. Tell everyone hi for me."

"I will. You'll see them all tomorrow."

All but Seth.

After Kelsey left, Natalie selected a mellow playlist, clipped her red waves up, and grabbed her book.

The heat, water, and sweet vanilla bubbles cured the remnants of a lingering headache. Settled in for a satisfying read, she wiggled her pink-painted toes in the suds, thankful for this old house and its oversized bathtub.

***

Seth ignored gnawing hunger while he reconciled another month of expenses. A knock on the outside window shocked him from his haze. Desiree's face, staring in from the shadows, rattled his nerves. She tested the handle and pushed the door open. Seth clenched his jaw while his ex-wife strutted into his space.

"Another Friday night and here you sit." She flopped onto the leather couch, put up her feet, and settled in. "I was driving by and saw the light. You know, I'm actually surprised to find you here. The rumor mill told me you had a new squeeze. I came to town to see her for myself."

Fuck, he didn't need this right now. "Desiree, go away. Go hang out with Paige. Or even better, pick up a tourist at the bar."

She stared at him evenly. "I'm not staying . . . unless you want to put that desk to good use."

He shook his head but didn't speak.

"Never mind. I only stopped by to talk, and I'm not leaving until we put a few rules back in place." Desiree spun one of her bracelets on her thin wrist, waiting for Seth to respond.

"Rules? When have you cared about rules?"

"When you broke one. You've never flaunted a woman in Ashwood."

"Flaunted? Desiree, we're divorced. Why do you care?"

"I'm not jealous. I don't give a flying fuck about where you put your dick. But I won't have my nose rubbed in it."

"Shit, Desiree. I live in Ashwood. I'm bound to find someone at some point. What do you expect me to do? Move?"

"No, but I'm warning you. If you break your half of the bargain, I'll break mine." She inspected her long, manicured fingernails, waiting for Seth to snap at the dangling bait.

"What bargain?"

Her shiny lip-gloss grin widened. "We've always had an unspoken agreement to keep our *hometown hook-ups* private. Obviously."

Desiree's gaze sharpened until he figured it out. Seth's eyebrows shot up. "Which one of my friends has been between those legs?" he growled.

Her head tipped and her eyes flicked to the dark workroom floor, but she didn't answer. Seth knew she was enjoying the guessing game, but he still couldn't resist her barbed lure.

"Did you sleep with Kent?"

She leveled a stare. "As if."

Was that disappointment he witnessed in her eyes? Desiree had probably tried with Kent and failed. "Carlos? Shit, he's married."

She rolled her eyes and huffed, waiting for him to guess again.

"Rick." Seth gritted the name past clenched teeth.

Her finger tapped the tip of her nose. "Bingo. We have a winner," she said on a mocking laugh.

Seth spread both hands wide open on the surface of his desk. "Desiree. We're done. Get out of my office and stay out of my life."

"Fine. Whatever. But consider the consequences. If you fuck this girl and parade her fat ass around town, I'll humiliate you. I'll find a way to spill the details about how rough you like it in bed. You know I can."

NINE

Bubbles mounded in white pillows around her, soothing every frayed nerve right to the tips of her toes, at least until the moment her phone rang. Natalie glanced at his name then let the call go to voicemail. Seth wasn't allowed to ruin this moment of perfection.

She extended her foot, twisted the knob, and a little more hot water spilled into her bath. A text buzzed. Proud of herself she ignored the message until another text followed.

"Damn. Now he's just being annoying." She didn't bother to read any of his messages before tapping the screen to return his call.

"Natalie, did you read my apology?" he blurted the moment she answered.

"Apology? No, I didn't bother. I'm just calling to stop you from blowing up my phone." Natalie's finger hovered over the red button.

"Tell me where you are—I need to talk to you," he said.

Her breasts tingled. *Damn. Why did it turn her on when Seth was pushy?* Natalie inched further into the warm water. Her knee caught the bottle of bubble bath, and it toppled in with a splash.

"Are you washing dishes?" he asked.

"No . . . I'm in . . ." Natalie blushed crimson and her nipples peaked.

"Oh. Damn. You're home. In the bath. I'll be right over."

"No, no, no," she said to dead air. He ruined everything. And now, she was all hot, wet, and tingly thinking about that primitive man speeding down the road, headed straight for her door.

She pulled the plug, dried off, and ran to her bedroom. The shopping bags were still scattered all over her bed. After stuffing them into the closet, she pulled on the ugliest baggiest sweats she could find.

A loud knock rattled the front door. "Crappity-crap . . . What did he do? Fly?" She yelped when the front door burst open.

***

"It wasn't locked." He struggled to breathe and took in her details. The entire house smelled like her sweet vanilla skin. She'd clipped her hair in a messy array and exposed her edible neck. Her oversized sweatshirt, fallen off one shoulder, revealed the fact that she hadn't put on a bra. Maybe she'd dressed so fast, she'd left off her panties, too.

He took a single step forward. "I'm sorry." He pulled in his lips when she didn't take a step back.

"Sorry for?" Her gaze demanded an answer. He loved that she wasn't going to let him off easily.

On another step toward her, he confessed, "For keeping you locked in my office . . . where I could see but not touch you."

Natalie's hands hit her hips. "And what else?"

Seth couldn't keep from smiling—she looked so damn cute when she was mad. "And for pushing you away. And for pretending like our first night together didn't matter."

Her teeth scraped her bottom lip. "It mattered."

"So much," Seth whispered. He closed the space between them and reached forward to stroke her jaw with the pad of his thumb.

Those first kisses, a week ago, had communicated how much he wanted her. Tonight, his lips had to demonstrate how sorry he was and how much he cared. Seth approached her carefully and claimed a tentative taste. He pulled away, giving her a moment to choose.

"You're so perfect, and I'm such a mess," he murmured before tilting his head again.

Her moan pushed the kiss from chaste to steady simmer. Pearled nipples pressed against his chest and notched the heat several degrees higher. Seth struggled to maintain a measured pace. His hands inched beneath the hem of her sweatshirt and found velvety skin, still warm and damp from her bath.

"I need to touch you, please" Natalie whispered against his mouth and tugged his shirt from his jeans. With one hand, he pulled the shirt up and off, and she smiled before running her fingertips over the dusting of hair on his chest. Her fingers trembled as she detailed his chiseled contours, drawing a line from one quarter-sized nipple to the other.

The rise and fall of his chest accelerated beneath her fingertips. Seth eased away to remove her bulky sweatshirt. His hungry eyes mapped each tempting freckle on her pale skin. "Natalie, words can't describe your beauty. I honestly can't breathe."

A crimson blush spread over her body before she bent forward to flick his nipple with her tongue.

Shattered by her exploration, Seth whispered, Bedroom or couch?" Her choice would dictate his pace.

"Kelsey might come home . . . so, bedroom," she said, her eyes dark with need. Lifting her with both hands, her warm breasts flattened against his bare chest as she straddled his hips.

"When will Kelsey come home?" he asked between kisses.

Natalie giggled. "I don't know, but I promise to be quiet."

"I don't want you quiet."

Never breaking contact, with her legs wrapped around his waist, Seth sank onto the bed. Tempted by her full lips, he thoroughly explored her with nips and a plunging tongue.

Natalie moaned, hungry for a more complete invasion. With shaking fingers, she slid her hands between them and popped the top button of his jeans. His larger fingers covered hers, halting her progress.

"Stand in front of me Natalie," he commanded.

She wound her legs off him and stood completely still while he slipped the sweatpants from her curves. He'd guessed accurately—no panties. Grasping her bare hips, Seth encouraged her to move one-step back, giving him room to drop to his knees at her feet. Not a position he normally took, but he had to worship this woman with his tongue.

Warm vanilla and her arousal invaded his senses. One strong hand cupped her ass. He pulled her forward and blew on the trim red hair that covered her sex, before parting the wet temptation with the tip of his tongue.

Natalie moaned when his touch invaded her hot wet center from behind.

"Ohhh," she exhaled as her hips canted, increasing his penetration. A second finger slipped in to move with her natural rhythm as she rode his hand. Either way she was rewarded—forward, her clit met his tongue, and back his invasion filled her drenched center.

Natalie gasped while attempting to find just the right slant to maximize the contact. Reading her, he angled his head and sucked hard on her pert bundle of nerves.

Thighs quaking, her coiling orgasm nearly brought Natalie to her knees as she detonated, flooding his fingers with her arousal. Seth supported her through the long, satisfying release and eased her gently to the bed. As she descended, his lips peppered her mound, stomach, and thighs with dozens of soothing kisses.

Taking extra time, he found a spot just below her belly button that coaxed her legs apart. He kissed his way back to her mouth, searching for freckles to taste along the way. Seth settled his hips between her thighs and lowered his head, his lips meeting hers in a tender, Natalie-flavored kiss.

The rough material of his jeans drew a gasp from her throat as he grazed against her sensitized flesh. He lifted his hips to remove the harsh pressure. The space gave Natalie room to reach down and open his jeans. "I need you to fill me," Natalie whispered.

With a nod, he moved to the foot of the bed, slid his jeans and boxers off, and stood with his erection jutting from his body. After locating a condom, he tore open the square package. Natalie's eyes were dark with anticipation, and perhaps a little concern. Watching him roll on the condom, she sucked in a breath and held it.

He balanced his weight on his arms, which flexed as she stroked his corded muscles with her fingers. Sleek and smooth, his broad tip teased her entrance. Wrapping her legs around his hips, she applied encouraging pressure to his muscular ass, drawing him forward.

Carefully watching to measure her reaction, Seth slowly eased inside, stretching her to accommodate him, and she moaned.

"Mm, sweetness, are you alright?" he asked.

She nodded, pivoting her hips to encourage his pace. Short measured thrusts pushed forward until he sheathed himself fully inside her heat.

Pulling almost completely out, he slid inside again, and inhaled her pleasured gasp. Retreat, then lunge, retreat again. The slow climb filmed his body with sweat as he struggled to prolong her bliss. When she adjusted the curve of her back, her legs quaked.

"Natalie, you're so tight, so wet, I'm not going to last." Seth's balls tightened. Her breath held. Her channel pulsed. "Come for me," he growled, thrusting even deeper.

With a keening cry, her explosive orgasm pulsated around his cock, increasing the tight sensation. He followed her, hips plunging, shouting his release.

Her body took everything from him, and he swallowed her still frantic pants with an immersive kiss. As she quieted, Seth took his weight on his forearms. Still hungry for her, he licked a salty path along her clavicle, savoring her flavor.

"Amazing," she whispered, while her fingertips painted the muscles of his back with her light touch. He hated that moment when he had to pull out of her warmth to dispose of the condom.

He asked if she wanted something to drink. "Water would be perfect." Keeping eyes on him, she rolled onto her side in a cat-like satisfied stretch.

Seth smiled, slid on his jeans and zipped, but didn't fasten the button. He still hadn't had enough.

After stopping in the bathroom, he wandered into the kitchen to grab a beer for himself and water for Natalie. Through the front windows, bright headlights panned like searchlights. Tires crunched gravel as Kelsey pulled up to the house.

Seth brought Natalie her water but found her already sleeping, curled, a thin blanket tucked under her chin. He wrapped her in the comforter, put on his shirt and went into the living room as Kels came through the door.

Her grip tightened on the knob the moment her eyes connected. "Seth? I didn't expect you. Where's Nate?"

"Sleeping."

"Huh. Do you have time to talk? Or did you plan to stay tonight?"

He should have known Kelsey wouldn't let him slip away. "Just let me say goodnight. I'll be right back," he said on a turn toward the bedrooms.

Natalie barely moved when he kissed her.

"I'll call you tomorrow," Seth whispered, and she stirred.

At the last moment, he sent a quick text in case she didn't remember his goodbye. *I'm tempted to stay, but you deserve to sleep. I'll call tomorrow.*

On the couch with a beer, Kelsey studied him as he sat. He nabbed his open beer from the coffee table and swallowed the cool drink.

Kelsey took her time, making him wait. "So, it looks like you patched things up?"

"I apologized and Natalie forgave me," he admitted, still not believing he'd managed to win her back.

"What are your plans?"

He bristled but understood Kelsey's concern. "Plans take time. We haven't progressed that far yet."

"Here's the deal." Kels spun the beer bottle between her hands. "Elsa asked me to keep an eye on Natalie. You're making my job difficult."

"I get that."

"She's trying to move past losing her grandfather and figure out her future."

"And I'm happy to help. I'm building her home."

"The last thing she needs is a messy breakup. Can you keep this summer thing casual?"

Deep down, Seth didn't believe Natalie did casual. "I don't plan to hurt her." In fact, when she left, he figured he'd be the one hurting.

Kelsey shook her head. "Could you at least try not to be a setback. We all want the best for her."

"We?"

"Me, Elsa, and Kent."

"She doesn't know Kent that well. What stake does he have in her future?"

"Kent was helping more than hurting. So far I can't say the same about you."

Seth's hard swallow pushed against his pride. "There's one person you failed to mention. Natalie. This is *her* future, after all."

"I just have to know that you won't stand in her way," Kelsey said with her typical blunt concern.

"I've never stood in anyone's way. I didn't stop Desiree when she left for Portland, and I won't stop Natalie when she decides to leave."

"Good. And thanks, Seth. Sorry about bitching you out, but I'm taking off on a trip next week and needed this settled before I left."

Seth absorbed Kelsey's concern. Beer in hand, he walked to her kitchen and dumped the rest down the drain. They exchanged quick nods on his way out the door.

Climbing into his truck, he promised himself one thing. He wouldn't tether himself too tightly to Natalie. She was just another person who couldn't wait to leave Ashwood behind.

TEN

Waking up sporting wood was not unusual. Seth lost himself in the memory of Natalie's tight heat. Rock-hard, he took himself in hand and stroked. With her image on his mind, his explosive orgasm took hold too quickly. His non-existent self-control irritated him.

The release should have taken the edge off, but Natalie continued to invade his thoughts. Hungry, he dug into his fridge and spotted a six-pack of Mosquito's IPA next to the eggs. His cousin's beer enhanced his obsession when he pictured Natalie at Rhythm and Brews.

It would be sweltering on the river. What would she be wearing? Maybe a tiny pair of cut-off shorts and a bikini top. Seth wondered if Kent's hands would be the ones to smooth coconut-scented sunscreen over her pale skin.

Sitting in his home office, he checked emails, but work was a thin distraction. After a cold shower, he found himself with damp hair sitting in the cab of his truck. *This woman is so damn distracting—I'll shoot myself with a nail gun if I go into the shop.*

When he set out, he pretended to have no particular destination in mind. Within the hour, he ground across the gravel lot at the county fairgrounds, skirting the wide Columbia River. Seth walked into the Rhythm and Brews festival determined to locate Natalie.

Under a canopy of cottonwoods, party tents overflowed with people devouring grilled burgers, bratwurst, and drinking Northwest craft beers. While some soaked in the summer rays, others sought the shade beneath the tents. Four music stages featured bands playing to pulsing crowds of tanned beer drinkers.

White tents, emblazoned with brewery banners, whipped in the breeze. Seth spotted the Mosquito logo halfway down the line. Wade brewed his award-winning beer with hops grown on a family-owned farm in eastern Washington.

Seth waved over a line of heads. "Hey, Wade! How are you holding up in this heat?"

His cousin filled another plastic cup with experienced speed. "Get your ass in here and pour!"

Seth slipped behind the counter. He grabbed a towel, wiped down the foam-sloshed surface, then went to work pulling out stacks of plastic cups for the next round of guests.

"Thanks, we're slammed. Are you here with family or friends?"

"On my own, for now. Have you seen anyone from town?" Seth bent to help one of Wade's employees switch out a keg.

"That guy who works for you stopped by, Kent I think, and he was with Kelsey. There was a cute little redhead with them I'd never met before."

Wade rambled about seeing their younger cousins, Jasmine and Rose, while Seth continued his visual quest for a cute redhead. His mind was as solid as the foam on the beer in his hand.

Wade snapped him with the end of a towel. "Why are you so distracted? Late night? Did Desiree show up needing a little something?"

A sharp glance shut *that* topic down. "Hell no. I'm done spending time with my ex." Shit, Desiree seemed to be feeding the rumor mill. He shook his head and searched the crowd again. If the pack from Ashwood had already stopped by, he'd better move on. "Hey, it looks like you have this under control. Mind if I catch you later?"

"Go. Have fun. And hey, thanks for helping out. You know where to find me." Wade turned his focus to a customer, another solid fan of his famous IPA.

***

Seth questioned his sanity as he passed tent after tent. Searching for anyone in this crowd had him feeling like a fool. He crossed the lawn to explore a mob of sweaty, sunbaked dancers fronting the main stage.

Before Seth reached the throng, Kent and Rick spotted him. Kent's determined steps closed the distance quickly, but Rick hung back. The dark scowl on Kent's face parted people blocking his path. Only one thing could have provoked that angry glint in his eyes. Kelsey had probably spilled everything about last night.

Seth backpedaled, preparing for the inevitable confrontation, creating space for the man to have his say.

With fiery rage in his eyes, Kent's words burst ahead of him. "Where the hell do you get off snagging Natalie? Just a couple days ago, you treated her like shit. Were you just waiting to get her alone before moving in for the kill?"

Hands held open, chest high, Seth jabbed in a word. "Whoa, Kent. What gives you th—?"

Rick moved in, grabbed Kent, trying to help. "Calm down. Do you want to get us kicked out?"

Kent jerked his arm away from Rick and spun back toward Seth. "On the ride down, Natalie had *taken* written all over her."

"She *is* taken . . . Natalie's *mine*." Seth cut in with whispered intensity. He stepped back, planting his feet preparing for anything.

Kent's neck glowed red, but he stared at the ground attempting to calm himself. He paced a wide circle and laid in again. "You don't understand. Her grandpa was all she had. Nate has about as much family as I do, and that's none worth having."

Seth raked his hands through his hair. "I know."

Kent stepped away and then spun back. "You don't know shit! When you look at Nate, all you see is a piece of ass. As soon as she leaves Ashwood, you'll keep right on banging Desiree."

Trying to stop his friend, Rick fisted a handful of Kent's shirt and yanked him away from a mass of interested onlookers. The three men faced each other again behind a row of trailers that were serving burgers. Greasy smoke billowed around them.

Seth wouldn't put up with any more of Kent's shit. "You've stepped way out of line."

Using both palms square on Seth's chest, Kent shoved him against the side of the burger trailer. A chorus of voices inside told the brawling men to move on.

"Damn it, Kent. Cool off!" Rick yelled. Kent bent in half, his hands on his knees, breathing hard.

"What did Natalie say to you?" Seth asked through gritted teeth.

"Nothing!" Chest puffed, Kent stood and snarled, "She didn't tell Kels shit. Knowing you, it's only a matter of time before she's trussed up in your office. I could practically see your stinging handprint on her ass right through her shorts."

No one talked about Natalie like this. "Enough!" Stepping into his fluid swing, Seth's right hook hurled Kent onto his back. He sprawled, limbs flying across the dusty ground.

A solid human wall, Rick stepped between them. "Seth. Dude, you've got to back off. Leave. I'll take care of Kent."

Seth pivoted around Rick and pointed at the jerk on the ground. "Don't talk shit about her. What happens between Natalie and me is private." Rage simmered below the surface. Seth struggled to maintain control. He turned from the pair with no destination in mind.

First Wade, now Kent—these details about his private sex life could only have one source—Desiree. She must be hard at work spreading her venom.

Perched over Kent, Rick offered his hand to lift him from the dust. Kent refused. "Back off. I don't need your goddamn help."

"Fine. Stay in the dirt until you find your sanity." Rick abandoned Kent in the shadow of the food vendors and jogged to catch Seth.

Still simmering with anger, Seth let his frustration fly. "Rick. I need to know . . . how many times did you fuck my ex-wife?"

Their forward momentum stopped. Rick raked his hands through his short-cropped hair. "I'm sorry."

"How many times?" He trapped anger between his teeth and waited for an answer.

"Just twice."

"When."

"Shit, you don't need to know that. Damn it. It won't happen again."

Seth just stared.

"It was a few months ago. Like I said, it will never happen again."

A careful study of Rick's face showed shame and something more. Pity. Rick hadn't been the only one.

***

Leaving Rick, Seth took a lap around the grounds and headed back to his pickup. Keys in hand, he lost the battle. Damn it, he couldn't leave her alone, not when the woman haunting him was so close.

Calmed by time and about a mile of rapid pacing, an invisible force drew him toward the main stage. It was strange how easily he found her. She shared a blanket with his cousins, reclined and radiant in the shimmering heat.

Seth wove toward them dodging through the sea of people, lawn chairs, and coolers. Jasmine spotted him first. "Hey, Seth, come sit with us." She patted a vacant spot on the blanket. "I can't believe we ran into you." The twins grinned and traded a knowing glance.

Natalie lay reclined on her back, eyes closed, her hands cradling her head. Her pale blue eyes popped open as soon as Jasmine spoke. She stretched, coming back from a sun-induced coma.

"Don't move, Natalie, you look too comfortable." Seth slowly drank in her languid body with his eyes, absorbing her curves as he claimed a spot on the blanket next to her.

She didn't move, only spoke. "It's the sun. We don't get super-warm days like this in Seattle."

After another song, the band wrapped up their set and announced a twenty-minute break. Sound techs swarmed the stage to switch out stacks of amps and gear for the next act.

Jasmine and Rose stood. "Can we bring back anything?" they asked before wandering off to leave the pair alone.

Natalie shook her head. "No, thanks . . . we'll hold down the blanket." Seth shifted to face her, hip to hip, the muscle of his thigh snug against her side.

A breeze gently blew her wavy hair, and he reached to tuck a red strand behind her ear. Gliding his knuckles, he burned a trail of desire past the edge of her breast and across her rib cage. Natalie shivered.

"I couldn't stop thinking about you." Seth loved the way her body responded.

A satisfied smile tipped the corners of her lips. "I'm glad you found me. It seems I'm already addicted to your touch."

"Addicted. That's the sexiest thing I've ever heard."

When she licked her lips, Seth brushed the pad of his thumb across her mouth. Natalie toyed with his muscular bicep. She slipped her hand beneath the skintight sleeve of his T-shirt and enhanced the heat of his skin.

To battle the swelling in his groin, Seth pulled their conversation to safer subjects. "Have you wandered much? I visited Mosquito Creek's tent. My cousin told me you stopped by."

"Yeah, but I have to confess, I'm having a hard time keeping track of your family. You seem to be related to half of the county."

"Not an exaggeration," Seth agreed with a chuckle. "Tons of kids run in the Michaels' clan. How about you?"

"My brother, Ben, is older, but I don't see him all that often. When my parents split, Ben went with my father and Mom got me."

"Your dad left Seattle?" Seth couldn't understand a man who would leave a child.

Natalie nodded slowly. "He moved to North Carolina. I haven't seen him in years. Mom remarried and has two boys with hubby number two. They live in Arizona."

Damn, Kent was right. Essentially, Natalie was alone. "How did you end up moving back to the Northwest?" he asked.

"I applied to schools in Seattle so I could be near Grandpa again." Natalie paused and Seth sensed sorrow in her hesitation. "I didn't mean to give you every boring detail of my life," she said with a strained smile.

He laced his fingers between hers. "Not boring at all. I want to know everything about you."

Those bright blue eyes closed, and she kneaded her lip with her teeth. "At first, when I moved to Seattle, I thought I'd help Grandpa. But he didn't need me nearly as much as I needed him."

Her hand flexed and tightened. "Grandpa Pete was fishing with friends when it happened . . . I guess he was tying off lines when he collapsed. His buddies said he had a perfect last day." A hint of a smile tipped the corners of her mouth. "They seemed to envy him, going quick like that, after a day on the water."

"I get that."

When she went quiet, Seth toyed with the edge of her shorts—the spot where her pale skin stopped and the line of her summer-tanned skin started. Her breathing hitched. "Natalie, Kent tracked me down. He wanted to make sure I was treating you right."

Her eyes met his as she absorbed the new information, "That explains a lot. He was strange today—I wonder if every detail I share with Kelsey makes its way to Kent."

He shrugged. "Probably,"

"I don't know how I feel about that." She closed her eyes again. Her dark lashes lay across her pale skin, the tips shiny in the bright summer sun.

All at once, everyone from Ashwood seemed to converge. Rick and Justin wandered back to the blanket bringing beer and goopy-cheesy nachos. Jasmine and Rose followed, now wearing matching tank tops from a local band.

Kelsey raced toward them from another direction. "Does anyone know why Kent tossed me the keys to his rig? He took off with some guys from Hood River and told me he'd find his own way back." She glanced from Nate to Seth, seeming to guess at the problem.

"I'm sure it's cool, Kels," Rick said quickly.

"Something's not right. He wouldn't talk to me. Later, I sent a text and it was the same crap. He only said that he'd see me Sunday." Kelsey collapsed on the blanket and huffed.

Seth didn't want to get into this again and pulled Natalie by the hand. "Since Natalie hasn't wandered around much, I'd like to steal her for a while." He stood as he spoke.

Pulled to her feet, Natalie laced her fingers with Seth's, and followed him to the art vendors.

***

The sun dipped below the horizon. Natalie led Seth through stalls selling tie-dyed shirts and cheap sunglasses.

He followed with his hand on her hip, and watched a smile spread when she spotted beaded earrings with a tiny hummingbird etched into a dangling glass disk. As she moved to open her purse,

Seth pulled out his wallet. He gave the vendor cash before she made a move.

She stared at him with raised eyebrows.

Seth shrugged and said, "What's wrong? The guy pays."

"Maybe in the 1950s."

When he laughed, Natalie planted her hand flat on the center of his chest and added, "Just for that, I'm going to buy you a tacky beer gift."

He chuckled at her flirtatious challenge.

"Don't try to stop me," she said.

"Stop you? I can't wait," Seth dared.

Natalie held his gaze. "You have to promise to keep what I pick out."

He nodded, eyes mockingly serious, mouth quirked with a smile. "Do your worst."

Vendors began illuminating their booths with glow-stick and neon knick-knacks as dusk approached.

Natalie wandered toward a booth selling tacky beer can hats with drinking straws attached. "This is perfect." She giggled and rose up on tiptoe to secure the hat to his head. "This might be the one. And when you wear it, you'll think only of me," she said laughing as he cringed.

"Maybe not. I'd be too wasted."

She pulled it off and set it back on the table.

Examining the next vendor's handmade leatherwork, she found a beautifully tooled leather bracelet with a metal clasp that doubled as a bottle opener. The design was masculine without trying too hard to be edgy.

After she paid the artist, Seth held his arm still while she secured it to his wrist. Her fingers trembled. Even in the low light, he could see her blush.

"Nice." He thanked her with a short kiss.

"It won't turn as many heads as the neon hat, but it will do."

"I don't need help turning heads with you by my side." He touched her chin, pulled her lips to his, and caressed her mouth. In return, she teased him with the tip of her tongue, drawing a moan from Seth.

Slipping his arm around her waist, they moved booth to booth, walking in time to music drifting from the main stage. Laughter and shrieks grew louder as the alcohol consumption increased.

Suddenly, Kelsey ran up to them from a dimly lit canopy. A game of giant beer Jenga had been set.

"Come be my partner, Nate. I'm designated driver and sentenced to soda. Drink beer for me!" Kels pulled Nate and Seth into the game where they found Wade mingling with the Ashwood mob.

***

Seth let Natalie's hand drop as she joined Kels.

He propped himself on the edge of a table near Wade. "Are you taking a break?"

"Yeah. I stopped serving alcohol an hour ago and switched the taps to root beer." Wade followed his cousin's gaze. "Hey, Seth. I don't mean to pry, well . . . yeah, I do. Are you here with Kelsey's friend?"

"I guess I am." Seth succumbed to the idea of having someone in his life.

"How did you meet?"

"She hired me to build a tiny house. I tried to keep Natalie at a professional distance but failed."

The tower of wood pieces swayed. Natalie eased forward with her arms lifted in a steadying movement, giving both men a long survey of her sensual curves.

Wade commented quietly, "At least you can count on getting laid."

A scowl crossed Seth's face but he didn't respond, confirming without words that this girl was different. When the silence between them expanded, Wade wandered the tent to clean up plastic cups.

Natalie pulled a Jenga piece out of the stack, almost toppling the tower, letting out a small scream as it teetered but did not fall. "You're next Kels, and you are so screwed, it's totally unstable."

"No way. I can't drink. If it falls, everyone else has to chug!" Kels slid the block carefully away, somehow managing to place it back on the stack. "You're up, Justin."

"Always up," Justin snickered.

"A couple of beers and he's thirteen," Jasmine said as the rest groaned. Justin's attempt failed, sending the tower cascading to the floor.

"Chug! Chug! Chug!" was chanted as he tipped his head and gulped. He punctuated the last slurp with an epic belch.

Snaking an arm around Natalie's waist, Seth tugged her away. "Kelsey, it looks like you have plenty of people to ride back with you. I'm stealing this girl." He kissed her cheek and she giggled.

"Figured you would."

"Kels, I'll see you at home," Natalie called over her shoulder.

Her comment sent a message. As much as he longed to, Seth wouldn't try to take her to his home above the lake tonight.

ELEVEN

Natalie nodded off five minutes into the drive. Seth stole dash lit glances—blueish light illuminated her pale skin. Her steady breathing and occasional sighs soothed him. After last night and a day spent in the heat she didn't wake, even on Kelsey's bumpy gravel drive.

He carefully parked and her body stirred. Natalie stretched and reestablished her bearings. "Sorry. I had no idea I was that tired." He smiled. She looked so damn cute when she was confused.

Seth opened his door and eased her across the bench seat. "I'm awake now, and I can walk," she said.

'I'd rather hold you." He loved carrying her and could get addicted to the way she nuzzled his neck. He didn't expect the nuzzle to turn into a bite.

"I thought you were tired," Seth said speeding his steps as heat surged to his groin.

"Not anymore." She grasped the back of his neck, pulling him in for a kiss. He broke away when they reached the back door.

He bent his knees so Natalie could turn the knob. "I can't believe Kels leaves her house unlocked," she said as he pushed the door open with his foot.

"Out here, most of us do."

Natalie already had Seth's shirt freed from his jeans by the time they made it into the kitchen. He placed her on the counter, in a room lit only by the light over the stove.

Centering her on the counter, Seth pivoted her between his hips, grabbed her round ass, and eased her forward to align her with his swelling length. Erratic breaths expanded Natalie's chest as Seth slid her shirt off, exposing her turquoise bikini top. That outline had distracted him all day. The tie at the neck unfurled and the triangles fell. He didn't bother with the knot at the back until his mouth covered a tempting peak.

He began sucking one nipple and teased the other with his fingers. Using his free hand, he pushed her round ass forward, and she circled his hips with her calves. Seth sensed her heat through his jeans and the thin fabric of her shorts. She ground against his erection, chasing her pleasure and heightening his.

Natalie's fingers knit into his hair as she kissed a path down his neck, then pushed him back to hop off the counter. The bounce of her curves bubbled a musical giggle as she cupped her full breasts in her small hands. Her joy and freedom lit places in Seth he didn't know had gone dark.

Pulling him to the living room, she tapped the couch and he obeyed. The playful dance of her eyes held his rapt attention and Seth sat, anticipating what Natalie had planned.

She lowered to the floor between his feet and unleashed his belt. "I don't have much experience with this, but after last night I want to . . ." One snick at a time, she lowered the zipper and his length sprang free.

"Wow." Natalie licked her lips and eased forward to take a tentative taste. "Tell me if I do something wrong . . ."

"Nothing's wrong when your lips are on me," Seth watched, eyes half-mast, as her hand pulled, her tongue teased, and her lips satisfied. Every long stroke took him higher than the one before.

His fingers wove into her hair, controlling her tempo. When he tugged the silky strands, Natalie moaned and Seth felt the vibration. Her confidence expanded and she tightened her lips as saliva dripped.

"Fuck yes," he groaned and lifted his hips encouraging her to take him a little deeper. A swallowing sensation pushed Seth closer to the edge. A few more pulls and he began to gasp. "Gonna come," he warned.

Her tongue danced as she stroked, unleashing an orgasm that Natalie relished, staying with him until he was tingly, sweaty, and spent.

She licked his softening shaft, then kissed a path across his abs. Still on her knees, Natalie rested her head on the inside of his thigh. Her swollen lips eased into a sexy grin. "That was fun," she whispered and giggled.

"You kill me, sweetness." He pulled her to his lap and their kisses lasted until Kelsey's headlights danced across the blinds.

With a shriek, she sprung from his lap. "Move!" She laughed as she gathered her clothes and sprinted naked to her room. Her curves bounced deliciously as she ran.

***

Last night was perfect, at least until he had to tell Natalie goodnight and drive home alone. Sleep came easily, and he woke at his usual early hour to check his email while sucking down his first cup of coffee. Kent's cowardly message stared at him from the top of the list. "Spineless. You couldn't talk to me face to face?" he mumbled at the screen.

Seth sent a quick reply, telling Kent his job would be waiting for him when he returned from the river. *Maybe it's best if we both cool off for a few weeks*. As one of the most respected river guides in the area, Kent predictably took off a few weeks each summer. Seth understood and shared a similar drive. Kent competed with the elements instead of business, and that translated into a hot temper from time to time.

Carlos met Seth at the coffee pot. His head tipped hello. "Looks like you had a good weekend."

"You must've heard I patched things with Natalie."

"Word travels." Carlos shrugged and Seth studied him, wondering if Desiree's trash-talk was also making the rounds.

Seth ignored a tingle of worry and dropped the inconvenient news. "Kent's taking off for a few weeks."

"Rafting again?" Everyone knew the routine.

"Yeah, for about three weeks on the Deschutes with Kelsey. Will that put your projects behind?"

Carlos shook his head. "Nah, you know I like working alone."

Rick and Natalie wandered in at about the same time. Today she carried a plate of homemade cookies in her hands.

"Where's Kent? I didn't see his car outside," Rick asked. Seth could see with a quick glance that Rick still had this weekend's shit weighing on his thoughts.

"He'll be out on the river for a while," Seth said accepting one of Natalie's oatmeal cookies.

"Strange, Kelsey didn't mention it." Natalie's eyes flicked between both men, trying to discern the source of the obvious strain.

Rick grumbled, "Typical."

Seth shrugged off the change. "It's cool. We shouldn't get behind schedule."

"Whatever." Rick grabbed two cookies and turned toward the shop. "I'll finish the work on the curved roof unless you have something else in mind." Seth nodded and Rick moved to gather his tools. Whitewater would be deathly quiet with Kent gone and Rick pissed. They'd probably get twice the work done after all.

Taking Natalie's hand, Seth led her through the door to his office. Blueprints for her home covered an ancient drafting table. Stepping to take a closer look, she couldn't seem to contain her happy dance. He liked that she was pleased, but realized she was admiring the visual proof of her future and the day she would leave.

Seth eyed her tempting wiggle, moved against her, and she stilled. Her head tipped against his chest as he savored the heat of her soft contours.

"Everything about you tempts me," Natalie said easing away. "Still, when we're surrounded by your employees, we should keep things professional."

A quick inhale and step away put a foot between them. "Professional. Right. No problem."

The physical distance didn't bother him too much. The emotional distance he'd created over the past week did. For the first time in years, he wanted to show off the woman in his life.

Seth was letting that unfamiliar urge sink in when a practical question turned his attention back to the home plans spread in front of them. "I've been wondering where I'll fit all the cups, plates, and lids?" she wondered aloud. "I guess I could sleep on the floor and the napkins can have my bed."

"Don't worry. Carlos will find the space. Just come up with a detailed list of supplies. I promise you won't be bunking with coffee beans."

Natalie took her spot at the computer researching commercial refrigerators, and Seth forced his feet out of his office. A few hours later, she located him where he was working on the plumbing in an almost-finished home.

"I'm going to take off for the day," she said standing over him. He put down his wrench and stopped tightening the fixture to enjoy her curves from this new angle.

"I could take you out for a late-lunch. You gotta eat," he said, propped with one elbow against the floor.

She shook her head. "Not today. I want to spend some time with Kels before she takes off for the river. Would you like to come over?"

"I can't. I need to focus on a few projects with Rick. See you tomorrow?"

Natalie nodded, seeming happy with the improved routine at the shop.

Seth couldn't let her escape so easily. "Let me walk you out," he said extending a hand. She reached to hoist him off the floor, but in one pull she landed with an oomph in his arms instead.

"I couldn't resist," he whispered against her neck. "No one will find us down here."

Natalie's giggle trailed away and she shook her head. "You're a terrible liar. It only took me about a minute to find you . . . anyone could wander in."

Seth rolled Natalie under him and kissed her until that moan he loved rumbled in her chest.

"I had to be sure you'd miss me tonight," he said against her mouth. She'd asked him to join the crowd at Northside, but he didn't want to fire off another blast of anger from Kent. One night on his own wouldn't kill him.

After another quick kiss, Seth popped to his feet and easily brought her with him.

Natalie blinked hard and gathered her scrambled senses. Using two hands, she planted his bulk against the wall. "Stay here. I don't trust you to walk me to my truck." He chuckled. She was wise to make him stay.

***

Kent slammed the rear door of his truck. "That's the last of the gear. We just need to add coolers tomorrow morning, when we leave at first light."

Kelsey stood on the running board to tighten the straps that secured her kayak to the top of his rig. "I always hate leaving at the butt-crack of dawn. How did Seth take your sudden change of plans? Did he fire your ass?"

"His email didn't say much. He's probably happy to slow the work on Nate's house. Now he can tap that all summer."

Kelsey jumped down from the running board. "Shut up, asshole, Natalie doesn't deserve that."

"Sorry. You're right—maybe leaving town will help my shitty attitude."

A cloud of fine dust floated in the air when Nate stopped next to his SUV. Kent regretted his decision to leave when he spotted her smile.

She flung her door open and yelled, "Darn, I missed all the fun." Slowly circling, she checked out the gear—kayaks, tent, gas tanks, and a tire secured to his lifted truck. "Add a gun turret and you'll be ready for the zombie apocalypse."

"Damn, it's already bolted to my other rig." Kent tossed an arm around Nate. "I'm crashing on your couch tonight."

"We're leaving before dawn," Kels added as she reached to check another strap.

Nate nodded. "Sounds perfect, but I'm not getting up before dawn to make you coffee."

Finished with the load, hunger drove them all inside.

"Have you made plans to keep busy?" Kelsey asked as she tossed together a sandwich.

"Yeah, Amanda and I are getting together to shoot the night sky."

"That's great." As Natalie typed a quick text to Amanda, nailing down plans for their night of photographing the stars, Kent realized he'd never stood a chance. Seth, with his perfect family, had so much more to offer.

Kels took a call securing details for the trip. When she pushed them outside, Kent grabbed two dusty lawn chairs from the shed. Nate followed with a half-empty bag of sour cream and onion chips. She passed it over and he took a handful.

"How often do you leave to get on the river?" she asked, wiping crumbs on her jeans.

"A few weeks each summer. But I get out on the Little White on the weekends when I can."

He lost himself explaining his love of paddling—days spent in the sun, reading the river cooled by the spray coming off the water. "It's a serious fucking rush. Only one other thrill compares . . ."

She giggled and waved off his teasing. He loved the way she blushed but knew her sly smile belonged to Seth.

**

Natalie headed to Northside Grill with the crowd for goodbye drinks. They piled into a large booth with another table pulled alongside. Laughter and pitchers of frosty beer flowed freely.

Jasmine leaned across her sister and raised her voice above the tumbling conversation. "Hey, Nate, Rose and I have this school orientation thing in Seattle. We've done Pike's and the Great Wheel, but don't want to see any more tourist traps."

"Jasmine, when are you going?" Natalie asked, pleased she could now tell the twins apart.

"Mid-July."

"Would you mind if I drive you both up? I need to make a Seattle run and would love some company." She simply couldn't put off sorting through Grandpa's things any longer and having friends along might alleviate some of her dread.

"We're staying in the dorms that week. Will that be too long? We could take the train back."

"No, a week is perfect."

"Cool. We'll pay for gas. Now I'm super stoked. Road trip!" Rose whooped and high-fived Natalie and her sister.

She was still celebrating when Kels waved Seth over. He'd turned down her invite earlier, but she hadn't given up hope. Her heart throttled when he claimed a chair on the edge. Jasmine and Rose bubbled with the details about their upcoming trip to Seattle. He asked questions about the classes they wanted to take and typed the dates when Natalie would be gone into his calendar.

***

Seth handed over three quarters he had in his pocket. The girls took everyone's offering and huddled over the jukebox, picking out music. He grinned as the women spilled onto the floor in a giggly mob.

"When do you leave?" Seth asked Kent, attempting to mend their fractured friendship.

"Tomorrow morning at the crack of dawn." With a lift of his chin, Kent added, "I'm crashing on Kelsey's couch tonight to get an early start. Do you have a problem with that?"

Seth clenched his jaw but moved past the irritation. "Nah, that's cool."

An order of nachos and a pitcher of Coke plopped hard in front of Seth. He turned his head, locking eyes with Desiree's sister, Paige.

"Nice to see you Seth," she lied, eyes cold and calculating, just like his ex-wife's.

"How's it going?" he asked, not caring if she answered.

"I visited Desiree in Portland last week. We hit the clubs."

He grunted then added, "Hope you had fun."

"More than you can possibly imagine." Paige spun and flounced back to the bar, her hips swaying. Seth groaned and watched as Kent elbowed Rick, sharing a chuckle as she left.

Needing a break, Seth stood as the girls tumbled back to the table. Before Natalie took her seat, he led her back onto the floor and pulled her close. Her movement soothed him with the warm push and pull of her soft curves against his body.

She shivered when his words puffed against her ear. "Spend the night with me, please." A moment of hesitation gave him enough time to turn her lips to his for a convincing kiss. With a nod and a tilted smile, she silently agreed.

The slow song finished. They returned to the crowd and slid side by side into the booth. Seth settled his hand on Natalie's upper thigh and eased it toward her warmth to tease a little pleasure. He shifted his hips and adjusted his jeans.

A conversation about river levels between Kent and Kelsey offered a meager distraction. Instead, Seth anticipated an entire night spent with Natalie in his bed. His hand inched a little higher on her thigh and Natalie squirmed.

Quickly downing the last of his beer, Kent slammed his glass on the table. "Gotta get up early."

Kelsey stood and tossed a wad of cash next to the empty nacho plate. "Hey, Nate, can we get home?"

"Sure." Her fingers dug into her purse, fishing for her keys.

The early risers in the group disbanded and headed toward the door. "Later Iris—we'll see you in a few weeks!" Kels yelled across the bar.

The owner of Northside Grill called back, "Paddle hard and stay dry."

Just outside, Seth pulled Natalie to his side and asked, "Do you mind if I follow and pick you up? We'll ride together over to my place from there."

"Sounds great," she answered. "See you in a minute."

***

Natalie divided her attention between the road and the shadow of the man in the rearview mirror. Her body heated, anticipating an entire night with Seth.

Uncomfortable quiet took over the ride until they were nearly home. Kent sat in silence, brooding, but Natalie couldn't think of a single thing to say that would improve the situation.

Kelsey finally filled the dead space. "If you need anything while we're gone, don't hesitate to call my parents."

Her quick response was distracted at best, "I'll be fine. Have fun. And be careful."

Kelsey leaped from Natalie's truck the moment they stopped in front of the house. She pulled Nate from the cab and trapped her in a hug illuminated by Seth's headlights. "I'm gonna miss you."

Nate gave her roommate a squeeze. "I'll miss you, too."

When Kels let go, the front door slammed. Kent had gone inside without saying goodbye.

TWELVE

Trapped by her seatbelt and his predatory gaze, Natalie's stomach clenched with anticipation. She slid to the center of the seat, re-buckled, and skated her fingers across his thigh. Her lips tipped into a smile when he groaned.

The delicate invitation had Seth's eyes searching, and he found an adequate spot for what he wanted to do. Seth pulled down an overgrown side road, unbuckled her seatbelt, and slid her to face him on his lap.

With a hip-rotation, she ground her heat against his prominent erection and moaned. Placing a hand on each side of her face, he leisurely explored her lips, nipping and sucking her tongue into his mouth.

Natalie responded, pulsing her soft heat against the hard ridge of his shaft through layers of clothes. Seth's hands slid under her shirt, shoving the demi bra up to pinch each nipple with his calloused fingers.

Her gasps increased along with the grind of her hips as she chased the tide of sensation. "I can't believe I'm already so close."

Answering her need, Seth eased the curve of her back across his muscular arm. He lowered his mouth to her nipple, teased with his tongue and sucked gently while increasing the pressure on her other rosy peak with his free hand. Just a little tighter, the pull on her nipple increased. With a slight scrape of his teeth across the tightened ruched tip, her body exploded with an orgasm that created stars behind her closed eyes.

Through layers of clothes, she rode him hard, wringing out each wave of pleasure. Gorgeous red hair lay tossed across his shoulder as her lungs heaved spent oxygen against his chest.

He stroked her back and nipped her lip. "I need you in my bed. This truck's inadequate for what I have planned for you tonight."

She shivered as Seth buckled her back into place.

***

Seth kept one hand on the wheel while the other grazed the inside of her thigh. She squirmed, so responsive. He pondered the edges of her limits and wondered what she could take.

After a few miles, Natalie broke the silence. "I've lost all sense of direction. Have we been climbing for a while?"

"Yeah. We're on a ridge over Osprey Lake. From my deck, you can see the lights from the homes along the shore." After a steep incline, he stopped at his home overlooking a deep valley.

Natalie jumped from his truck to take in the view of the vast heavens. When the lights in the cab extinguished, she sighed. "Oh, Seth, it's absolutely stunning. I wish I had my camera. The sky's actually a deep purple, and the stars are unreal." Lifted into his arms again, she tipped her head back, studying the inky night sky.

After carrying her across his driveway, he used one arm to open the front door. She pushed it shut, but Seth didn't let her feet touch the floor. With ease, he moved up a broad staircase that overlooked a great room, dominated by floor-to-ceiling windows.

He moved directly to his simply decorated bedroom and placed her on the thick mattress of his four-post bed. Seth prowled over Natalie, planning to savor every inch of her body and memorize her desires, especially those she had not yet discovered.

He tossed her sandals onto the floor, and his deft fingers shimmied every scrap of fabric from her curves. Seth stretched her out and caressed her from fingertips to toes.

Beginning at the arch of her instep, he kissed, licked, and nibbled a winding path. Warm and wet, his tongue discovered each erogenous point. Natalie squirmed as her body replied to his physical exploration. Sucking at the inside of her wrists made her moan. Dragging his day-growth beard between her breasts charmed a cat-like flex from her spine. Flicking the tip of his tongue against the dent at her throat coaxed a delicate cry.

Seth had not completed his exploration. She giggled when he flipped her to her stomach to explore the opposite side. The backs of her knees, the hollow of her back, and the cheeks of her rounded ass ignited under his touch. Each nip and suck tightened the tension that Seth would unleash. . . when *he* was ready.

"Please," she begged.

Fully clothed, he stood at the foot of the bed, seeming to savor every inch of her bare body.

Still on her stomach, she squirmed against the bed when his heavy buckle fell to the floor, followed by the rustle of his jeans and shirt. His weight dipped the mattress before his naked contours covered hers. Hard and hot, his cock nestled against the crease of her rounded ass. Natalie arched her back to grind against his length.

Seth went to his knees on either side of her torso, flipped her over, and overwhelmed her mouth with kisses designed to scramble her senses.

"I need to taste you," he murmured as he made a slow glide from her throat, pausing for a moment to suck on each nipple. Her stomach jumped as his tongue slid south.

Broad shoulders pushed her thighs apart. He closed his eyes and inhaled the sweet heady scent of her arousal. Using the pads of his thumbs, he gently parted her and slid the tip of his tongue along her dewy seam. "Love your sweet honey," he said as he lifted her hips and plunged his tongue deep. He lapped and sucked, then moved in for another penetrating dive. With each pass, he gave extra attention to her sensitive bundle of nerves.

"So close, please, Seth, make me come," she pleaded. He increased the velocity of his attention, but backed off again, making her wait. She cried in protest, and he smiled before beginning again.

The teasing was intoxicating, and her responsive movements too addictive. When he felt her channel pulse around his tongue, he moved away and inserted two curved fingers inside her instead. Her body trembled as he plied hot kisses over her mound.

His tongue danced. She writhed and squirmed. One final flick to her clit sent her bucking against his plundering mouth. His name flew from her sweet lips and it echoed from the lofted ceiling.

Open-mouthed kisses followed the downward crest of her release. Sated and sweaty, Natalie collapsed across the mattress, stretching her boneless arms above her head. Instinctively, she grasped the rail of his bed, just above the cloud of red hair spread in messy disarray across the mattress. The submissive vision halted his breathing.

"Don't move." Seth simply lost the power to wait another moment. He needed to plunge into her wet, swollen sheath.

Quickly covering his girth with a condom, he pressed her fingers tighter around the rail of his bed. She kept hold as he pushed into her passage in one hard drive. Sweat glistened down his back as his balls drew tight. Seth struggled for control. Slowly in. Even slower out. Each pass set up a measured pace that prolonged his satisfaction.

Natalie panted. "God, Seth . . . I'm going to come again." Her breath felt cool against his chest. She writhed beneath him and adjusted the angle of her hips, but she never removed her hands from their grasp on his bed. Each pass over her internal nerves increased the fist-like hold her body had on his shaft.

Reality left him when her channel pulsed in another explosive release. Natalie's abandon brought him over the edge with a roar. He tried to hover above her on extended arms, but she released her grip on the bed to pull him down and savor the protective feel of his weight.

Seth's breathing slowed, and the night-air cooled his heated body. Natalie's delicate fingertips made him shiver and they laughed together, still connected.

"Oh my God," she said with a giggle.

"I never—" he agreed, still struggling to think.

Softening, he pulled free and had to take care of the condom.

While he was in the attached bathroom, he grabbed water for himself and brought some back for Natalie. She thanked him, drank, and curled into his body as he toyed with her hair.

His room was so dark that she could see the Milky Way in a wide swath through his bedroom window.

The cadence of Seth's breathing changed, and she whispered, "Seth, are you still awake?"

When he didn't answer, she risked a quiet truth. "Everything is moving so fast, I'm afraid of needing you this much."

Seth barely woke and murmured, "Scares me too. I'm powerless when it comes to you." His breathing slowed and he turned in his sleep to pull her closer. She was comfortable but couldn't find sleep.

Natalie listened to the ticking of a distant clock and imagined what the rest of Seth's house actually looked like. She suspected it was stunning and looked forward to seeing it in the morning.

Uprooted and replanted here in Ashwood, it would be easy to let Seth fill an empty void. He was so strong, so sure of himself, so easy to need. But that would defeat her purpose.

Leaving Seattle had opened her eyes, and she wasn't willing to narrow her vision. Like a wide-open aperture on her Canon, she wanted to flood herself with life-altering light—something that would expose her weaknesses and ignite change.

***

Morning light slanted into his room, and Seth opened his eyes to find Natalie watching. "You snore," she said. He faked a scowl, and she poked his stomach playfully. "Don't worry, I liked it. I've never slept better." Her delicate fingers traced a path across his chest.

He realized he hadn't slept better either. "Me too, I feel great."

Her hand stroked his shaft. "Great . . . except maybe for this," She purred as she stroked his urgent erection

Lazing against the pillow, Seth pulled her over him to nuzzle her breast, teasing her pink peak. When he nestled her over his jutting cock, she gasped.

Natalie moved, gliding her wet arousal over his shaft. She slipped the tip into her body. "I'm on the pill. Never been with anyone without a condom . . . it's actually been more than a year."

No wonder she was so tight. Seth didn't want to think about her with anyone. He'd been tested, used condoms meticulously, and knew he was clean.

"I want your heat surrounding me," he said.

With a nod, she sheathed him, skin to skin. His growl spread a self-assured smile across her face. Taking a patient pace, he felt her gaze as his desperation increased. She timed each lift of her hips with his guttural groans and followed the ascent with a slow impale down the length of his shaft.

On his back, Seth memorized the bounce of her breasts, the arch of her torso, and the dewy glow of perspiration that gathered on her chest. Natalie's body took them on a slow climb to release.

"I need more, please," she pleaded. He reached and pulsed his thumb on her begging clit.

"Yes, oh God—" Head arched; her heartbeat pulsed quickly at her neck. She slammed down, riding his length, her sex tightening around him, drawing him in.

"Sweetness, I'm not going to last. Come for me. Now," he moaned, responding to the onslaught of friction. A powerful thrust lifted her body as his orgasm shot liquid heat.

The jolt added the sensation she needed to find her release. Her hips pressed, took everything from him, then rose slightly before anchoring onto his shaft again.

Moaning, her spent frame collapsed onto his muscled chest. They breathed together, intimately connected in her slick heat.

***

She didn't ever want to separate her body from his. However, the view out his window and the need to visit the bathroom made her move. Natalie wrapped herself in a blanket and disappeared for a bit. When they traded places, she had a moment to enjoy the view from his bedroom window. French doors opened to a second-story deck. Clad in the blanket she shuffled out to take in the view.

Tall pines swayed sweet and crisp in the morning breeze. Honeybees zipped past, and darting birds held tree-to-tree conversations. Sparkling in the sunlight, Osprey Lake dominated the broad valley below. Tucked in one alcove, she recognized the collection of buildings that made up the Fisher farm.

Out of the bathroom, she was disappointed to see Seth wearing a towel slung low on his hips. She'd be showering alone later. Barefoot, he moved silently across the deck to join her in the morning sun.

"Did you build this home? It's absolutely perfect."

"Not all of it. The exterior was almost complete when the previous owner sold the place. They thought they wanted a vacation home in the Northwest but underestimated our rain."

She turned to Seth. Droplets of water sparkled in the sunlight on his freshly showered hair. "I made an offer on the house and they accepted. At the time, the place was just a shell with a roof, so the price was right. To save money, I lived here while I completed the home the way I wanted."

"It reflects you," she said while pushing a messy, golden curl out of her way. She looked toward the house, worried her hair was on end. "I'll grab a shower before you drop me at Kelsey's. If I spend time on the supply list, I should have it for you in a day or two."

A hint of irritation tightened Seth's brows. "Why aren't you planning to work on that from my office?" he asked.

"You might get tired of having me underfoot," she admitted.

"Underfoot?" His grin relaxed his features. "Not how I picture you under me, Natalie." He scooped her up and carried her toward the shower.

She squealed as he tossed her blanket-wrapped body over his shoulder. Her round bottom begged for a firm slap. He gave her a smack—once, twice, three times on the way to the bathroom.

With each tingling strike, she moaned and wriggled her ass. Seth's towel dropped and Natalie took in the delicious upside-down view of his chiseled butt from the perch across his shoulder.

He laughed. "We're gonna be late to work."

***

Showered and starving, Natalie made toast while Seth scrambled eggs. As she waited for the toast to pop, he tasted her neck.

"Damn, you're like a drug. I could spend days just exploring all the ways to make you come."

She shivered and blushed, tilting her head to savor the sweet caress. He flinched away when his cell buzzed. "Shit. Let me see who this is." He strolled across the room to take the call.

She turned to the eggs and scraped the pan. Consumed with making their breakfast, she tried to ignore his half of the conversation.

"Hey, Mom, what do you need? Is everything okay?"

Toast sprang up and she buttered the bread.

"Oh, you ran into Wade in town? Yeah, he had a nice setup at the river."

There was a long pause, and she opened three cupboards before finding the plates.

"Yeah . . . Wade met her. Her name is Natalie." He turned to her and grinned with a shrug. "Yes, Mom, we've been spending time together."

She pulled the pan from the stove and warmed her coffee with the half-full pot.

"Mom, I need to go to work." Seth began to pace. "She'll be in Ashwood most of the summer." His steps stopped, but his back was to her, and she couldn't read his expression.

"I don't know, Mom. Okay . . . I'll ask . . . No problem. Gotcha. Love you too."

Leaning against the counter, she wondered if he felt cornered by the conversation with his mom. When he turned to face her, he said, "If Mom spots you around town, be ready for a round of questions."

Her stomach tightened as she battled fresh nerves. "No problem."

"Thanks for wrapping up breakfast," he blurted.

"Mm, hmm." Now not as hungry, she grabbed a single slice of toast and nibbled the corner.

Seth finally really looked at her and asked, "Sweetness, how would you feel about dinner with my parents next week?"

Natalie almost laughed when she realized he was more nervous than she was. "Oh, that would be great."

A whoosh of air hissed past his lips. "Awesome. I'll let Mom know."

Relief hit, and she was suddenly starved. Natalie hid her grin as she scooped up a generous helping of eggs.

THIRTEEN

"Does this skirt look okay?" Natalie spun in front of the mirror. After three outfits, she still couldn't decide what to wear to dinner with Seth's parents.

The palms of her hands felt sweaty, and she knew her nerves were showing. Seth's grin put her at ease. Almost.

"It's gorgeous." He answered with a smile. Seth closed the distance between them, took her face in his hands, and planted a quick kiss. "Damn, you're cute."

That kiss helped more than he knew. Feeling a bit more confident, she went back to the mirror and spun to get a second look. Her skirt flew up a bit as she whirled.

"If you do that again, we'll definitely be late."

Warmth flushed her skin. "Stop teasing. Now I'm overheating for different reasons."

"You're beautiful, sweetness. Even if you wore a burlap bag, Mom would be thrilled to meet you. Remember, Amanda will be there, so you won't have a chance to feel awkward."

"Right. Good. Amanda and I can hang out." Natalie held two different earrings near her face and checked her reflection. A few others lay scattered in a small saucer on his master bath counter. Seth liked the things she'd scattered across his house. After spending the past five nights together, she'd started to relax and settle in.

Following him downstairs, she grabbed her purse and glanced around the room, certain she'd forgotten something.

"I'll never remember everyone's name. I'm *really* nervous."

Seth shook his head, "Oh, crap, I almost forgot, Amanda wondered if you'd bring your camera."

"Camera, camera, camera." She took the stairs two at a time then called over her shoulder, "Don't forget the flowers for your mom."

"Gotcha. You ready to go?"

"In a minute. Just wait for me in the truck." At the last moment, she switched from her heels to flat sandals—so much easier to wear outdoors.

Glancing again at her reflection, she bit her thumbnail, huffed, and gave in to the sacrifice. She'd be the shortest person in the room without those three extra inches. Still, the camera bag at her hip brightened her mood.

To welcome them, Amanda launched from the porch the moment Seth's truck stopped in front of his parent's spacious craftsman home. She bounced while waiting for Natalie to exit the passenger side.

"We're so glad you're here. Come in . . . Mom can't wait to meet you." She took Natalie's camera bag and rushed toward the house.

Seth grabbed Natalie's left hand and she cradled the fresh flowers in the right. Amanda glanced back from a few steps ahead. If possible, her grin was even more animated than usual.

The commotion pulled Seth's mom to the front door where quick introductions were made. Sandy accepted the flowers, inhaling the scent. "Thank you, these are lovely."

On her way to the kitchen, she pulled an antique vase from a cupboard, snipped off the stems with a pair of garden shears kept under the sink, and perfected the arrangement while Natalie admired the unfussy kitchen. The space was a seamless blend of simple function and nature. Herbs grew in a sunny window, and homegrown fruits and vegetables filled a large bowl on the butcher-block island.

Sandy placed the flowers on a tiger maple sideboard and directed Seth and Natalie to the backyard. "Owen and Traci are playing with the kids on the swings. Let's all go outside so Natalie can meet your brother's family."

The yard had obviously been a center of activity when the Michaels' kids were young. Faded lines for basketball took up a wide concrete pad in front of a three-bay garage. Beyond the swings, a tall fence built to deter deer caged an expansive garden.

"Mrs. Michaels, your garden is beautiful." Natalie secretly wished for a yard as beautiful someday.

"Call me Sandy, please, and Seth's dad, call him Bill. We only get Mr. and Mrs. Michaels from our Sunday school kiddos at church. Owen!" she hollered across the lawn.

Owen gathered his family to meet his big brother's girl. Propelled by pre-school energy, Will and Kellie streaked across the yard and tackled Uncle Seth's legs. He scooped them up, football style, one under each arm. His sprint around the yard had the kids squealing.

Sandy introduced the pair. Traci didn't hesitate and drew Natalie into a quick hug. "We'll let Uncle Seth wear out the kids. Hopefully, he'll run off their energy before we eat."

Traci kept an arm around Natalie's waist. "Come on, let's have some iced tea and sit in the shade. We want to hear all about what brought you to Ashwood."

After talking for a few minutes, Bill left the women to join Owen and Seth with the kids. He pulled chunky colorful chalk from a bin on the porch. Will and Kellie decorated the concrete with pink, yellow, and blue indiscernible shapes.

When asked, Natalie explained what brought her to Ashwood, and to Seth. Sandy questioned where Natalie planned to spend her time and how her business would run.

"That's so exciting. Life on the road," Amanda envied aloud. "Natalie, please start a travel blog. I'd love to follow it."

Dinner came out of the oven, and the youngest brother, Neil, showed up to join the family meal. Seth popped a couple bottles of wine, then settled next to Natalie at the table. After dinner, he slid his hand around her chair and toyed with a curl of her hair.

Teasing and laughter popped around the dining room, like a game of pinball. Natalie gave into the simple joy of the close family bonds and wondered if all families joked this way. Even on their best days, she didn't remember her family ever feeling this close.

***

Warm leather seats clung to the back of Natalie's legs on the drive home. She happily talked about the evening, then began to toy with the edge of her skirt. "One thing worries me," she said quietly.

Seth glanced her way and Natalie bit her lip before she spoke. "Does your mom know about all the nights I spend at your house? When that Sunday school thing came up, I worried she might not approve."

His chuckle pushed her nerves aside. "No worries. Owen and Traci lived together for a while at Mom and Dad's before they even got married. They had just found out that Traci was pregnant with Will and hadn't quite decided if they really wanted to tie the knot. Mom and Dad didn't push, but begged Traci to stay during the pregnancy."

"That's sweet. I'm not surprised. Grandpa loved like that—unconditionally. You're lucky."

Natalie gazed at the trees speeding by. "My dad, on the other hand, attaches strings to what he believes is affection. . ."

"And your mom?"

Her head tipped to the side and rested against the window. "Mom loves me, but her world shifted when she remarried and had my little brothers. I don't resent it—she deserves another chance at love." Natalie closed her eyes, forcing her emotions out of reach.

"When we get home, I'm going to get you a glass of wine, babe. How does a long bubble bath sound?" She loved how easily Seth read her moods and gave her time to work things out for herself.

"Perfect. But after a hot bath and a glass of wine, I may slide into bed and crash."

"Whatever you need . . . a bath, wine, a backrub, even a chick flick on TV. I aim to please."

***

She fell asleep while he locked up the house. Seth slid under the covers and watched her sleep. The scent of lavender bubble bath clung to her skin. He listened to her steady breathing as he lay in the dark, wondering how he'd let himself fall so fast.

***

Breakfast together turned into her favorite routine. Their mornings weren't complicated. He'd make eggs while she experimented with new coffee concoctions. Seth tasted her efforts and was honest about the results.

Yet, each day passed too quickly, at a speed that was impossible to savor. At Whitewater, Natalie chose materials and placed orders while watching the shell of her little house come together on the large gooseneck trailer.

The crew grew comfortable with her presence on the job site. She dared to take a few pictures, capturing the progress of her house and two other homes. Sitting at her laptop, editing the shots, Seth gazed at her work over her shoulder.

"Your photos are fantastic. Carlos looks so connected to his work."

"The camera loves Carlos. He's unguarded when he builds. If you want to choose your favorites, I'd be happy to add them to your webpage."

Seth pointed to three images with one hand and stroked her hair with the other. "I like them all, but these are fantastic."

"Nice choices." Natalie closed her eyes and leaned into his affectionate touch.

A scream of a saw coming from the work floor broke the trance, and her eyes sprung open again. "Who set up your webpage?"

"Jasmine and Rose put it together initially, but I've let it slide."

Natalie nodded then glanced up from her computer screen as she recalled her trip with the twins. "I'll be leaving for Seattle soon. At least it's only for a week." The thought of leaving at the end of summer was beginning to terrify her.

"Do you want me to come along?" he asked.

She appreciated the offer. Seth knew how much she dreaded this. "No. I have to face letting go on my own. You'd just be bored while I sell off Grandpa's things." Her voice wavered as she thought of Grandpa Pete.

"Will Elsa be around?" he asked, concern wrinkling his brow.

"Yes, and I can't wait to see her. Summer's flying by so fast. I almost forgot Kelsey and Kent come back Saturday." The past few weeks had been perfect, but she didn't want to assume too much. Natalie wondered if their short-term living arrangements needed to come to an end. "If you want, I could pack up my stuff and be ready to head back to Kel—"

Seth spun Natalie around in his office chair, planted himself on his couch, and rolled her forward between his parted legs. Her eyes locked on his intense, almost frightening, cobalt-gaze. "I've been thinking about something, Natalie."

Her heart throttled and she prepared herself for the impact of his rejection. His hesitation increased her anxiety. "Alright, I'll just say it. I want you to move up to my place. You know, when Kelsey comes home. Not that you can't spend as much time as you want with your friends. Oh God, now I sound like a control freak."

Seth stared at the floor, then his intense gaze pinned her again. "It's just, we've been together every night, and I don't want that to change. I like waking up with you and, and . . ." He flopped back, let out a strained breath, and stared directly into her eyes. "Please don't leave, Natalie. Not yet."

His eyes widened when a little burst of laughter she couldn't suppress surprised him. "Seth, that's not what I expected. You looked so stressed. I thought it would be, you know, something *bad*."

He leaned forward and covered her hands with his. "No, sweetness, I'm falling—" The word he couldn't say hovered between them.

"I'm falling too, Seth, falling hard." Grasping his face between her soft hands, she kissed him and whispered, "Of course I'll stay with you."

***

The drive home that evening felt more permanent, and Natalie indulged in a moment of belonging to one person and to one place. She loved it here in Ashwood—balanced on a high point between the east and west side of the Cascade Range, where lush forests faded into harsh arid desert.

Tonight, the mountains were the battleground between hot and cold air, and Natalie studied an approaching storm. "Those clouds are building. I hope we get a display . . . I haven't had a chance to take shots of lightning in a long time." To gain a better perspective, she leaned forward in her seat. Black clouds billowed over the foothills. By the time Seth pulled into the drive, the clouds were stacked in pillars of energy.

She rushed to set up her camera on the back deck. With her gear surrounding her, she sat perched behind her tripod waiting for the impending show. Her foot tapped. Impatient, she pulled out her digital camera, and captured a hawk skimming the treetops.

Still waiting, she checked the satellite feed for recent lightning strikes with a weather app on her phone. Rapidly moving from eastern Oregon, the storm rolled along the Cascade Range heading north in a counterclockwise spin.

"Shouldn't be too long," she said from behind her camera.

***

Seth gave her space to do her thing and grilled chicken and potatoes on the barbeque. "Wine tonight, sweetness?"

"Yes, please." He poured as Natalie followed the path of a hummingbird with the lens of her Canon. His girl smiled like the little bird was a friend. It darted and investigated her, visiting the flowers that Natalie had planted in a large ceramic pot on his deck.

Guiding her lens, she followed the metallic shimmer of the hummingbird's iridescent wings. Her camera's high-speed shutter snapped rapidly, taking multiple simultaneous shots. He recognized the magic in her photographs, her effortless connection to the environment and her subjects.

From behind the camera, she said, "Next summer, even more hummingbirds will come, as long as the flowers are here."

Will you be here with your hummingbirds? He thought as he watched her bend to capture the shot. Her movement calmed him. Daily life with Natalie had an easy pace that Seth sank into.

The camera clicked, and her words continued from behind the lens. "In Seattle, some hummingbirds overwintered, but most left in September. It always made me sad to see them go."

By September, she'll be gone. Seth watched as she panned the flight of the hummingbird, capturing fragments of time with her lens.

The bird's path zipped past Seth, bringing his face into the field of the viewfinder. Without forethought, the shutter trapped everything he felt—the intense fear of losing a woman he was growing to love.

Seeing the bird more than the man, Natalie only sighed as the hummingbird disappeared.

***

"I'm so full. That grilled chicken was so perfect, I ate way too much." Natalie carried a stack of plates into the kitchen. One moment later, a loud rumble rolled across the valley.

Seth smiled. "Great timing. I'll clean up. Go, get behind your camera." She squealed and danced with childlike excitement when a bright bolt severed the sky. Stacking dishes in the sink, Seth joined her on the deck for the show.

Natalie captured several bolts far in the distance before the storm rolled overhead. The lightening snaked white-blue tendrils across the entire horizon. Her face brightened and she yelled, "Did you see that!"

"Were you able to get the shot?" Before she could answer, a bolt streaked and a simultaneous boom shook Seth's entire house.

"Shit!" he yelled as she squealed. Seth had found at least one thing that didn't faze his woman. "That was close."

He fought the urge to drag her inside. "Natalie, please, at least scoot closer to the house," he warned as another bolt parted the horizon. All she did was giggle and dance.

"And miss this?" Evidently, she lost all common sense when it came to thunderstorms. A gray haze curtained the sky in the distance and the air cooled rapidly.

"Looks like rain!" The din of approaching hail swallowed Seth's words.

The first of a million hailstones bounced off the wooden deck. Tall trees bent and swayed as wind pushed in from the south, carrying with it the scent of wet earth. Natalie scooped up her camera and tripod while the gray onslaught curtained the horizon.

Rain and hail pelted her back as she stooped over her camera and dashed through the door.

Trapped indoors, Seth was now determined to take advantage of the confinement. "Let's watch the rest of the storm from upstairs." She smiled and needed no encouragement. A trail of clothes littered their scrambling path.

The power went out. Another lightning strike cast a blue flash across the bed where Seth and Natalie made love. Slick with sweat, seared with heat, his slow penetration was lit by nature's show.

Patiently, he brought her with him on a slow ascent. Breathing as one, their release united them in a moment of perfection, souls permanently imprinted upon the other.

Locked inside her heat and already hardening again, Seth spun their bodies, bringing her over him to worship her breasts. Natalie took control, rocking down, pulling almost completely away to impale herself again. His fingers dug into her soft hips.

Erratically breathing, her gaze became desperate. One final thrust propelled a tempest of sensation. Thunder mingled with her cries before she collapsed against his chest. They dozed connected. Natalie woke to Seth's slight tickle across her cool back. The touch returned her from a dream-like state.

The dark sky lit and thunder rumbled far in the distance. Caged in his strong arms, she slipped deep into sleep, and deeper into his heart.

FOURTEEN

Amanda shared Ashwood's latest gossip while she prepped their sandwiches. Natalie begged her to join all the girls at the park for an impromptu picnic, but Amanda couldn't get away from the Stop-n-Shop, the line at the sandwich counter was too long.

Kelsey led their little group to the small park near the river that ran through the center of town and found a table beneath the shade of a cottonwood tree. Natalie looked forward to sharing a meal before their schedules took them in separate directions.

Inside a plastic container, Nate hid a dozen snickerdoodles she'd made fresh this morning using Elsa's recipe. She'd already dropped another batch off at Whitewater for the guys. The thank you kiss from Seth still had her smiling.

"What's hidden in the Tupperware? I hope it's for me," Kels asked as Nate pulled the lid away.

"Ta-da . . . cookies! And I used Elsa's recipe."

"You read my mind. I love you, Nate," Kels said as she bit into the tender cookie and moaned with pleasure. "If you still lived at my house, I'd beg you to make these every damn day."

"What are you talking about? Where are you living?" the twins questioned simultaneously, their mouths falling open.

Shooting Kels a steely glance, Nate admitted, "Seth asked me to stay. I guess I'm up at his house most nights."

"Finally. Thank God. We wondered if he would ever—" Jasmine paused mid-sentence, cringing when she overstepped an invisible line.

Natalie waved off their concern. "Don't worry about it. I know about Desiree and the divorce. Anyway, we're keeping this casual. After my house is finished, I need to move on."

The twins and Kelsey traded looks. None of them believed anything about the relationship between Seth and Natalie was casual.

The conversation moved to plans for this weekend's road trip. "I wish I could go with you three to Seattle. What do you have lined up?" Kelsey asked.

Natalie pointed with her sandwich as she spoke, "The fair at Lake Washington will be in full swing and the crowds totally insane."

"I'd like to see the torchlight parade. What do you think?" Rose asked.

Jasmine's plans took a different spin. "Forget the parade. Seattle will be crawling with guys in uniform for fleet week."

Nate laughed. "You two are dangerous and can't help looking like some guy's twin fantasy. I'll need a Taser to control the masses of testosterone."

"Never ever going to fulfill a twin-fantasy," they said in unison a little too loud, and at just the right moment.

Kent prowled from behind and draped his muscular arms loosely around their necks. "Damn, I'm disappointed. Why do you think I've hung out with you two all these years? I've only been biding my time."

"For you Kent, anything." Each twin pulled him down to plant a kiss on an opposite cheek.

"When do you three leave for the big city?" he asked squeezing between the twins and grabbing two cookies.

"Tomorrow morning. You won't even notice we're gone."

"Seth will notice," Kent said as he chewed. "He's been moping around the shop all day. How about you, Kels, what trips do you have planned?"

"More family float-trips. Nothing exciting, but that's where the money is. We do have a group that needs a guide for a paddle on the Sandy. I'd love to snag that job."

"Shit Kels, the Sandy?" Kent's brows rose. "That river won't tolerate errors. Let me know if that pans out for you."

"Jealous?" Kelsey asked.

Kent tightened his grip on the twin's shoulders. "Not for the Sandy trip. No. I have to admit, I envy the lucky guy who finally gets his twin fantasy realized."

"Shut up. Perve!" Rose and Jasmine landed a couple of solid smacks as he scrambled out of his seat between them on the bench, laughing.

"Ladies, it's been a pleasure. Thanks for the cookies, Nate. See you all soon."

Kent wandered off, but when he glanced back Natalie caught a look of concern. She couldn't tell if he was worried more about the twins partying in Seattle or Kelsey landing a spot on the trip down the Sandy River.

***

Seattle traffic gave Natalie a headache. She took two aspirin and felt even better when she sent Seth a text. *We made it. Headed to a concert at Gasworks. Miss you.*

***

From his perch on a stool at Northside Grill, Seth texted back. *Miss you too.*

Feeling a little lost, he decided to order another beer. "Hey, Iris, can I have another IPA?"

She glanced at the two empties. "Sure thing, Seth, what can I get you to go with that?"

He took her not-so-subtle hint. "I guess I better get chili fries to soak it up."

Iris filled another pint for him as a woman snaked forward. Seth refused to respond when Desiree took the seat next to him at the bar.

"Hey, Seth, I already stopped by the shop for a visit. I'm surprised to find you here this early."

"So, you stopped at Whitewater? Weren't you looking for Rick?"

"Oh, baby—I didn't know how much you still cared," she whined with pseudo-sweetness.

Seth lifted his eyebrows when she reached over and helped herself to a drink of his beer, her mouth lingering on the edge of the glass.

"I heard you lost your girl and need some company," she said and bit her lip hard enough to leave a dent, her usual hint for hot, tied-up sex.

Seth shook his head and pushed his beer toward his ex-wife, unwilling to share her spit.

With a shake of her head, Des added, "Fuck, Seth. This girl has you by the balls. This won't last. You're never the one who wears the shackles." Desiree grinned while she pressed his buttons with sniper-precision, amused by his pain.

Buzz ruined, he spotted his broken reflection between the bottles of booze in the mirrored-wall behind the bar. "I don't need this," he muttered to the face staring back at him. Seth hated that man. Damaged and twisted by his failures, he knew that Natalie deserved better. It was a good thing she planned to escape him soon.

Desiree stood and scraped her fingernails over her ex-husband's shoulder. "Call me when she's gone, and we'll hook up like we always do. Because, baby . . . you need me.

Seth didn't bother to respond. "Shot of Jack," he said when the chili fries arrived. *Might as well get shit-faced drunk.*

***

Natalie and the twins parted ways after the concert. With an orientation starting early the next morning, Jasmine and Rose needed to get back to the university.

Hidden in her darkroom, Natalie exhaled a long, satisfied sigh, having forgotten how much this place centered her. Chemicals, paper, dark and light—the simple magic dazed her every time. The black and whites she took of the lightning storm were vibrant, and she couldn't wait to frame one for Seth. Happy about the photos, she sent him a goodnight text but it wasn't answered. *Strange.*

Starved after a few hours in her darkroom, Natalie toasted bread and slathered on a layer of peanut butter then hopped onto the kitchen counter to devour it. The time alone infused her with energy, and she found herself in the doorway of Grandpa's office. She took a deep breath and decided to tackle the chaos hidden in his desk.

Music drifted through the condo from a classic rock station. She opened drawers and sorted through piles. Important documents sat to her left, personal stuff to her right, and in the center, a large cardboard box overflowed with a strange assortment of trash.

Sifting through his desk, she found a stack of personal cards and letters from Elsa. She placed the letters in a pile to return to her friend in the morning.

Dozens of photos she had shot filled an entire drawer. Grandpa loved her photography. All around his condo, her best photographs still hung in simple black frames.

Maybe Amanda could help her sell those at the farmers' market in Ashwood. She simply didn't have enough room to keep them all.

In a crushed shoebox, Natalie discovered a stack of yellowed letters, postmarked 1962, the year Grandpa and Grandma began dating. Tears welled. She couldn't read those personal messages . . . not yet. Still, leaving them in the condo seemed wrong.

Glancing around, she spotted an ancient hatbox tucked in the back of the closet. Opening it, she found it stuffed full of old seed packets and shook her head. "People keep the strangest things." She dumped the seeds into the trash, wiped out the round box, and put the precious letters inside to read another day.

In a filing cabinet, she found a manila envelope beneath another heavy stack of *National Geographic magazines. Osprey Lake, Ashwood,* was neatly typed on the top left corner of the wrinkled envelope.

Prying the metal clasp with her fingernail, she opened the envelope and removed a stack of papers—a title for land, a faded hand-drawn sketch, and a few Kodak pictures of the lake. Unfolding the drawing, she traced her fingers over her Grandfather's writing. He'd labeled boundary lines, a small outbuilding, and plans for a cabin.

"Oh my God, twenty-two acres of waterfront property." She stared at it for a long moment, set it aside, only to pick it up again three separate times. She wanted answers, but this late, there was no one she could call.

By two fifteen in the morning, after sorting, researching, and more sorting, she could scarcely see straight. Natalie brushed her teeth and crawled into her old bed. Seth never texted, but all the clutter in Grandpa's office kept her from obsessing.

***

Seth woke with a puddle of drool pooled between his cheek and the warn leather of his office couch.

What the hell?"

The pounding of nails in the shop matched the pounding in his skull. He moved his head just enough to peer through the window, but he didn't find his truck parked outside. *Thank God I didn't drive here.*

A note from Kent was stapled to his shirt.
Stapled? Seriously.

Seth read the note slowly hoping to find clues.

—I hauled your sorry ass over here before you made a bigger fool of yourself – YOU'RE WELCOME - KENT

Events pieced together in his mind. Multiple shots of whiskey, a grinding slow dance in front of half the town with his ex, and he'd capped his night off by trying to pick a fight with two big-ass tourists who were hitting on Desiree.

The last thing he remembered was Kent and Wade dragging him out of Northside Grill. They must have dumped him here to sleep it off.

He felt like a steaming pile of crap. *How could I do this to Natalie? I need to talk to her before she hears the embellished version from Kelsey.*

Seth grabbed his phone. *Of course*, the battery was dead. Finding a charger at his desk, he plugged it in. Once it powered up, he discovered that sleeping until eleven gave half the town plenty of time to blast his phone with messages. "Shit, Shit, Shit."

Natalie left two text messages, one last night and one this morning. She wanted to share some news. There was also a missed call from her, but no voicemail. "Maybe she hasn't heard anything. Please, God—let me have one free pass."

He glared at two calls from his mother. She definitely had the scoop and wanted to make him suffer.

His brows furrowed trying to decipher a cryptic text from Desiree, peppered with strange symbols. He didn't have the first damn clue what those emoji meant and did not care.

Last, he read a single text from Kent. **Kelsey's out of town. I Don't know how much time you have to fix this. Good luck, asshole.**

Seth staggered into the small bathroom attached to his office, brushed his teeth, splashed water on his face, and tossed on a baseball cap. He heard his office door open and shut and returned to find his mother sitting in his chair behind his desk, waiting.

"Mom, I'm barely awake. Can I call you later when I can think clearly?"

"No," she said, too loud. "Silence is perfect. You need to *listen*."

"Fair enough," he mumbled, blinking hard to bring her into focus.

She folded her hands on the top of his desk. It reminded him of those times he'd been sent to the principal's office. "What happened last night at The Northside will blow over, just like all gossip in this town. But it's time for you to take your life off the shelf and start living. Natalie and I went to lunch last week. I like her . . . I like her for you."

That got his attention. "Natalie didn't say anything to me about having lunch with you."

"Does she have to run every detail of her life by you, son?"

"No. Point taken." He nodded and pressed his lips shut.

"Natalie likes Ashwood and feels a connection to the people and to this town. Her eyes light up when she talks about you. She's falling in love with you, Seth. If your unusual behavior is any indication, you love her, too."

Her pause was long, but he wasn't sure he could get a sentence past the disgusting cotton mouth.

"Tell me, does that terrify you?" she asked.

"I'm not terrified, Mom."

"Do you love her, Seth?"

"Yes."

"Have you told her?"

"No."

"There's your first mistake. How do you expect her to make decisions about her future when she doesn't have any idea how you feel?"

"Mom, she's leaving."

"Son, she doesn't want to wander the Earth selling coffee out of a camper."

He pinched the spot between his eyes. "For the hundredth time, I don't build campers."

"Can you really see Natalie living like a nomad? Do you intend to let her drive off, pulling that house on wheels behind that giant pickup?"

The only place Seth could picture her making coffee was in his kitchen, wearing one of his cotton T-shirts, with her hair tossed on her head in a messy bun.

"Seth, I love you, and I want the best for you. You deserve another chance at love. Build a future with Natalie."

He glanced up, bleary-eyed but determined. "Okay. I got this."

FIFTEEN

Natalie knocked and in a few moments Elsa's door opened. While twisting a tendril of her wet hair, Natalie apologized with a smile. "It's too early, right? I'm sorry. I can come back later."

The scent of cinnamon, rich and sweet, drifted from Elsa's kitchen. No wonder Grandpa Pete had loved her so much.

"Sweetheart, I was just spreading frosting on the coffee cake. Come in and help yourself. It looks like you have something on your mind."

"I've missed you." After a long hug, Natalie cut herself a slice of the warm crumbly cake and added cream to her mug of coffee. She sank into the rose-patterned floral chair and snuggled into the comfortable cushions.

"Oh, Elsa this is so delicious," she moaned, savoring another bite.

"Thank you. I'll give you the recipe. Now, I know you didn't show up this early on the off-chance that I made coffee cake." Elsa chuckled, and Natalie felt completely at home. "Dear, what's on your mind?"

"Last night I was going through Grandpa's office, sorting through his papers, and I found something unexpected. He had property on Osprey Lake in Ashwood. Did you know?"

"My goodness, yes, he bought property up there years ago. In fact, he camped up there and used it as a base for fishing. I thought he sold it about the time you started college."

"Have you ever visited? I couldn't tell where it is on the lake."

Elsa closed her eyes imagining the scene. "If you stand on the property, facing the water, the Fisher place is about a quarter of the way around on the left."

"Just a second, let me find a map." Natalie opened Elsa's old laptop and pulled up a satellite photo. Taking a moment to locate the collection of buildings that made up the Fisher property, she pointed them out on the screen.

Elsa leaned in. "These details are just astounding. This section of taller timber must be Pete's property. The owners next door thinned their trees to open up the view. I think your grandpa's land made a narrow rectangle that extends toward this ridge."

Just above her property, sitting on top of that steep incline, Natalie saw the green metal roof of Seth's home reflecting the sunlight in the satellite photo.

Why hadn't he called or sent a text? She desperately wanted to share this news with him.

"Isn't that something?" Elsa continued, "I was certain Pete sold that land."

"I'm not even sure the land is mine. Maybe Grandpa left it to someone else." Natalie sank back, confused. "Oh, and one more thing . . . inside his desk were letters that I need to return to you, but I don't have them with me."

Elsa's cheeks flushed and she pressed her hands to her face. "He kept those?"

"Don't worry. I didn't read them. Those thoughts are for the two of you. Why don't you come by later, and I'll return the letters?"

"Thank you, dear. I'll stop by this afternoon."

"I better get going. I have an appointment with the lawyer. Come by around two, if you have time."

Natalie gave Elsa a long hug and left to catch a bus downtown. Seattle rolled by through the large filmy windows. The buildings and parks zipping past were familiar, but the city didn't feel like home anymore.

***

Seth paced the vast gravel lot attempting to clear the alcohol-induced haze from his mind. Battling dehydration, he took another long swig from his sports drink and pulled his phone from his pocket. Fingers shaking, he worked up the nerve to call Natalie before she heard a more lurid version of last night's events from one of her friends.

The phone rang three times before she picked up. "Hi, Seth, I'm sorry, I'm on the bus and running late. Can I call you back?"

He cursed his bad timing and tried to sound relaxed. "No problem, whenever you have a minute."

The rumble of the bus made her words difficult to understand. "I have news. I guess it's good. I'll call as soon as I can. Need to go."

"Bye, miss you," he added as her phone beeped off in his ear. Nausea pushed its way to the back of his throat, but it wasn't from the lingering effects of the alcohol.

***

The aroma of roasting coffee mingled with pungent salty air as she hurried from the bus. Jogging the block, Natalie climbed the brick stairs leading to the lawyer's office near Pikes Place Market. The assistant looked up to find her panting in the doorway.

"Sorry . . . I'm a little late."

"Go right on in. Ms. Evert's expecting you." She brought Natalie a bottled water and shut the door as she left.

Miss Evert nodded as Natalie took a seat. "Good morning, Natalie. This shouldn't take too long. After we get the boat paperwork squared away, I have another matter to discuss with you."

"Thank you for your help. I have a question as well." Natalie signed where the small sticky arrows indicated, and Ms. Evert closed the file. "Why don't we begin with your question?"

"When I was cleaning out Grandpa's office, I found some documents about property on Osprey Lake. Is this a place he still owned when he passed?"

"Let me see." Ms. Evert tapped a few keys and her eyes roamed back and forth across the computer screen. "Yes, here it is. The land on Osprey Lake is listed among the assets you inherited. When we met a few months ago, we may not have gone over that specifically. I'm sorry. I just assumed you visited there in the past. Do you have any questions about the land?"

"No. When I found the paperwork, I only wondered if Grandpa had sold it." Natalie sat back, taking in her new reality. "At least this is property I can keep."

"Yes, the condo needs to go on the market soon to meet the requirements of that community. And it should sell quickly. Do you plan to build something on Lake Osprey?"

"It's too soon to decide. I guess I could park my tiny house at the lake, but I already reserved a spot in a community on the Oregon coast." Natalie nibbled her bottom lip, considering the possibilities. "Hmm, now I have two options."

She took a long swig from her water and asked her lawyer, "What was the other matter you wanted to discuss?"

Ms. Evert's smile faded. "I don't want you to be alarmed. A letter concerning your grandfather's estate was received by our office."

Natalie eased forward to listen to her lawyer. "The correspondence was from Malcolm Journey."

A gasp tightened her throat. "Oh, no. Not my father."

With a short nod, Ms. Evert continued, "Apparently, he's exploring the possibility of contesting the will to secure assets from the estate for your brother."

The unexpected news smothered her with thoughts of guilt and anger, and tears pressed against the back of her eyes. "Is this something I should worry about?"

"No. Pete wanted you to be the sole beneficiary. These matters were discussed years ago during your parents' divorce proceedings. Your father does not have any legal recourse."

"Have you talked to my brother?" Natalie hadn't heard from Ben since the morning of Grandpa's funeral.

"No, all correspondence went through Malcolm's attorney. Please, don't worry. When the will was signed your grandfather was in perfect health and had made sound decisions."

Natalie sat back in her chair and finished her water. "Is there anything you need me to do? Would you advise that I reach out and talk about this with my father or brother?"

"Actually, I would advise against that. If Malcolm contacts you directly, please let me know. Peter's wishes were followed as he directed. His greatest concern was your welfare."

Natalie sighed softly. "That does sound like Grandpa."

Ms. Evert nodded as Natalie picked up her backpack. "Thank you so much, Ms. Evert. I know you're busy. I'll be in touch when I'm ready to move forward with the sale of the condo."

"Please call anytime."

A storm of feelings buffeted her thoughts. Should she give some of the inheritance to Ben? Her father had all but abandoned her. Even a call on her birthday was a rare event.

Heavy steps scuffed to the bus stop where she waited in a hazy emotional fog. She wanted to talk to Ben, and needed to talk to Seth, but her bus pulled up too quickly for either.

Headphones on, she blotted out the tempest with a thumping bassline. With property on Lake Osprey, Natalie could finally belong to one place. That choice came with a heavy price. Everyone told her Seth never dated women from Ashwood. She didn't know if her heart could survive living in a small town with Seth after he decided to move on.

Increasing the volume on her headphones, she sunk down on her seat, gazed out the window of the bus, and waited for her stop.

**

Seth's crew avoided his office, and no one approached him in the shop. Almost a ghost, his employees functioned just fine without him.

"To hell with this waiting," he mumbled. Seth grabbed his jacket and shut down his computer. He popped his head into the home where Carlos stood on a ladder installing trim. "Hey, I'm leaving for a few days. Give me a call if anything comes up."

"Got it. Good luck," Carlos added with a quick nod.

With a full tank and some thick coffee from the gas station, he left for Seattle to find Natalie.

***

Finding time to return Seth's call was impossible. Elsa met her at her door with a lasagna ready to go into the oven. They worked together, sorting documents and cleaning out the entire office while sharing memories, laughter, and tears.

The lasagna came bubbling from the oven. Red wine, hot French bread, and a fresh salad completed the delicious meal. After dinner, Elsa and Natalie sat at the dining room table, sorting pictures into piles.

"Look at this one. Ben looks so much like Grandpa. Is this Grandma in the picture with him?"

Handing the faded black and white to Elsa, she smiled, reliving a memory. "Actually, dear, I'm the girl in this photo. I'm not surprised you don't recognize me. It was such a long time ago." Elsa blushed recalling the summer she met Pete. "Did you find any other photos with these?"

Natalie piled a stack of pictures between them, and together they studied each image.

"Right here, this is your grandmother, she's standing with me and my sister—Kelsey's grandmother. We had so many wonderful times."

Natalie studied the photo. Three laughing teenage girls, dressed in skirts and sweaters, standing in front of a muscle car.

"Your grandpa was so proud of that car—not many boys back then owned one. Around Ashwood, like now, most just drove old pickups." Before Natalie could ask if Elsa and Grandpa dated when they were younger, a loud knock rattled the front door.

Pushing back from the table, Natalie said, "I don't know who that could be . . . everything I planned to sell right now is already gone."

***

The lock clunked before the knob turned. Seth couldn't breathe. When the door opened, he snagged Natalie's waist, pulled her close, and plundered her mouth with a thorough kiss. Coming up for air, Natalie stepped away from him by a fraction. He studied her carefully, looking for any evidence that she had heard the shitty news.

"Well hello, Seth," Elsa teased from the living room. He tipped up his chin as Elsa gathered her sweater to leave. "Natalie, we accomplished plenty this evening. Give me a call tomorrow, dear."

Seth pulled Natalie to his side, unwilling to lose her touch. "Nice to see you," he said. "It's been a long time."

Elsa slipped by, chuckling as she pulled the door shut.

Natalie eased from Seth's arms and pulled him toward the living room. Carefully, her eyes searched his face. "What are you doing here? I would have been home in a few days."

"We need to talk. And it couldn't wait."

Natalie's breath hitched. "Is everything all right?"

"I think it will be." To order his thoughts, Seth roamed the half-empty living room and inspected the black and white photographs hanging on every wall. "Did you take these pictures?" he asked while tucking an arm around her waist.

She nodded as he glanced from her shot of Mount Rainier to a black and white of the Space Needle. "I developed them here in my darkroom. I guess I won't have room to hang these in my tiny home." A shadow of sadness shifted her expression. He pulled her tightly against his side, knowing he was bound to add more pain.

"Seth, I love that you're here, but I still don't know why. What's happened?"

He pulled her to sit close to him on the sofa and kept her hand trapped in his. "When you left on Saturday, I went over to The Northside. My first mistake was sitting alone at the bar instead of hanging out with the guys. My second mistake, several shots of whiskey." Pacing himself, he watched his thumb stroke the back of her small hand.

"My ex showed up. I didn't know she was in town." Natalie attempted to pull away, but Seth gripped her hand tighter. "We have a history. Desiree and I kept in touch after the divorce."

Unshed tears crowded Natalie's words. "Kels told me about Desiree . . . warned me I guess."

"Nothing really happened. I mean, nothing that half the town didn't witness. You'll probably hear versions of this from your friends, but I need you to hear it from me. After I drank several shots, I vaguely remember dancing with her."

Seth stared at the floor, avoiding the pain in her eyes. "Later, Des danced with some tourists. You know, grinding on the dance floor. And shit, I really couldn't care less. She probably left with them later that night. These guys, there were two of them—they had her pressed between them."

Head dipped; his voice rumbled with shame. "Anyway, hell, I was wasted, got pissed, and tried to pull them out of The Northside to beat the shit out of them in the parking lot."

He raked his free hand through his hair, his gaze locked on the floor. "I'm such a fucking idiot. Wade and Kent pulled my ass out of there and dumped me off at the shop. I woke up this morning, on the couch in my office, with a pounding headache, feeling like . . . like I betrayed you. Natalie, please, let me make this up to you."

This time when she tugged, he let her hand slip from his. Natalie stirred beside him on the couch. She moved over him and settled on his lap, straddling his hips between her thighs. Sliding her hands to his face, she kissed Seth and waited for his eyes to meet hers.

"So, let me get this straight. You protected a woman, one you have a history with, from scumbags who were grabbing her ass in front of half the town?"

His eyes lit. He didn't deserve her compassion. "Yeah, but—"

Natalie covered his lips with her fingers to finish her thought. "Seth, I won't play second to her. If you decide to see Desiree while we're together, what we have is over. But what happened doesn't come close to crossing that line."

His hands smashed her entire body against his, and he kissed her as if his life depended on it.

"She's nothing but a memory," he said against her lips, "completely locked in the past. My future belongs to you."

Natalie's mouth soothed his fears, but he had more to promise. "I'll do everything I can to deserve you," he said, intending to keep that vow.

Her caress passed from his lips to the hollow of his neck, meeting her fingers to trace the line of his jaw. Those beautiful delicate fingers gave him a gift. She teased open each button on her blouse and let the fabric drop to the floor. But she wasn't finished. Natalie coiled her hands behind her torso and found the hooks on her bra. As the soft lace fell away, her pale skin erased his fears and replaced the emotion with passion.

Standing, Natalie held her hand for Seth to take. She led him to her bed. Seth gave himself to the soothing balm of her forgiveness.

Natalie shared every part of herself, and he gave her his unconfessed love in return.

SIXTEEN

The rich aroma of coffee and bacon woke Seth. He blinked at the confusing surroundings until he recognized her feminine touches—the purple bedspread, a delicate jewelry box, and stunning photographs on the wall.

Seth slid on jeans, went to the bathroom, and found a toothbrush before locating Natalie in the kitchen. "Smells fantastic." He grabbed a hot slice of bacon and ate it in two bites.

She smiled up at him as he slid a hand around her waist. "You slept late."

He glanced at the clock. "Wow, eleven! You wore me out last night, sweetness." He gave her shorts-clad butt a caress. "I feel fantastic. Will it be a day in Seattle, or should we entertain ourselves here?" Seth snagged another slice of bacon.

"If you want, we could spend the day at Alki Beach. I checked the schedule, there's a home game. What do you think?"

"The beach and baseball with my girl? Couldn't be better. Maybe we could find a secluded spot on the beach where I could have my way with you."

She giggled as he wriggled his eyebrows. "In Seattle? Impossible." She loved this playful side of Seth almost as much as the dominant streak he showed her again last night.

"Are fried eggs okay?"

He nodded yes, chewing bacon while he sat on a stool to watch her move around the kitchen.

Natalie slid three eggs onto his plate just as wheat bread popped from the toaster. He buttered her toast as her eggs sizzled in the pan.

After they cleaned up and she turned on the dishwasher, Seth realized that he hadn't seen the entire condo. "Why don't you show me your darkroom?" he asked.

"You really want to see it?"

"Yeah. It's where the magic happens." He pulled her down the hall and felt her fingers twitch when Natalie's nerves jumped.

He waited at the door to her darkroom for Natalie to lead him into her private space. She grasped the knob, turned, and pushed the door open.

In the converted bathroom, empty trays waited on a long counter. Over the tub, photos hung from a cord by clothespins. "The storm pictures," he said staring, but not touching. "These are stunning."

"Thanks." Her quiet reply seemed almost embarrassed. Seth admired her careful organization. She had removed cabinet doors to allow for easy access. Paper, chemicals, and plastic bins were stacked neatly, waiting for her to use them.

"What's this black contraption?" he asked.

"An enlarger. It takes the negative and projects my image on light-sensitive paper."

"Cool." He nodded and touched the knob but didn't change any of the adjustments. "Do you work in the dark?"

"Sometimes." She reached around and flipped two switches. The light changed from white to red. Her breathing hitched. "I'm going to give this up."

"Sweetness, why?" Everything about that decision seemed wrong.

"Carlos told me he can't make it fit. Not in a way I'd be happy with. And I have to sell this place by the end of August. It's okay—I'll still shoot with film and send it to a lab."

Seth felt like he'd failed. He shook his head and struggled to find a way to fix this.

Natalie forced a smile. "I have a buyer lined up, and he's a friend. At least it won't be too bad seeing it go."

"Who?"

"A customer. He's a regular at Elsa's coffee shop. A photographer who retired from the Seattle P.I."

Seth nodded, determined to find a way to fit a darkroom into her life.

***

After his shower, Seth emerged from the bathroom with a towel slung low on his hips. Natalie recognized that gaze. He intended to mess her up.

Already dressed, she turned and found him stripping her bare with his eyes.

"There's no way I'm keeping my hands off you in that string bikini. Let me get this out of my system now or the beach could end in disaster."

He peeled away her tank top then traced the tiny triangles cupping her breasts with his fingertips. "Beautiful."

As Natalie giggled and squirmed, he kissed each creamy swell then nipped her taut peaks through the thin fabric. Seth's eyes hooded. He took a few steps back and sank into a chair. Her eyes landed on his bulge tenting the thick cotton towel.

"Strip for me," he said with a sexy grin.

Natalie turned her back to him. An inch at a time, she eased the zipper down then shimmied her snug shorts over her full hips. Adding a wiggle, she bent at the waist and slipped one leg at a time out of her shorts but left the bottoms of her skimpy bikini in place.

"Fuck," he muttered.

She giggled, but she wasn't finished yet.

Spinning to face Seth, Natalie's eyes danced as she slid the strings open first at her neck and then at the back, but she held the triangles in place. In one move, she let the bikini fall and dangle from her finger and thumb. Twirling it, she tossed the turquoise scrap to Seth.

He caught it with his left hand, as his right moved his towel away from his engorged length.

Widening her stance, Natalie slowly untied and stripped the bottoms away, dangling them again from one hand.

Seth's erection jumped and her naked body heated.

"Come here," he growled.

Natalie moved closer, her skin prickling with the heat of his gaze. She stood in front of Seth, waiting for his touch. He guided her legs and hips over his torso, delaying contact for a single controlled impale. Natalie climbed aloft and carefully lowered, taking him inside her slick heat with one smooth, almost painfully slow, slide. She hissed as her body took him in.

"So damn tight," Seth growled and gripped her hips to control the pace. He lifted her from his length only to plunge her against his hips again.

Tension spiraled. She wrapped her heels around the legs of the chair, and her arms encircled his shoulders to gain purchase and pitch the angle exactly right. Her hips canted. The pulse around his girth increased as her slick arousal enhanced the connection.

"Harder, Seth," she cried against his neck. He took each globe of her ass in hand, lifting to increase the velocity of her frantic ride. Her fingers clawed into his shoulders as she came, and he shivered when her teeth grazed his skin.

Still shaking, Seth resumed the measured thrusts, lifting her hips and impaling her center as his release built at the base of his spine. A final penetration bathed her channel. When he finally stilled, she wilted against his chest. She matched his slow inhale and exhale until their gasps flipped to uninhibited laughter.

***

With her camera aimed across Puget Sound, Natalie snapped pictures of Seattle from their spot on Alki Beach. When hunger gnawed, they found a restaurant with a walk-up window and ordered fried clams, oysters, and fries. She followed him with oversized drinks as he carried paper-lined baskets to a beachside picnic table.

After they munched their way through the seafood, he nibbled on fries and asked, "Do you ever miss Seattle?"

"Not too much. With the high cost of living, I felt like I was constantly working just to survive."

"But is that still a problem?" She hadn't cut corners on her home and he figured she was set.

"I guess not. After living in Ashwood this city isn't so tempting." She grabbed a fry and was aiming for her mouth when she suddenly grinned. "Oh, I completely forgot that I have news. A couple of things have happened in the last few days. One is great. The other, not so much."

When she revealed her father's letter, Seth clenched his teeth, wondering how a man could neglect his family, ignore his daughter, and then expect money.

Natalie found her smile again when she revealed better news. With it came Seth's first glimmer of hope—she had a reason to settle in Ashwood.

"The lakefront property is so unexpected," she said. "But I wish Grandpa had told me about the land. I would have loved seeing him there."

"Who knows, we might have met sooner," Seth pointed out.

"I hadn't thought of that. What do you think seventeen-year-old Seth would've thought of twelve-year-old Natalie?"

"Scratch that idea. I'm happy you didn't know me then. I was such an ass."

"I don't believe it."

He stared and nodded *yes* until she laughed and gave in. "Okay. I believe you."

Seth shrugged. "I guess my past doesn't matter. I'm not really the same person since I met you." He never realized until this moment how much Natalie had changed him.

As she stared out over the water, Natalie toyed with the settings on her camera. "I don't know what I should do. I've never had so many options."

"There's no need to rush."

"Then I'll take my time and enjoy this moment." Natalie lifted her camera to snap a photo of a ferry repeating a trip across Puget Sound. The boat left a long wake in the water—an imprint that wouldn't last long.

Seth wondered if the impression he made on her life would be just as temporary.

***

Baseball, the glass museum, and canoeing on Lake Washington filled their next two days. Seth played the role of tourist while answering an occasional email.

Whenever Natalie was busy, he rushed to Elsa's place. Two days were scarcely enough time to iron out the details of his complicated plan.

He couldn't have done it without his enthusiastic helper. Elsa agreed that Natalie would definitely regret giving up her darkroom. Working with the retired photojournalist, Seth asked this potential buyer for a huge favor.

The man, a romantic at heart, seemed to enjoy his part in the clandestine transfer. He agreed to pack Natalie's dark room, pretending to buy the entire lot, and with help, relocate the contents to Whitewater Homes. Seth's family, working in Seattle and Ashwood, was more than willing to assist with the relocation of her darkroom.

Rose and Jasmine's presence in Seattle now seemed like fate. And Amanda couldn't wait to help unpack everything in Ashwood. With so many moving parts, Seth didn't know if he could keep the whole thing a secret, though, he was determined to try.

One concern wormed into his mind—a gesture this big might be too much too soon.

When Thursday night rolled around, he had to find a way to nudge Natalie from the condo and transfer his truck to Rose and Jasmine. It wasn't too difficult—this city was already grating on his nerves.

"Are you okay?" Natalie asked as he slouched on the couch, exaggerating his sulk.

"I'm fine . . . why?"

"You're just really quiet." He was more than quiet. All morning he'd kept his hands off Natalie. The cool distance might be an act, but it was still torture.

He rubbed his temples, wondering if the gesture was too much. "I guess I've had enough of the city."

"Come here," she said, moving him so she could massage his shoulders. It took all his self-control to keep from pulling her beneath him.

As her fingers kneaded, she admitted, "I'm anxious to get out of here, too."

Seth held back a grin when she suggested, "Why don't I call Jasmine and Rose? Maybe they can bring my truck back to Ashwood, and I'll ride home with you."

"Are you sure?" he asked.

"Absolutely. The condo's so hollow now . . . it's sort of, I don't know, sad." Only a few of her favorite things were still around. She still hadn't decided if she should sell or store these cherished last reminders of Grandpa Pete.

"How would you feel about a side trip?" he asked, needing her on the road an extra day for his plan to work. "I spotted Pete's camping gear, and it's pretty sweet. We could take an extra night on our way home."

"Perfect. I can be ready tomorrow morning." Natalie almost glowed. "I can't wait. I haven't camped in forever."

With the last element of his plan in place, he stretched his arms and pretended to relax.

"Sweetness, that backrub was heaven. How about I return the favor?" In one fluid move, he tackled her to the couch and plundered her with his fingers, lips, and tongue.

SEVENTEEN

Just after dawn, they drove into the sun, traveling east on Interstate 90. Within an hour, the landscape transitioned from lush green to arid. This stark contrast never ceased to surprise Seth's senses. He'd always felt like the stark beauty on the east side of the state was a well-kept secret.

While Seth gassed up the pickup, he answered Jasmine's final text, and warned her that he'd be losing cell service in the wilderness.

Seth: *Elsa has the keys to Natalie's condo and my truck.*

Jasmine: *Cool. We'll pick everything up in an hour.*

Seth: *Just head to Whitewater. Amanda's handling everything in Ashwood. She asked a friend from Hood River to help set up the darkroom.*

Jasmine: *This is off the charts romantic.*

Seth: *Feels right. I hope Natalie likes it.*

Jasmine: *Are you kidding? It's perfect.*

Seth: *Gotta go. Text Amanda if you need anything.*

Jasmine: *Got it. And have fun - we'll take care of everything.*

Amanda knew the spot where he was headed. With no cell service, he'd given her thirty-six hours to pull this together. Thrilled to be trusted with so much, his sister had promised to handle every detail of his perfect surprise.

***

A few miles outside of Ellensburg, Seth turned south. He drove narrow two-lane roads Natalie never knew existed. By noon, the air prickled with heat.

Eventually the blacktop transitioned to graded gravel where he stopped and opened a gate, drove his truck through, and closed the gate behind them. Following a creek, they passed twisted pine, cottonwood, and prickly pear cactus.

Seth parked off the road on a wide bank overlooking a deep spot in the river. "I hope you're okay roughing it. We'll need to boil water and there aren't any bathrooms."

Natalie grinned. "Not a problem. I love how remote this feels. Where are we, anyway?"

"On the western edge of a parcel owned by Wade's family. It's passed from one part of the Michaels' family to another for generations."

Seth chose a sheltered spot beneath a gnarled cottonwood to make camp. The dappled shade took the edge off the blazing sun. Setting up didn't take long, but the work was still enough to send a trickle of sweat down his back. The arid heat quickly whisked away the moisture, and he was thirsty no matter how much he drank.

Digging in a cooler, he pulled out two bottles of Gatorade and tossed one to Natalie. "Keep hydrated."

"Thanks. I better put on sunscreen or I'll be miserable tonight."

He smoothed sunscreen on places she couldn't reach and was tempted to touch her everywhere, but the water looked just as inviting.

A deep calm pool on a bend in the river offered an escape from the sweltering sun. Natalie dove beneath the cool water and popped to the surface on the opposite bank where Seth sat watching her from a wide, flat boulder.

She joined him, layered on sunscreen, and let the sun dry her hair into a cloud of red curls. "It's hard to believe we're anywhere near Seattle. The contrast is so dramatic and beautiful. It's strange . . . I find it's almost easier to breathe."

"Maybe it's the low humidity," he said.

"No, I think it might be the open space."

Natalie seemed to understand why he loved this place, and her appreciation of the stark landscape pleased him. Lacing their fingers together, he brought her hand to his lips and kissed each knuckle one at a time.

Natalie sighed and turned to face him. "Maybe the hope of an escape just like this drew me to the tiny house idea. The city, with crowds of disconnected people, feels lonelier somehow. I don't know, Seth, maybe I'm not making sense."

"I get it. I'm relieved you feel it, too." Seth had never been this unguarded, and she didn't seem to hide anything from him.

Yes, she would leave this fall, and it would hurt like hell, because she would take something of him with her. Yet, he'd come to realize she'd also leave a bit of herself behind. The exchange would be even. He was willing to give her everything in the time they had left.

The hot sun forced Natalie into the cool river again. She stepped out onto the other bank and found her camera to shoot pictures of two red-winged blackbirds in the tall grass.

Scrambling higher on the boulder, Seth studied her as she patiently waited for the perfect shot. Black and sleek, the birds stopped noticing the girl with the camera and Seth barely heard the shutter click. Satisfied, she straightened, and the birds flew away. Natalie crossed toward camp, stowed her camera, and pulled a bottled water from the cooler.

After drinking half, she glanced in his direction and grinned playfully. Arms behind her neck, she untied her bikini top, and pretended to ignore his gaze as she smoothed sunscreen over her palest skin. Seth could scarcely breathe. Her golden body, with lighter triangles on the soft mounds, held his attention for a long moment.

Her name left his lips in a whisper, "Natalie." *So stunning. So beautiful. So mine.*

With a quick smile, she shimmied out of her cut-offs and walked nude into the river. The water swirled around her waist, caressing her curves.

From his perch on the boulder, Seth jumped in, stripped, and tossed his shorts on a rock. She giggled as cool water, hot sun, and his kisses worshipped every inch of her warm skin.

The taste of her skin wasn't enough. Seth needed more. He lifted Natalie to the edge of that same smooth boulder where it dipped into the water near the bank. Touching her curves, he nipped deliberate bites on her breasts, stomach, and legs. Saving the best, he lifted her hips to relish her soft pink center.

Tickling his scalp with her fingertips, she closed her eyes as his tongue danced and lapped at her core. As her breathing raced, he flicked her bundle of nerves but stopped the moment her legs began to quake.

"Torture," she moaned and lifted her head. She blinked at his back lit silhouette in the bright sunlight.

"Trust me?" he puffed against her sex.

"Always."

With a slow nod, he dove again between her thighs. He began as he had before, sucking the tender flesh into his mouth then plunging his tongue into her heat.

He pulled away a fraction, but this time his tongue slid lower, exploring the sensitive bud.

Natalie froze but had promised to trust him and didn't hitch her hips away. His lips moved up again, returning to her clitoris for a more thorough taste.

Desperate eyes measured her reaction as his fingers dipped into her drenched heat, stroking her within. Slowly he explored. His wet fingers caressed her rosebud and she lost herself in new sensations—flicks on nerves, tongue in her cleft, and a slow new penetration.

Owned, she cried out, eyes bright with surprise. The cresting orgasm ripped through her body as Seth created fresh paths for bliss that belonged only to him.

After he coaxed her last wave of pleasure, he grasped her waist and lifted Natalie into the water again. Wrapping her legs around him, he moved a few steps deeper into the clear pool for a tangled kiss.

"Thank you for sharing this with me," she whispered as she collapsed against his chest. Purple light bathed their naked bodies. The air cooled, forcing them to leave the water and dress.

Against the edge of the mountains, dark followed sunset quickly. Seth built a fire as sounds of scurrying animals mingled with the murmur of the river. Leaning together near the fire, Natalie drifted. "How can I be so tired? It's not even ten."

"Come on. Let's stretch out in the tent. We'll wake up at first light and head home."

Naked again in the warm tent, Natalie woke enough to climb over his hips and wring another climax from their sunbaked bodies before falling asleep.

At first light, Seth woke, legs tangled with hers. Half-asleep, he didn't want to leave the spell of his recent perfect dream. In his sleep-induced fantasy, he had the courage to tell Natalie that he loved her, and she had echoed his words in return. Now that he was awake, he knew that confession would only cause unbearable pain on the day she chose to leave.

***

Following breakfast, Seth cut across his uncle's land to reach the highway and headed south toward the Columbia River. As they moved out of the arid hills, irrigated crops took over. Eventually, green fields gave way to apple and cherry orchards.

Closer to Wade's family farm, trellises towered high above them, supporting acres upon acres of hops. Angled lines ran up the tall poles where heavy bines already ran along the top.

"Why didn't Wade start his brewery here?" Natalie asked, straining her head to see the top of the trellis.

"Wade and his dad don't see his future playing out the same. It's a family farm, and his dad expects him to take over."

"Complicated."

"Families are like that."

Seth considered whether having a family with Natalie would be complicated or not. Either way, he knew he wanted all of that with her, but only if she would change her plans and decide to stay.

***

"Do you mind if we stop at Whitewater?" Seth asked a few miles outside of town.

"No problem." She wondered why he seemed suddenly guarded. Over the past few days, all walls between them had disappeared. Yet something shifted as the miles drew his truck closer to Ashwood.

When he stopped the truck, she noticed his hands were shaking. Something was wrong. Seth asked her to come inside Whitewater. Nervous, Natalie almost decided to stay in his truck.

Avoiding this shift in Seth, she escaped to the safety of his office and tried not to worry.

***

After he checked on Amanda's work in Natalie's new darkroom, Seth smiled and turned off the light. Everything looked perfect.

"Sweetness, could you help me?" he called, enticing her toward the back of his shop.

"Seth, where are you?" Her voice echoed as she searched the dark.

"In here," he coaxed her forward. "The switch is by the door, could you get it?"

She flicked on the light and froze.

Seth watched her, waited, and watched some more. He needed a reaction. Words. A scream. Anything.

Natalie stood perfectly still and held her breath.

"Sweetness?" he asked and that was all it took. She flung her hand over her mouth as a sob burst through her fingers.

"Oh, Seth. How did you know?" Relief swept over him as she collapsed into his arms. "No one has ever done anything this wonderful." Her body shook as she wept against his chest and he grinned.

Thank God. She loves it. He held Natalie, kissed the top of her head, and knew making her cry shouldn't make him feel this happy.

EIGHTEEN

Oysters sizzled above a fire Seth built down by the lake. Releasing the shell enough to pop it open, Kelsey squeezed a bit of lemon over the mollusk, tipped the oyster onto her tongue, and let it glide down her throat.

"Wade, I love you for bringing these to the party." She wasted no time and slid another taste of pure ocean into her mouth.

Wade joined her, downing two in a row. "Fresh seafood is the best part about the brewing festivals on the coast."

Kent grimaced, refusing the slimy sea creatures. Seeing his face, Kels chose the largest oyster and made eye contact before she downed it with a slurp. He shuddered and turned away as Kelsey laughed.

"Hey, Seth, when should we put the salmon on the grill?" Wade finished off his third oyster while waiting for an answer.

"No hurry. Jasmine and Rose are still on their way." Seth couldn't wait to thank the twins for their help with the darkroom. Natalie's happiness had bounced off her that night, making Seth feel high.

Adirondack chairs circled the fire. Kelsey grinned at the small spontaneous party. Kent, Rick, and Justin had worked together to set up several tents. Wade brought up a keg of his new batch to test out and no one intended to drive home tonight.

The connection to Natalie had solidified Seth and Wade as a permanent addition to these gatherings. Come September, when Nate moved her tiny house to the Oregon Coast, the bonds might weaken, but the small town of Ashwood always held their community close.

On a large old blanket spread over the lawn, Seth held Natalie between his legs, reclined snug against his chest. When a light breeze brushed the water, she shivered in her tank top and shorts.

Wrapping her tighter in his arms, he whispered, "Are you cold? I can grab your sweatshirt from our tent."

"No. Don't move. I'm way too comfortable," she said and nestled further into the rise and fall of his chest.

Jasmine and Rose arrived, carrying a giant pan of rice crispy treats. "Hey everyone!" Rose called. "We cooked."

"Dessert before dinner—awesome." Kelsey held out her hand and took the pan. Her sweet tooth was so easy to please. She took two, giving one to Nate, and sprawled out on the blanket with the couple.

"Delicious." Nate tore off a piece and fed a bite to Seth. He licked and sucked the sticky marshmallow off her fingers, moaning.

Wade took aim and chucked a pinecone at his cousin. He laughed when it bounced harmlessly off Seth's head.

"What? Dude, she was sticky." Seth laughed, not caring about his shameless show of public affection.

Wade snorted. "Have mercy, there are single guys suffering over here."

"Not my problem, dude." Seth kissed the top of Natalie's head then stood. "Let me get you that sweatshirt before I prep the salmon."

***

Natalie wanted to hold him in place, maybe even keep him on the blanket all night. Instead, she settled for watching him walk away, admiring the easy way he moved. She sly-grinned when Kelsey caught her lusting over the way Seth's jeans hugged his muscular butt.

Seth emerged from their tent and threw her rolled up sweatshirt in the girls' direction like a football. Kelsey caught it mid-air, turned and gave it to Nate. A line of concern wrinkled Kelsey's forehead.

"You and Seth make so much sense. Are you sure about your plans?"

Nate whispered and kept the conversation close. "I'm trying hard not to overthink it. Reality may change everything."

"Reality? What's not real about Ashwood?" Kelsey asked.

"This small town feels like a big vacation. I need to leave and grow my business. If the coast doesn't have enough winter tourists, I may be forced to move again."

Kelsey frowned, reached for Natalie's hand, and gave it a squeeze. "At least keep Ashwood in mind for summer. We get enough tourists here to keep you busy. Or if you get tired of serving coffee, you can plant your ass at the lake and take a break."

"This ass needs space." Natalie giggled as Kelsey tackled her and playfully slapped that ample butt cheek.

"Seth's not complaining." Kelsey laughed and Natalie blushed, wondering if her friend had *any* idea. Next summer in Ashwood seemed more tempting every day.

When Nate gave up the wrestling match, Kent crashed their blanket and declared Kels the winner. She accepted her reward—another beer.

"How's she doing with the trailer?" Kelsey asked, shifting the conversation to safer territory.

"We worked on backing the trailer this week. Nate will be ready by September . . . if Seth ever finishes her house."

"The components for the kitchen are on back order." Natalie explained.

"Yeah, right." Kent capped his chuckle with a huff. "Seth's dragging his feet. We've never had so many delays."

To shut him up, Kelsey tossed the pinecone missile at the center of Kent's chest. "Never mind the delays! I'm just glad Natalie's going to be around a little longer. I'll miss you so much when you leave." Kelsey gave her beer to Kent and launched across the blanket, pinning Natalie. "Kent, I have an idea. We could sabotage her tiny house to keep Nate here all winter!" Kelsey and Natalie tumbled, giggling. "Please, help me hold her against her will."

For a brief moment, Natalie got the upper hand and pinned Kelsey's wrists. "This is all part of your evil plot to increase the population of Ashwood."

Twisting and giggling, they rolled again, and Nate almost managed to break free. Kelsey won the wrestling match by pinning her friend to the blanket.

Kent shook his head and closed his eyes against the tangle of tanned legs and jiggling parts. As he stood to escape, he adjusted his shorts and groaned.

After dinner, everyone pulled out canoes. Jasmine and Rick explored a nearby alcove. Justin and Rose paddled away and disappeared for an hour, leaving a long V-shaped wake on the surface of Osprey Lake. Kent and Seth tossed horseshoes and later sketched a loft idea with a stick in the sand.

By the fire, Wade strummed a familiar song on his guitar while Kelsey hummed along. Natalie sat near the fire, picking flowers from a patch of little daisies. Using her fingernail, she sliced a hole in the stem and strung the flowers in a long chain. Kelsey grinned when Natalie placed the pretty wreath of flowers on her white-gold hair. Surrounded by friends, Natalie couldn't imagine a better moment. She belonged.

Natalie and Seth were the first to crawl into their tent. Everyone chose to ignore the random pairs that emerged among their group of slightly drunk friends. Temptation took over, and Seth could not resist a make-out session with his girl. Sleeping bags zipped together, their bodies tangled. They touched, explored, nibbled, and kissed, attempting silence when their bodies connected.

***

Natalie pushed her cart laden with groceries across the Stop-n-Shop parking lot. After one final stop at the farmers' market, she'd have everything she needed to make Seth her chicken enchiladas.

Rounding her truck, she was surprised by a tall attractive woman's quick approach. With her long, manicured nails and false eyelashes, the dark-haired woman seemed out of place in Ashwood.

"Hello, do you need help finding something?" Natalie asked politely.

"Oh, I think I've found it. You're Natalie, aren't you."

"Yes. I'm sorry, have we met?"

The woman's eyes narrowed. "No. You don't know me, but I know exactly who you are. I'm Desiree Michaels—and, bitch, you don't belong here." Her pointed finger invaded Natalie's personal space. "I'm taking back what isn't yours."

Oh, God. I can't believe this woman kept Seth's name after the divorce. "Desiree, I haven't taken anything from you," Natalie said, standing a little taller.

Desiree leaned forward, nearly touching Natalie chest to chest before she stopped and canted her hip to one side. "You might have Seth distracted with some missionary position summer fling, but I understand exactly what that man needs."

Natalie blinked. "But I know what he needs."

When she backed a step, Desiree claimed the space. "You don't know shit. Seth always comes back *to me* to get exactly what satisfies him. In *my bed.*"

Natalie shook with anger and refused to budge. "I don't need to manipulate a man to keep him. Get out of my way and stay out of Seth's life."

"Don't waste your time. Seth and I have history," Desiree jeered and laughed.

"Only ancient history—*I'm* Seth's future."

Finished with this woman, Nate pushed past Desiree and ignored barbed taunts as she loaded her groceries. While trying to control her trembling hands, Natalie climbed in her truck, clung to the steering wheel, and drove away spitting anger. "Desiree thinks she can scare me away with that load of crap? Game on, bitch."

***

Hot spicy scents greeted Seth at the door. He'd hurried home, knowing Natalie had come home early to make dinner. His mouth watered. A pitcher of margaritas waited for him on the counter, but she wasn't anywhere in sight. "Natalie, sweetness where are you?" he called.

Movement at the top of the stairs captured his attention. He thought he was hungry for dinner—until he spotted her red heels and taut tan legs stretching beyond the shortest black skirt he'd ever seen. She'd tied a button-up shirt at the waist to showcase her curves. The way she wore it pushed her soft delectable mounds above the confines of her red lace bra.

Without seeing, Seth knew a matching thong was hidden beneath that skirt. Natalie's hair was in that messy bun he loved, worn high to grant him full access to her sensitive neck.

Mouth gone dry, Seth could not form a sound. She prowled like a cat down the stairs and toward the bar to pour him a cool margarita. Her delicate hand held it out for him to retrieve, waiting for his senses to return.

"Thirsty?" she purred, watching as he took hold of the glass.

Draining half of the tequila-laced elixir, Seth set down the glass, lifted Natalie onto the counter, and parted her legs to step between them. His lips scrambled her senses with a bone-melting kiss.

While her tongue slid along his lower lip, she pulled his shirt up, snaked her nails across his ridged abs, and lightly scraped his sensitive nipples.

"Natalie, all of this is coming off." He groaned. "But not the heels. Baby, those heels stay on."

"Whatever you say, Seth. Whatever you want," Natalie promised.

"Mine." He'd never meant anything more.

Seth took his time removing her clothes, savoring every layer of eye candy. First, he slipped two fingers under her skirt, moving her thong aside. Panting, she rode his hand to her first release.

Next, he revealed her body, clad in only the red bra, red thong, and red heels. That image almost had his cock exploding in his jeans. Carrying her from the kitchen, he only made it as far as the stairs before he deposited her on the treads with her legs spread while he feasted.

He tore the thong from her body, needing nothing but bare skin. Natalie moaned and writhed while his tongue explored, dipping deep into her channel, lapping as she climbed to a second orgasm. Seth controlled her pleasure—it was his to own.

Entering his bedroom, with Natalie still trapped in his arms, Seth stopped cold. Arranged on his bed, laid out like an invitation—ropes and straps were neatly coiled on each corner of the bed. The clasps were already attached to the bedposts. He had designed the bed specifically for this purpose. Seth's erection pulsed. How did Natalie know?

The summons to share every part of himself brought a growl of anticipation. "Natalie, I need you."

"Please," was her single response.

***

Seth ran a bath for Natalie the following morning. He added vanilla-orange bubble bath to the tumbling water. On a sigh, she slowly eased in, loving the creamsicle scent and the way the warmth soothed muscles that ached in the best possible way.

"I'll only be a minute." Seth ran downstairs and came back with fresh-squeezed orange juice. "As much as I want to join you, if I slip into that water, we won't make it out of this house today." He gave her temple a kiss and added, "I'll get breakfast going. Take all the time you need."

Natalie soaked, feeling cherished and wonderfully tender. Last night and again before dawn, Seth had teased, tied, and satisfied, while making her feel completely claimed by his potent need.

Keen hunger and the smell of food eventually drew her from the bath and led her downstairs. She appeared in a bathrobe, her toenails in a fresh coat of bubblegum pink.

Seth stood at the counter cutting up peaches. A toasty smell rolled from a waffle iron. He hadn't noticed her yet, and she watched as he opened the iron and caught the waffle with a fork.

"Damn," he muttered when he burned his finger on the hot metal edge. Sticking his finger into his mouth, he finally noticed Natalie and smiled with his index finger still trapped in his teeth. "I burned myself," he muttered.

"Let me see." She pulled his finger from his lips and ran it under cold water.

"Better?" she asked, kissing the center of his hand.

"Mm-hmm. Damn you smell good. As much as I would like to pick up where we left off, I'm putting your comfort first. You need recovery time."

"Are you sure?" she asked with a pout.

"Positive," he answered and kissed her forehead.

"I guess that's probably wise. You have clients coming in today around eleven—that young couple from California." She stole one more kiss as he lifted her to the kitchen counter. "Yum, you taste like peaches," she moaned, licking the sweet taste from her lips.

Seth shook his head and backed away. "Stay right there and watch me from a safe distance."

***

"Shopping shouldn't hurt this much," Natalie groaned while following the twins to their car.

"Seriously, my feet are killing me," Jasmine said as she stuffed a bag holding fall sweaters on top of goose down bedding, a blender, and bo-go shoes.

"I hope we're done. I'm starving." Kelsey checked her phone. "I found a spot with margaritas and an outdoor patio."

Natalie's stomach rumbled as if on cue. "Kels, you had me at margaritas."

"Shotgun!" Rose yelled. Nobody had enough energy to fight her for the spot.

Natalie's mouth watered as they parked. They found a table under a bright red umbrella and ordered drinks after salty chips appeared on their table.

Kelsey sipped and moaned. "This is too good. Are they better than the ones you made for Seth?"

Natalie blushed. "I don't know . . . I never had a chance to try one."

"Damn." Kelsey laughed.

"I can't believe Desiree got in your face at the Stop-n-Shop," Jasmine said and Natalie smiled, loving that the twins had her back.

"What did Seth say about that awful confrontation?" Rose asked.

"I didn't tell him. What difference would it make? If I said something, he'd just call his ex, and I won't give that witch the satisfaction."

"Perfect call." Rose went on, "I bet her sister, Paige, ratted you out. She probably saw you at Northside Grill and told Desiree."

"Desiree's sister works at Northside Grill?" Natalie asked as another puzzle piece of Ashwood slipped into place.

"Yeah, nights. And on Saturdays she works at the farmers' market with Annie." Kelsey filled in the layers and Natalie rolled her eyes.

Jasmine grabbed a chip and accentuated her point in the air with the triangle. "I never trusted her. Desiree probably can't wait to sharpen her nails, fly her broom to Ashwood, and claw her way back two seconds after you leave."

Natalie shrugged. "I don't have a reason to be jealous. Seth and I haven't talked about our future."

The twins shared a look, and Kelsey filled the silence. "Well, I admire that you're sticking with your plans. Too many women have given up their opportunities just to please a man."

"True," Natalie agreed, and she believed it to an extent. Still, it wasn't like she had her future mapped. Her greatest fear was choosing Ashwood, only to discover that Seth hadn't made room for her in his long-term plans.

NINETEEN

"That's right, ease the wheel a little more to the left, take it slow, and now put the truck in park." Kent finished her test run towing the biggest trailer in Whitewater's fleet with a high-five. "Nate, that's awesome and exactly where you planned to put it."

Kent's confidence-building maneuvers had her driving like a pro. "I like these lessons better with you. Seth worries, and I get jittery and make stupid mistakes," Natalie admitted.

"Seth's worried, but not about your ability to handle the tiny home behind your truck. He's concerned about you living on your own. Promise me, if you get in a bind, you'll give one of us a call. We're all going to miss you." Kent's sincere smile contained a different kind of magnitude than when they first met.

"I'll miss you, too. But if I don't launch this business, I'll feel like I failed."

"Don't say that. I've never met anyone with your courage."

Natalie blushed. "Thanks." She kissed Kent's cheek before they climbed out of her truck. All the awkwardness between them had evaporated. He still flirted, but she now realized he was only masking how deeply he cared about all his friends.

As they walked toward the shop, a sleek sports car crunched across the gravel lot. Two men emerged from the low-slung vehicle, unfolding as they stood. Natalie recognized them and froze.

Standing thirty feet away, her father pulled off his sunglasses, tossed them on the black leather seat, and slammed the door.

"Ben!" Natalie screamed and raced toward her brother. She wrapped arms around his neck and pulled him down to her petite height.

After the hug, Ben grasped her shoulders and held her at arm's length for a close inspection. A massive grin spread across his face. "Wow, Sis . . . you grew up."

Malcolm Journey scrutinized the emotional greeting with cool disdain. "Natalie, aren't you going to say hello?"

As Seth came outside, his eyes darted between the new faces. Natalie took courage from Seth's presence and cleared her throat, preparing to speak to a man she hadn't seen in eight years. "Seeing you surprised m—"

Abrupt words cut her off. "I'm Malcolm Journey, Natalie's father." Seth stared at the hand thrust his direction. He shook it once, hard, then dropped it.

"How did you find me?" Natalie asked, shoulders squared, boldly facing the bulldozer of a man who had once been her father.

"Well, isn't that polite?"

"Polite? I haven't seen you in years," she snapped, unwilling to bend to his arrogance.

Ben crowded into the midst of the confrontation. "I'm just so happy to see you again. When Dad said he was flying out, I invited myself along. Natalie, I've missed you so much."

Her weak smile accepted his concern. "I've missed you, too. Ben, I want you to meet my friend, Kent. And this is Seth, the owner of Whitewater Homes. We're seeing each other." She moved to Seth's side, sliding her arm around his waist, the simple touch borrowed a bit of his strength. Her eyes looked anywhere but her father—he didn't deserve her time.

Seth extended a hand toward Ben. "Happy to meet y—"

"Well, isn't this opportunistic?" Malcolm sneered, cutting off the friendly introductions.

Ben angled his body to deflect the escalating anger. "Dad, come on, you don't—"

Malcolm stepped past his son and yelled, "Fucking brilliant! I should have known my daughter would blow the inheritance on this frivolous fad."

Natalie stood taller. "What I do with my inheritance is none of your business. I know Grandpa wanted to see Ben, and you wouldn't allow it. If this is anyone's fault, it's yours."

Malcolm puffed his chest. "It's a good thing I kept Ben on the East Coast. You're just as stupid as your mother."

Her fists tightened, and she took a slow, deep breath. "How did you know I was here?"

The sneer on his face curled into a smile. "The internet is a wealth of information. It took me about ten minutes to find this hole."

Seth stared squarely at the man. "Mr. Journey, I'm going to have to ask you to leave. This is private property. Get off my land."

Malcolm fumed, "Natalie, I'm not leaving town until we settle this."

Her voice trembled with barely controlled fury. "Not happening. Talk to my lawyer and stop wasting my time." She pulled Seth close as tears stung her eyes.

"Fine, hide behind your hack of a lawyer," her father said with a venomous snort. "Let's go." Malcolm Journey opened the door to his lavish rental car and barked, "Get in the car, Benjamin, we'll deal with this nuisance later."

Malcolm got in, revved the motor, and rolled the window down, but Ben didn't move. Spit flew from Malcolm's mouth as he yelled, "What are you waiting for? Get in!"

"Dad, I came here to see Natalie. You've already stolen too much time from us. I won't let you do it again." Ignoring the rude sputters coming from inside the car, Ben turned to his sister, his eyes shadowed by embarrassment. "I'd like to start making up for all the time we've missed. Can I stay . . . just for a week or two?"

Tears rolled down her face. "Of course, I can't imagine anything better."

"I can't believe this shit!" Malcolm shoved the car in gear, gunned the engine, and fishtailed. Everyone backpedaled to avoid the spraying gravel. Seth sheltered Natalie to protect her from the barrage. The sports car left a cloud of dust and two snaking skid marks on the highway when the wheels hit the pavement.

Ben's shoulders sank and he asked, "Is everyone okay?"

Silent and shocked, Natalie stared blankly while Kent paced off his anger. He pounded a fist into his open palm. "Shit, if he shows here again, I don't care what happens, I'm kicking his ass."

With a gentle touch to her chin, Seth turned Natalie's face to his. "Don't cry sweetness," he whispered as his thumb caressed her tears away.

"I'm sorry," Ben apologized. "Dad won't come back now that he knows I won't play by his rules."

Natalie felt terrible for her brother and for all the years he'd endured that awful man.

"Hey, I've got two weeks of vacation. Let's see if you get sick of your big brother by then." Ben's teasing found Natalie's smile.

"Not possible—it would take at least three." Laughter shattered the tension and Natalie put her free arm around her brother. "Let's erase what just happened. How would you like to see my new home?"

Holding Seth's hand, Natalie led the tour, thrilled to show off her place.

"Everything seems perfect," Ben said with a grin. She knew he was talking about more than the tiny home.

***

"Natalie, why didn't you tell us your brother was so hot? And that little hint of southern drawl . . . damn," Kelsey whispered as Ben bent over to take a shot at the pool table.

"Seriously, Kels, he's my brother."

"Separated from your family," Jasmine said to her twin, "I can't imagine anything worse."

Natalie watched while Ben joked with the guys. "He's changed so much."

"Must be for the better." Rose took a slow visual survey.

Natalie stood, needing to escape the ogling. "I'm buying the next pitcher." She painted the air with her hand. "While I'm gone, get all this *admiration* out of your system."

Her friends laughed. "You better take your time."

She rolled her eyes and dodged tables while making her way to the bar. Natalie turned to find Seth leaning against the wall with his pool cue in hand. He watched as she waited for her order. Paige poured, but didn't bother with any friendly banter. Natalie didn't care, it gave her a moment to watch her friends from a distance.

Kelsey inspected Ben as he moved around the pool table. She didn't get it. Her brother seemed too clean-cut to appeal to Kels.

A little beer sloshed when Nate clunked two heavy pitchers down for the crowd. They thanked her for the round and helped clean up the mess with a stack of napkins.

On the last swipe, she leaned in and whispered, "Hey Kels, can I beg a favor. I'm not sure about sleeping arrangements now that Ben has arrived. Could we both stay at your place if we need to?"

"Fine by me." She nodded, "But, with that temptation at my house, I may sneak back early from my next guiding trip."

Natalie smiled. "Thanks, Kels."

When hot pizza arrived, arms crowded in and grabbed a tasty slice. Everyone relaxed, sharing laughter, food, and beer—a miracle considering how the day began.

Her brother pushed back from the table. "Natalie, I need to ask a favor . . ."

"Name it."

"Dad left my luggage at a hotel in Portland. Can I borrow your car to pick it up?"

"No problem."

"I'll arrange for a rental, but I'll probably need to pick it up in Hood River."

"Don't worry about a rental, we can share," Natalie offered.

Seth slid his hand across the back of Natalie's chair. "We share rides most of the time anyway. It will be easy, especially with both of you at my place. I hope that's what you had in mind."

"Seth, are you sure?" she asked.

"Absolutely. Ben's family."

***

Seth watched Ben leave for Portland then counted three seconds before he rushed back inside his house. As he scooped Natalie into his arms, she wrapped her legs around his waist. On the trip up the stairs, they both glanced at the clock above the fireplace, calculating Ben's drive time to Portland and back.

He grinned as Natalie hastened the pace. She stripped her shirt and then his, lost the bra, then traced a path straight to his buckle.

His girth strained against the faded denim as she slipped the strip of leather from the loops. Each click of the zipper hastened his breath. Natalie fell to her knees and licked her lips while preparing to swallow his shaft.

With his jeans at his feet, he stepped out of the bunched fabric. His legs shook while he stood naked before her, anticipating her first move. Natalie's eyes flicked up, and she gripped his muscled legs, holding tight while she leisurely licked his length.

Moving lower, Natalie rolled his balls with her tongue and dared to suck on them playfully. Seth took himself in hand and stroked. Fisting her hair, he eased her mouth to the tip, painted her lips with a bead of cum and controlled the increasing pace. He tugged her hair, and his legs started to quake.

"So close," he warned as electric bliss raced down his spine. Three slim fingers gently stroked behind his balls. That extra sensation scrambled Seth's control.

"Ah fuck," he shouted as his seed shot hot bursts down her throat. She gently prolonged his climax until he collapsed onto the bed, panting, spent, and sated.

Huddled together, Natalie traced the slanted-V near his hips and licked his contoured chest. Salty with sweat, she climbed over him and carefully nibbled each tan nipple.

"How would you feel about being tied-up?" she asked eyes dancing, begging yes.

"I'm all yours, sweetness." He winked, stretched, and presented his wrists and ankles for Natalie to buckle into the leather cuffs. While she worked, Seth realized he'd never trusted anyone with this much control.

Natalie stood at the end of the bed with a finger hooked over her lip. "What are you dreaming up for me sweetness?" he asked, intrigued by the naked woman and that playful glint in her eye.

"I'll be right back." She giggled, her round buns bouncing as she hurried away.

Seth stared at the ceiling and said, "Hmm, I may have to spank her later for leaving me like this. Well, that might be fun."

Cupboards slammed in the kitchen moments before her bare feet ran back up the stairs. His brows lifted when she walked through his bedroom door with a large glass full of ice cubes.

The mattress dipped beneath her climb alongside his tethered torso. "Let me chill that heat rolling off you," she said as she settled between his legs.

Please, not the balls, he willed with a stare that made Natalie pause. And as if she read his mind, she grinned and said, "I promise not to torture you . . . too much."

Melted water dripped from the ice cube in her hand. It ran down her arm and fell from her elbow, dotting his ridged stomach as his muscles tensed and jumped. Straddling Seth, she teased her way up the center of his chest, drawing cold circles with the ice.

"Ahhh, shit," he growled, and his nipples tightened as the sensation shot directly to his balls—a cold and hot contrast that throbbed with aching perfection. On hands and knees, Natalie caged him, leaning over to suck one nipple, scraping it lightly with her teeth.

Natalie popped an ice cube in her mouth, cooling her tongue and lips. As it melted, she trailed another icy shard from the center of his chest. She traced his ridged stomach on her way down the arrow of hair which angled toward his jutting arousal. Each time she moved the ice, his erection bobbed.

Seth watched from hooded eyes as she planned her next move. "I promise to be really nice," she said with a wiggle of her hips as she avoided his most sensitive places.

Now that the shard of cold on her tongue had melted, she opened her lips and took his arousal fully into her chilled mouth.

"Damn, that's seriously cold," he said as her icy fingertips explored. Each point of chill heightened his need. Natalie sucked, driving the head of his cock against her soft palate.

Straps straining, the bed creaked when his wrists and ankles pulled against the taught restraints. She pumped and swallowed to squeeze his crown with the back of her throat. His hips lifted from the mattress in time with the plunging of her head down his shaft.

"Not going to last much longer. Fuck. That's so deep." His body thrashed, begging for release.

"Not yet, Seth," she whispered raising her eyebrows, seeking permission.

His body protested, but he nodded and took a deep, steadying breath. Natalie straddled his hips and nestled his length against her heat. She rode his cock and claimed her pleasure, dragging his crown across her nerves. He canted his hips, attempting to slide inside. He hissed as she pulled away.

"Please, Natalie," he said—a command more than a request.

"Just want to try one more little thing." She chose two half-melted ice cubes from the glass. On her knees hovering over his hips, she slid each cold sliver gently inside her already drenched cleft.

"Ooh, yes," she hissed at the chilled invasion. Her beautiful, reckless abandon sent another surge directly to Seth's rock-hard rod.

Grasping his shaft, she aligned and impaled her chilled channel in one swift move. His hips lifted off the bed while she ground and writhed.

Hot and cold, hard and soft, urgent need balanced on a knife's edge. Hungry carnal thrusts crested in blinding simultaneous pleasure mixed with a small bite of icy pain.

Panting, she collapsed on his outstretched body, languid and gloriously spent. Still bound, Seth never felt so content.

Imitating the care he always demonstrated, Natalie released each restraint with kisses and soothing massage. Receiving rather than giving, Seth fought a tide of unexpected emotion and silently filled vulnerable spaces with her unspoken love.

***

Natalie finished dinner prep later that night, feeling entirely at ease in Seth's home. She sensed Ben's eyes on her and wondered if he would ever ask the question that seemed to hover in the air between them.

After dinner, a project called Seth to his office, and he left Ben and Natalie to catch up. She led the way outside to share the rest of a bottle of wine with her brother out on the deck. The night was warm, and the moon gave just enough light to talk.

Ben finally brought up what was on his mind. He asked if Natalie was sure about her plan to take her tiny home to the Oregon coast. She pretended to have her mind solidly made up. Yet, with each passing day, the life she was building in Ashwood lashed another pleasant cord that bound her to this place.

The cooling night air finally forced the siblings inside. Ben asked for the Wi-Fi password and went to his guest room early to answer a few emails.

Natalie found Seth in his office, going over plans for a new client. "I had so much fun tonight. Thanks for letting Ben stay."

"Happy to, sweetness. I like him. How he managed to emerge from your father's home this balanced is a credit to his character. Do you think it's good genes?" he asked.

"Well, obviously." She popped her hip and chuckled. "Just look how I turned out."

Seth took Natalie's face in his hands and brought her lips to his. "Sweetness, I really love how you turned out," he whispered against her mouth then gave her a tender kiss.

TWENTY

Two canoes rested side by side on Lake Osprey's pebbled shore. Natalie couldn't wait to show her brother Grandpa Pete's lakefront property. She hadn't mentally taken ownership of it yet, and she hoped today's outing would help the reality sink in.

Kelsey had invited her and Ben to a small family dinner. The moment Elsa heard Ben was visiting, she'd shifted her plans and made time for an impromptu vacation.

While Elsa was making pies, Kelsey, Ben, Natalie, and Seth climbed into canoes and took a break from the Fisher family gathering. They planned to return in a couple of hours—right around the time Elsa's pies would come out of the oven.

Natalie wandered near the shore, amazed by how much had changed in her life in just a few short months. She'd met Seth, established friendships with Kelsey and the rest of her crowd, and reconnected with her brother.

The crimson maple leaves, succumbing to crisp fall nights, reminded her that everything was about to shift again.

"What do you think of the property, Ben?" she asked as Seth and Kelsey pulled the canoes onto the bank.

He wandered the shore and took it all in—the tall trees, calm lake, and something undefinable. "It's peaceful. Grandpa must have loved to come here and escape."

A bright blue feather tumbled past Natalie's feet, carried on a warm windy gust. She hurried to catch it and twirled it between her fingers. "I can't figure out why Grandpa kept this place a secret. Even Elsa assumed he'd sold it years ago."

"Maybe someday you'll figure it out. Until then, just enjoy this place from his past Grandpa saved for you."

"It's here for you, too. I mean that." She couldn't shake the strange feeling they'd been here together, long ago.

Ben picked up a bright white stone, then tossed it into the lake. "I'm glad Elsa drove down from Seattle for a visit. She feels like family."

"Elsa knew Grandma and Grandpa for years, and she remembers when we were kids."

He shrugged and huffed. "Such a small world." For a long moment they stood side by side, staring across the water. "I love it here," he said.

"If I bring my tiny home back next summer, would you think about coming for a visit?"

"You bet." Ben glanced toward her access road. "Will your home fit through those trees?"

She nodded. "It shouldn't be a problem."

Ben spun and shaded his eyes from the sun as he stared over the tree line. "Is that Seth's place?"

"Yeah. You can just make out the roof." Staring skyward, she realized that when the leaves fell, his house would be in full view.

"Promise me you won't sell it." Ben's sudden urgent tone surprised her.

"I don't think I ever could. I feel more connected to Grandpa here. Does that sound crazy?" Natalie wrapped her arms around her middle then Ben caught her in a one-arm hug.

"Not crazy at all. I know he kept it for a reason."

Seth and Kelsey wandered back from an inspection of the dock. "Everything about the dock looks sound. Now, all you need is a fishing boat." Seth said with a smile.

Kelsey raised her hand. "I vote for jet skis."

"I think a rowboat is more my speed." Natalie laughed as Kels snagged her away from Ben and pulled her toward the lake.

"Take off those shoes. I want to get my feet wet." Kelsey toed out of her shoes, stuffed socks inside, and abandoned them on shore.

Natalie squinted at the sun bouncing from the lake as she followed her friend into the knee-deep water.

***

Seth led Ben down a narrow path. The dense forest surrounded them as they melted into overgrown deer trails and explored the property.

Lifting a broken branch and tossing it aside, Seth stopped to make sure Natalie's brother was keeping up. When he spotted Ben's face, he wondered what was on his mind.

"I know it's none of my business," Ben said. "But don't you want Natalie to stay?"

The abrupt question didn't shock Seth, not too much. He'd ask something similar if someone was dating Amanda.

"Of course, I want her to stay. Hell, everyone knows I've been stalling the tiny home build to keep her around. But I can't get in her way. This business and this home . . . damn, it's her dream."

Ben shifted foot to foot. "It worries me."

"Worries me too, but Natalie lights up when she talks about her plans. If I asked her to stay, I think she would." Seth forced air into his lungs. The thought of her leaving made it hard to breathe. "But I don't want her wondering *what if* because of me."

"I guess I understand. Do you think she'd mind if I check on her after she moves to the coast? You know, to make sure she's okay?"

"How? Won't you be in North Carolina?"

Ben grinned. "I've put in for a transfer to our Portland office."

That news pushed Seth back a step. "Wow. Big move."

"These past two weeks have shown me how much I've missed my sister. She's worth this change."

***

Natalie's toes splashed along the pebbled shore. "The water is so much warmer than when I first arrived in June."

"I think it's warm enough to go for a swim. What do you say we all take a midnight skinny dip?" Kelsey asked.

"Uh, Kels, I don't think so. I don't want my brother to see my birthday suit."

"You mind if I ask him to join just me?" Kelsey asked with a sly smile.

"Go for it. You're running out of time."

"Then I better make my move."

Nate raised her eyebrows. "Ben won't know what hit him."

The clear water around their feet distorted the rocks and their toes. Small fish swam close, investigating. Kelsey reached for Natalie's hand. "Everyone's moving. First Jasmine and Rose, then you and Ben. Do you really have to leave?"

Natalie stared at the horizon, fighting a flash of heat behind her eyes. She didn't want to cry, but knew she'd miss everyone deeply. "It's inevitable. The stock for my coffee shop has finally started to arrive." She squeezed Kelsey's hand. "Will you help me get everything organized?"

"I'll help, but I won't be happy," Kels said with a hip-bump.

"I'll visit Ashwood. I promise. We'll always be tied together by this place."

"Love you, Nate."

"Love you, too, Kels."

She couldn't picture life without Kelsey. It was equally difficult to imagine her future without Seth.

The crashing of branches turned them around just as Ben and Seth pushed their way through the tall underbrush. Leaves and moss hung in their hair and clung on their clothes. A boyish grin lit up Seth's face. "We lost the trail."

"And had to blaze one of our own," Ben hollered with a manly growl. The country suited him. Natalie noticed the extra layer of muscle Ben put on while spending time outdoors. And in only two short weeks, he'd carved a niche for himself in Ashwood.

"Is anyone else as starved as I am?" Seth asked, raking the brush off his shirt.

"Famished," Natalie agreed.

The girls settled in the front of the canoes as the guys steadied the boats. Pushing theirs farther into the water, Seth jumped in, then easily found his seat. Ben rocked the canoe when he attempted the same maneuver. Keeping them balanced, Kelsey laughed and screamed as they nearly went over.

"Slick moves, city boy," she teased.

"Watch it or I'll tip us in," he warned grabbing the edges and giving the canoe a shake with a broad smile plastered across his face.

Natalie laughed as she and Seth paddled ahead. She could barely hear Kelsey's voice as it echoed across the surface of the lake.

Bold as always, Kels asked her brother for a late night swim, promising the water was warm enough.

The sound of their paddles stopped, and Natalie could hear her brother easily. "Another time?" he said, and Kelsey didn't answer.

Silence disappeared into the smooth splash of Kelsey's paddle. Natalie didn't turn around, but she knew her friend was disappointed. She could have sworn her brother was into Kelsey. Maybe she didn't know him as well as she thought.

**

"Dinner was fantastic," Natalie groaned, full to the point of pain.

"Aunt Elsa, oh my God, the pie was delicious." Kelsey stood and smoothed her hand over a distinct food baby. Only crumbles remained in the two empty pie pans.

With hunger a distant memory, everyone pushed back from the long dining table as Nate and Kels gathered the dishes. "We're on cleaning duty, Mom."

"I won't put up a fight. Would you put decaf on?"

Kels nodded. "On it."

Ben and Seth stood at the sink, rinsing and loading the dishwasher as Nate and Kels put leftovers away.

Elsa wandered into the kitchen. "Do you kids mind if I steal Natalie for a while?"

Seth tossed a glance over his shoulder. "I think we can manage without her."

"Come find her outside in a bit and you can have her back."

Natalie held Elsa's arm as she navigated the steps in the dim light. Together they wandered away from the house into the late summer evening.

"You've been in my thoughts, especially with Ben's visit. How are you handling all the changes?"

"I love my temporary home in Ashwood. I'm so glad you gave me Kelsey's name." Natalie dodged the subject she knew Elsa wanted to explore.

"Are you sure about your plans? Seth seems like a good enough reason to stay. But I guess that depends on how you feel about him," Elsa prodded.

Natalie stopped, turned back to the house, and saw her brother, Seth, and Kelsey hanging together on the deck.

The dark hid her face from view, yet Seth must have felt her watching. He glanced into the night, seeking her gaze.

"How do I feel about him? I've fallen in love. But if I stay, I'll just crowd his life. I wonder, too, if staying would just be another safe choice." The weight of her words left her feeling weak. Natalie headed for a bench a few yards away and sank onto it with a ragged sigh.

Elsa settled next to her. "Have you told Seth how you feel?"

"No." She shook her head and sighed. "It's too fast. I know he needs time. He doesn't want to repeat the same mistakes he made with Desiree."

Elsa sighed. "My dear, you are nothing like Desiree."

"Yes, I know . . . I met her and it was very unpleasant."

They both chuckled. "I can imagine." Elsa reached out and squeezed Natalie's hand. "Trust yourself. Trust Seth. When the time is right, promise me, you will tell him how you feel."

"I promise."

"Good. Why don't we walk back together? Seth seems torn between giving us space and wanting to find you."

Natalie smiled when she saw Seth standing on the deck, patiently waiting. He met them half way, helped Elsa up the steps, and she went inside.

"Is everything okay?" he asked with a whisper before they sat across from Ben and Kelsey.

"Mm-hmm. Elsa worries, you know, since Grandpa passed. I think she feels . . . responsible for me." The admission filled the center of Natalie's chest with a pit of loneliness. If only Grandpa could have known Seth. She grabbed his hand and pulled him to sit across from her brother. The move distracted him enough to miss the single tear rolling down her face.

As she settled, Ben drummed his fingers on the tabletop. "Nate?" She smiled when he used her nickname—it seemed that Seth was the only one who never did. Ben waited until she met his gaze. "Do you think you could get used to having your big brother around?"

"What? That would be fantastic! Are you thinking of looking for work out here? I'll help with the job search if it will speed things up."

"Actually." He glanced quickly at Kelsey. "My company has a branch in Portland. I start in two weeks. I just need to find an apartment." His grin spread wide.

"This is so perfect. Kelsey, isn't that the best news!" Nate's thrilled smile met her friend's shocked expression.

Seth chuckled. "See? I knew she'd be happy."

"Wait. . . You knew?"

"He told me earlier today."

Natalie stood and hauled her brother's unwilling limbs into her happy dance. Kelsey sat in stunned silence until Natalie yanked her to dance to a nonexistent song.

Ben collapsed in laughter and turned to Natalie. "Would you have time to help me find a place? I know I sprung this on you at a busy time."

Natalie found a seat on Seth's lap. "I'll help. It sounds like fun, but I don't know Portland's quirky neighborhoods like Kelsey and Seth do."

"I'll call a property manager I know," Seth offered. "When do you fly back?"

"Thursday."

"Damn, you're cutting it close." Kelsey grinned, always loving an impossible challenge.

***

After checking out four different properties, Ben chose a two-story brick duplex. The two-bedroom oozed character—built in the 1940's when craftsman touches were common.

Natalie went from room to room. "You have a Mount Hood view from the master," she pointed out. Calling it the master was a stretch, but it was the larger of the two bedrooms, which shared a jack-and-jill bath.

Seth inspected under the sinks, checking the plumbing. "The bones are solid, and the maintenance is top notch. You shouldn't have any issues."

"I'll send in the paperwork from that pub down the street. Let's celebrate! Dinner's on me." Ben locked the door as they left. Natalie hoped he would be satisfied with this new direction in his life. She never dared to dream that her brother would live so close.

Standing on the front porch, Ben turned to her and groaned about the cost of shipping his furniture. "I think I'll just sell it all and buy new stuff once I'm settled out here. Nate, do you have time to go shopping?"

"I might have a better idea. I knew there was a reason I couldn't part with Grandpa's most beautiful things. Just take a look at what's left in his condo. It's gorgeous furniture, I promise you'll love it."

"Are you sure?" he asked with a grin. The thought of owning those family heirlooms seemed to make Ben happy.

"Absolutely."

"Aren't you keeping any of it?" he asked carefully.

"I can't fit it in my tiny home. This is great—it will be like Grandpa's housewarming gift to you." Natalie fought happy tears as Ben accepted.

Once Ben settled, she would be ready to put Grandpa's condominium on the market and finally close the Seattle chapter of her life.

With her fingers laced in Seth's, Natalie followed Ben and Kelsey to a nearby pub.

"That was generous," Seth said as he squeezed her hand.

"It feels right, and I'm happy Ben will have some of Grandpa's things."

"You know your darkroom has a home at Whitewater for as long as you like."

Natalie studied Seth and considered the offer. "Thank you. I'll accept so long as Amanda agrees to use it when I'm gone."

Sharing the space made sense. Amanda had helped to set up all the equipment in Ashwood and loved developing film. Each time she stopped by to process her work, their laughter echoed throughout Whitewater from behind the darkroom door.

"Have you talked to the owner of that community near Otter Rock?" Seth asked, while slowing his steps and increasing their distance between Kelsey and Ben.

"Yes, I sent my deposit last week," Natalie said, as her stomach sank.

"I'd like to follow you out, if that's okay. You know, to make sure everything looks solid after the first move."

"Are you sure? Ben will be back and already offered to help." Natalie glanced ahead and watched as her brother disappeared into the pub with Kelsey.

Seth tucked Natalie against his chest. He claimed a quick kiss then eased away. "I'll talk to Ben. I don't think he'll mind shifting his plans."

TWENTY-ONE

Time sped so quickly, Natalie didn't have time to worry about leaving. They emptied Grandpa's condo and moved the furniture into Ben's place.

After helping her apply a fresh coat of paint, Ben hopped a plane to Charlotte. One final project needed his attention before he made his move to Portland. Eager to leave Seattle, Natalie met with the realtor and put the condo on the market.

The day finally arrived for the last test drive of her completed tiny home. Seth sat in the passenger seat, ready to help, but only if she asked. Natalie took a deep breath, and let the significance of the moment seep in.

Painted olive green and trimmed in white, her home filled the side mirrors as she pulled onto the highway. A broad grin stretched across her face. "Seth, I've got this!"

"Never doubted it, sweetness," he said, giving her knee a squeeze. "Where are you taking us?"

Her confidence swelled. "The farmers' market has a nice-sized lot. Let's show this house off and see if anyone wants a tour. What do you think?"

"I'm your wingman." Seth nodded and relaxed in his seat, watching as she took control.

She pulled into the lot and a crowd gathered around the home in minutes. Natalie opened the large window. Her only regret? Not stocking the kitchen—it seemed like everyone who wandered over wanted a coffee.

Seth texted Carlos, Kent, and Rick and asked them to lock Whitewater Homes and come over. No one was prepared for the impact their work had on the community.

A line formed for impromptu tours. Seth stood outside, answering questions while Natalie revealed the details of her home.

Carlos arrived. It wasn't long before he had a fan base of potential customers.

Amanda, already at the market selling her photos, spotted her brother and rushed over. She pulled Natalie into a big hug. "Do you have your camera with you, Nate? I'll take pictures in case you decide to start that travel blog."

"Great idea." She dashed inside her home, found her camera, and placed it in Amanda's capable hands.

After the market closed for the day, the crowd disappeared. Natalie finally had a moment to take a breath. "This surprised me," she said with a satisfied grin.

"Everyone wanted a closer look," Seth said, amazed by the interest.

"Why haven't we tried this before?" Rick asked.

"How can we keep this interest hot?" Kent grinned and winked at Amanda. She giggled and moved a few inches closer, drawn by his magnetic smile.

"Nate could serve coffee at the Octoberfest celebration," Carlos suggested before he caught himself. Everyone knew by then, this home and Natalie would be gone. Carlos tried to shrug off the sobering suggestion. "Maybe we can take one of the other models...it's something to consider."

Natalie didn't let that little slip diminish her enthusiasm. She still glowed with the exhilaration of the afternoon. "I just love this town," she said. "This was the perfect way to wrap up my project, don't you think?" Her glance darted from friend to friend. Then her smile faded as the moment sunk in. This was the beginning of goodbye.

Seth took her hand and kissed her knuckles. "Why don't we get your house back to base and celebrate at Northside Grill? My treat."

"I'm in," Kent shouted. "How about it, Amanda. Can you join us?"

She beamed and blushed. "I'd love to."

Carlos shook his head and declined, "My daughter has soccer practice, so I'll have to pass. I do have something in my truck for you, Natalie, to commemorate your launch."

Trailing Carlos, Natalie couldn't imagine what he had planned. Lowering the tailgate, she gasped as he peeled a moving blanket away from a handcrafted 'Little Latte' sign, complete with a hand-carved coffee cup.

"I'm proud of you, kiddo. Damn, I wish you weren't leaving."

"Thank you. I love it." She hugged the quiet man and he flushed.

Seth slid his hand over the beautifully crafted sign. "Great touch, Carlos."

"I installed hooks under the eaves and used teak. It's light, so you can lift it on your own."

Natalie nodded. "Thank you." She'd miss him so much, along with the rest of the crew.

Kent and Rick secured the windows, doors, and latches for the short trip back to Whitewater Homes.

Seth drove this time and was satisfied with the way the gooseneck trailer handled. The worry, deep in his gut, had nothing to do with Natalie's ability to manage the rig. Managing life without her, that was a different concern.

***

Early the next morning, Seth came into his office to warm his coffee. He found Natalie uploading a few of Amanda's best farmers' market shots to his webpage.

He stared over her shoulder as she worked her magic, effortlessly adding a slideshow with cascading graphics and mixing in text. She peeked at him over her shoulder. "I can help with this sort of thing remotely if you'd like."

Seth settled his hands on her shoulders, squeezing. "Amanda's pics are great, but if you want to come back and take shots of every finished home, it would be just fine with me." The offer was sincere, and as close as he would come to asking Natalie to stay.

Seth was relieved Natalie was so distracted by the screen. If she had locked eyes with him, she would have sensed his mounting pain.

Natalie kept the mouse clicking and added, "Amanda can handle anything you throw at her. I can't believe some of the work she's doing in the dark room." Once she was pleased with the changes, she hit save.

She'd missed his offer and the jagged sensation of rejection bubbled from a forgotten well of pain. His jaw clenched, and Seth had to find a quick escape. "I've got work to finish on the floor. If you changed any passwords, put them on the orange pad in the top drawer so I can decipher this again on my own." With his back to Natalie, Seth pulled his office door firmly closed behind him.

All afternoon he maintained a distance, pushing Natalie away for his own protection.

Later that evening, Seth knocked on her locked darkroom door. "Still need the dark," she called from the other side.

"Everyone's gone and the shop lights are off, can I come in?" he asked.

She turned the lock and opened the door. The shop, completely dark, left the pair bathed in only the darkroom's red light.

"I'm sorry," he said with a gentle kiss. She sighed, accepting the balm meant to soothe all the emotions he had left in disarray.

"I'm sorry too . . . but I have to leave Ashwood, even if it's difficult. I need to do this, Seth, for me."

He kissed her again. "I understand. But you might find me chasing you, Natalie. And I'm fast." He smiled trying to mask his fear.

"God, I hope so," she said before he captured her giggle with his lips and toed the darkroom door shut. The counter looked like the perfect spot for what he had in mind.

TWENTY-TWO

Natalie packed the last of her clothes in a small suitcase. Most of her belongings were already on board.

She stole a moment alone on Seth's deck overlooking her property. The crisp morning air crackled. A first frost would soon strip the rest of the leaves from the trees. The flowers she'd planted still bloomed in large pots on the deck, but her hummingbirds were gone.

She turned to find Seth waiting. He held out his hand, and they walked with fingers entwined to his truck.

***

Even though the drive was exhausting, Natalie pulled her home for the entire trip to Driftwood Shores. Seth offered to take a leg of the journey, but she wanted to do this on her own. Climbing down from her truck, Natalie stretched and moaned. Shoulders tight and legs heavy, she propped her foot on the running board, stretching to work out the kinks in her hips and thighs.

When his truck pulled alongside Seth sprung out, unaffected by the six-hour drive.

"I'm so sore. I almost wish I'd had you build something smaller." Her back popped as she stretched side to side.

Seth closed the distance and wrapped his hands around her shoulders. "Oh, sweetness, I found a knot. Is that better?" he asked. "I know pulling a big trailer can take a toll."

"Mmm, that's nice." She tilted her head forward, closed her eyes, and moaned. When he added extra pressure with his thumb, her knees sagged.

Her muscles had just slacked, when out of nowhere a woman said, "Welcome to Driftwood Shores."

Natalie tensed again as her eyes popped open. "Oh, hello."

"You must be the new addition to our community. Natalie, I'm Faye. Looks like you'll need my yoga class tomorrow."

The woman wore a faded denim skirt and a tie-dyed shirt. Her lack of shoes and the long braid plaited down her back gave her the illusion of perpetual youth.

"Great to finally meet you." Natalie bent to pet the orange cat circling her feet. "I wondered if I missed an email. Is there any final paperwork that I need to sign?"

"Oh no. I'm not that formal . . . I don't even own a computer. Everyone here is month to month. When the winds change and someone has an itch to move, I won't stand in their way."

A bug scurried in the sandy soil destined to become the next victim of Faye's cat. Stalking like a predator, it pounced. With a laugh, Faye scooped up the orange-striped kitty and stroked him between his ears.

"Don't be surprised if Bramble leaves a gift on your porch in the morning. Most new residents find a dead mouse the first day or two."

"I look forward to it, Bramble." Natalie scratched between the cat's shoulders. It tolerated the attention for a few seconds and then jumped to the ground.

"Let me know if you need anything at all." Faye's gaze swept across the tiny home neighborhood. "Everyone lends a hand and watches out for each other. It's all part of our communal adventure."

"Thanks, I'll be happy to pitch in where I can." Natalie went to shake Faye's hand but found her body pulled in for a quick hug instead.

"Welcome home," Faye said then swept away on steps as light as her cat's. Bramble followed, seeming connected by an invisible string.

"I like her," Seth said as she left.

"Me too, and after that drive, I may need her yoga class." Natalie turned, stared at her home with her hands on her hips, and took on a personal challenge. "Let me level this thing on my own."

"It's all yours." She knew he was tempted to help, it was his nature, but he only stepped in at the end, securing the home on sturdy jacks.

She brushed her sweaty hair away from her face and sighed. "I did it."

"Like a pro," he said with a proud grin. "Hey, those waves are calling. After dinner, I want a sunset walk on the beach with my girl."

Dinner prep for their simple meal heightened their awareness. Each light touch felt like a game of domestic foreplay.

Following the grilled cheese and tomato soup, they abandoned their dishes and headed toward the beach. They walked barefoot across the wide dunes that rose in drifts between her community and the ocean. After a final climb, the turbulent waves came into view. Skirting the edge, bare feet splashed the shallow surf, and a stiff breeze carried seagulls on a rollercoaster flight.

Natalie turned, her red hair tossing in the wind. "When Ben and I were little, before our parents split, we spent a week at a musty cabin on the coast. We built sandcastles, went horseback riding, and roasted hot dogs over a campfire on long sticks. That was the best."

"So, some of your memories of your Dad—"

"Are really good."

"Nice. I'm glad Ben made this move."

She squeezed his hand. "He plans to visit in a couple of weeks."

"I will too, if that's okay."

"I'll count the days." She stopped for a moment and avoided his eyes, watching the surf instead. "Seth, I'd like to keep what we've built, but with the distance, I'll understand if you need to give this up."

When he pulled her close, the waves swept over their bare feet. "Sweetness, you're too important to give up." The kiss that devoured her lips might have seemed desperate, but he didn't care if it revealed how much he hurt.

A couple of barking dogs passing by with their owners ended the public embrace. They pulled apart and walked on, drawn toward immense tide pools. Purple sea stars and green urchins clung to black weathered rocks. Natalie waded into the deep water up to her knees. "It's really warm."

"I believe you," Seth said from the dry sand.

When she could see he wasn't willing to wade in, she yelled, "Chicken!" and swept her hand through the pool, sending a curtain of water cascading over Seth's head.

She regretted her action when he chased her screaming and giggling down the beach. Seth caught up and swept Natalie's legs from under her, carrying her kicking and laughing into the churning surf. He waded deeper and deeper until his shorts were completely soaked. "What are you going to do now, sweetness?"

"Beg for mercy?"

"I'm merciless when it comes to you." Still holding her in his arms, he pressed his lips to hers and trailed kisses down her neck. She squirmed and screamed as his nibbles and bites crept lower.

Snaking her fingers through his hair, she stilled in his arms and pulled his mouth to hers. A searing tangle of tongues, lips, and teeth brought them both to the point of moaning.

Coming up for air, Seth remembered that the beach was dotted with people. He walked toward the dunes and set Natalie back on her bare feet in the sand.

"How do you feel about finding a quiet place in the dunes?" he asked. Natalie nodded, and it didn't take Seth long to find a secluded spot hidden in the hilly sea grass.

They covered the ground with their clothes, and the autumn sun warmed their skin. He took his time, loving Natalie as the cool breeze tickled their bodies with a light dusting of sand.

***

"I have sand there too?" Natalie laughed and stood still in the shower as Seth used the wand to rinse every grain down the drain.

"That's all of it, I think," he said, but he knew sand was bound to appear for days.

"Thanks. Now I'll do you." She blushed as the wand hit low places.

"Sweetness, you're shivering," he said, then teased the wand from her fingers. "Why don't you wrap up in a towel and I'll join you in the loft in a second."

Natalie kneaded her lip as Seth climbed the ladder with a towel wrapped around his hips. Her gaze lingered on that muscular V at his groin. The desire in her eyes swelled his cock even after the hour they'd spent on the beach.

The bed dipped as he joined her. She seemed surprised when he said, "Let me comb out your hair." After he arranged her cross-legged on the bed, he straddled her hips with his knees. Slowly, he stroked the red waves and sopped up little drops of water from the end of the summer bleached tips.

His fingers swept her hair to the side, giving him a few inches of skin to taste with a tender kiss. While his lips were close to her ear he whispered, "Lay down on your stomach."

Straddling her thighs, he kneaded lotion into her skin, and followed her spine to the sexy dimples at the small of her back. After the long drive she had endured, her shoulders deserved the same attention. He massaged her outstretched arms, out to the very tips of her fingers.

Crawling down her frame, his work began again with her feet. His hands devoted time to the muscles of each thigh and squeezed the beautiful globes of her butt. Her body was boneless in stark contrast to his restless steel shaft.

Natalie melted into the mattress as his fingers pressed closer and closer to her heat. Spreading her legs, Seth settled on his knees between them. Pink and glistening, her arousal begged for a taste. He teased her hips higher, placing her in the perfect position to dip his tongue.

"So sweet and hot for me," he said. Natalie tucked her knees under and lifted her hips, begging for attention against her pulsing clit. Seth's slick fingers drifted forward, drawing slow circles.

A throaty moan quickened the pace of his attention on each erogenous point. Riding the sensation, Natalie begged, "Inside me, please."

He grasped her soft hips, aligned his velvety head with her heat, and surged forward in one strong stroke. In response to the deep invasion, Natalie exhaled a satisfied moan. Seth pulled back, drove forward, and repeated his path again.

"Harder," she begged, and pressed her hips against him. His balls drew up and legs quaked as tension built at the base of his spine.

"Mine," he growled, losing himself in the visual overload, watching his length emerge, only to disappear again.

"Come for me, sweetness." His words seemed to unleash her explosive release, and she came with a keening cry. Overcome with a need to mark her, he pulled out, fisted his shaft, and shot cum in white arcs, painting her ass.

Her body sank to the bed in a sex-drunk haze. Grabbing the damp towel, Seth carefully cleaned the white pearls from her butt and lower back. Her eyes fluttered and she smiled as he sank down and hitched his leg over her thighs.

"Sleep, sweetness," he said, as his fingers danced until she faded into a dreamless sleep.

***

Seth woke in the dark loft, alone. He blinked, adjusting to the dim light, while listening carefully to locate Natalie. A clink drew his attention outside, just beyond the half-sized door that led to the rooftop deck.

He rose and found Natalie snuggled in his oversized Ashwood High sweatshirt, tossed on over her yoga pants. When she'd found that high school relic in a bottom dresser drawer, he'd asked her to keep it. The way his girl looked wearing his name in bold white letters appealed to his possessive nature.

When Natalie spotted him at the threshold, she said, "Grab a mug if you want cocoa. I brought the carafe up here."

In a moment, Seth returned with a cup. "I must have been dead to the world if you made cocoa and snuck outside without waking me."

She giggled. "You might have been snoring, just a little bit."

"Did I wake you?" he asked.

"No. I was hungry and needed a sugar fix." She took his cup and poured cocoa. The dark, rich liquid steamed in the cool night air. As he took a sip, Natalie gazed into the complete darkness that seemed to swallow the dunes. "It's so mild, I wonder if it will even freeze here this winter."

"It might. I've seen pictures of snow covering that big rock on Cannon beach." Seth yawned, still sleepy. She caught the tail end of his contagious yawn then kneaded the back of her neck. He waited for Natalie to tell him why she was so tense.

Finally, when Seth couldn't take the silence he asked, "Are you okay?"

"I'm wondering how I'll settle. New job, new home, new people. It's normal to be nervous, right?"

"Absolutely. But, Natalie . . . you know you have a home in Ashwood." If he thought it would work, he'd drop to his knees and beg her to change her mind.

"I can see myself there. Still, after all the effort, all the planning, I have to see this through."

"I understand," he said, but part of him didn't. And he didn't try to disguise his deep disappointment. On a long slow exhale, Seth stared into the dark, quiet.

She reached over with her toe and touched the top of his bare foot, coaxing a smile. The moon chose that moment to emerge from a gap between the clouds. "Look," she said. "I have a million-dollar ocean view!"

"Damn. How about that . . . You can see the surf from up here."

As Natalie watched the moon bathe the ocean with an iridescent glow, Seth turned and memorized her details—her profile, the curve of her hand, the slow rise and fall of her chest as she breathed. And he let himself slide into love by increments.

***

Early the following morning, Natalie heard a commotion and opened her door to find a small brown bird on her doorstep.

"Oh, no, it's dead." She covered her mouth and asked through her fingers, "Do you think that orange cat left me a housewarming gift?"

Seth joined her at the threshold. "It sure looks like it."

He tucked her against him, and her shoulders curled as she sighed. Movement in the tall grass brought her eyes up where she spotted Bramble warming himself on the sand, his tail flicking.

"Seth, what am I supposed to do?" He smoothed the hitch in her voice with a slow stroke up her spine.

"I'm on it." He jumped over the top step on his way outside and grabbed a shovel from the storage space beneath the tiny home. The small creature didn't move at all as he scooped it up.

"Sorry little guy," Seth mumbled as he scouted the dunes for a burial site.

Natalie stood a few steps back while he concealed the tiny carcass. "I know I should have taken care of that myself," she said, but depending on Seth came so easily. "Am I high-maintenance?" she asked, knowing the answer before she'd even finished asking the question.

"Sweetness, if I like maintaining you, what difference does it make?" His eyes softened and conveyed so much — tenderness, caring, and love. Love she accepted, even if he wasn't ready to proclaim it.

The rattle of metal turned her head. "Good morning, kids." Faye waved and closed in with a wagon in tow, wearing a wrap-around skirt that resembled a patchwork quilt.

When a wheel hit a bump, a box tumbled from the stack in the red wagon. "Your supplies have been arriving all week. This is about half of it."

"That's great! I'll be able to open Monday morning." Natalie hopped with anticipation, already digging through the parcels.

"I'll get the rest," Seth offered, and in a few minutes returned to her home with several more boxes. When he put the most important on top, Natalie squealed and tore into the package right away.

"What did Elsa send?" he asked when she ripped away the tape and flopped the top open.

"Snickerdoodles and a card." Smiling, Natalie read a note that wished her good luck while Seth devoured three cookies.

***

Over the screen of his laptop, Seth watched while Natalie organized her kitchen. Her little red apron was secured around her waist by a bow that landed just above her heart-shaped butt. It looked so damn sexy. The emails couldn't hold his attention, not with the string of illicit thoughts that stubbornly invaded.

His cargo shorts tightened every time she bent to store supplies on lower shelves. Just when he began to gain a little focus, she stretched to stow a sleeve of paper cups in a high cabinet, showing off every curve.

Seth stood quickly, took the cups from her hand, and stuffed them into the shelf for her. "Enough, woman," he howled.

"What?" She yelped when Seth pulled her hips against his hard length.

"Watching you move around this kitchen—porn, baby, pure porn." His searing kiss put an end to her work, and they tumbled into the loft to work up an appetite.

***

Dinner reservations gave Natalie a reason to dress up. Seth placed a kiss at her nape as he zipped her into her favorite green dress—a color that brought out the red in her hair. She only needed a touch of lip-gloss and mascara after so many walks on the beach had flushed her cheeks.

"So beautiful, sweetness."

"I think you're beautiful, too." She covered his slow chuckle with a tiptoe kiss.

Their table showcased a perfect sunset, but the meal and view were just a distraction. Natalie watched Seth's thumb stroke back and forth across her hand.

"These past three days have seemed like a vacation," she said. "A perfect beach getaway before . . ." Her goodbye caught in her throat, and she couldn't speak. A single tear found a path down her cheek where Seth caught it with his free hand.

"Don't cry. The distance might be difficult, but what we've started is worth everything." Seth reached into his jacket pocket. "I want to give you something to celebrate your new beginning."

"You didn't need to do that, but I'm so happy you did," she said as her fingers toyed with the earrings she wore tonight, the one's he'd bought for her at the festival.

She held her breath, tore away the ribbon and paper, and lifted the lid. Inside the flat box Natalie found a silver necklace with tiny flowers dotting the links. From the chain, a delicate silver hummingbird hung mid-flight.

"I know you have a thing for those little birds."

"Seth, I love it."

When he stood, she lifted her hair, giving him room to clasp the jewelry around her neck. She closed her eyes when Seth pressed a warm gentle kiss to the sway of her shoulder. "Beautiful, sweetness, so beautiful."

Hoping the night would never end, they aimlessly wandered the boardwalk that paralleled the beach. Seth slid his hand over the sway of her hip and gave her a gentle squeeze. "I don't think I'll sleep very well without you in my bed."

She sighed. "If we keep busy, time will fly. Kelsey plans to visit right away, and Ben is coming the week after." Her words didn't convince either of them. They weren't even apart, and it already hurt.

Seth nodded. "I'll be busy, too. Wade asked for my help with a festival in Boise. I hope it's okay . . . it's on Halloween weekend."

Her shoulders lifted in a disappointed shrug. They'd thought about meeting at Ben's for Halloween.

"He needs another driver," Seth apologized.

"That's okay. It sounds fun. You should go." She leaned into him as the night air seeped past her coat.

"I'll drive out the week before," he promised.

"Or I can come to Ashwood. I might need a break. Let's give it a couple of weeks and see how it goes."

That night, they touched more than talked and savored slow kisses. She absorbed his unspoken love, as his hands seemed to memorize her curves. Seth pressed deeper and she received him, giving herself completely until they could be together again.

TWENTY-THREE

Awake before dawn, Natalie prepped her kitchen for coffee service. She chose bright green chalk to boldly write her featured coffee drinks on a portable blackboard. At the last moment, she scrawled a vine design along the bottom. Standing back, she admired the touch of artwork with a smile.

Seth tore his eyes away from the window and ignored that familiar angry hurt. Too much of this reminded him of that day he left Desiree in Portland. After his bag was packed, he leaned outside and asked, "Do you need help hanging your Little Latte sign?"

"I'm not quite ready." Natalie climbed the steps and pulled him close. "First, I want to steal a kiss from you." Up on tiptoe in her white canvas sneakers, she held him tight. Her lips teased until Seth responded. He wrapped one arm around her waist as instinct took over and he stole her senses with a desperate embrace.

"I'm going to miss you," she said against his lips.

His arms ached as he let her go. "If you plan to serve coffee today, we better open that window. Then I'll get on the road, and leave you to it."

When he took a final glance in the rearview mirror, she'd already gone inside.

***

Each mile increased the bitter taste in his mouth. The muscles in his forearms twitched, desperate to turn around. Every fiber in his body knew this was wrong. Still, he could not bring himself to chase a woman and become an afterthought. Not again.

Familiar misery erupted without warning. A jagged scar ripped open, and he re-experienced the anger that had never really healed when Desiree shoved him out of her life.

Pathetic. He was just a small-town guy, satisfied with small-town dreams. And nothing could change that fact. Yet, he seemed destined to attract women who wanted more than he could give.

Trapped in a bitter version of himself, hollow fury took over, intensified by Portland's grinding traffic. Seth gripped the wheel and wondered how much whiskey it would take to recover this time. The bottle had numbed his senses before—until Wade had towed him back from the edge. Back to work, back to things that mattered when a woman didn't give a shit.

Seth didn't know what he could have done differently this time. Fuck this. He didn't have the power to change Natalie's mind.

Without forethought, Seth eased to the right and took the next exit. Three stoplights later, he found himself in a familiar neighborhood.

Lined with gnarled hawthorn trees, his former street stretched ahead—exactly the same. Small homes and duplexes, some with peeling paint, sat in tight, even rows. More cars lined the street than he recalled and forced him to take the last vacant spot near the corner, four houses down from Desiree's front door.

A faint tick, tick, tick from the cooling engine blended with the swish of his racing heartbeat. He peeled his fingers from the steering wheel.

Seth inhaled, closed his eyes, and opened his door. A frigid blast couldn't sharpen senses that had dulled more than one hundred miles ago. He climbed out on heavy legs that staggered toward something he desperately needed, a quick fix for this nauseating ache.

Sex. Owning Desiree's body, even for just an hour, would patch this cannon ball-sized hole in his chest. Her car waited at the curb. She was home.

As he stepped from the gutter to the sidewalk, a shout turned his head. "Hey! Asshole!"

The words exploded from a pot-bellied man walking a scruffy mutt at the end of a long leash. Seth's eyes widened as the wire-haired mutt lifted his leg. The little turd looked right at Seth just as a stream of urine arced, splattering a fire hydrant and the side of his truck.

What the hell?

In his mental fog, he'd pulled to the curb and parked directly in front of a fire hydrant.

"You can't park there. Move your goddamn truck," the guy grunted.

Seth grinned. How could he have been so blind? He gave the guy a one shoulder shrug.

"Wipe that grin off your face. Do you think I'm kidding?" The dog yipped, shrill and high. When it wouldn't shut up, Seth tilted his head back and laughed.

"I ain't gonna tell you again—move your fuckin' truck. You want my house to burn to the ground?"

Seth lifted both hands and took a step back. "Hey, man. Sorry. I only wanted to say thanks."

Two bushy eyebrows furrowed. "What did you say?"

"I said, thanks." Seth circled his truck.

"My dog takes a piss on your rig, and you're thanking me?"

"Yup. You and your miserable dog kept me from making the biggest fucking mistake of my life."

"Are you crazy or something?" the guy yelled back as he yanked his dog down the sidewalk, suddenly in a hurry.

"Or something." Laughter filled the cab when he slammed the door. Freed from his momentary insanity, he turned the key and pressed the accelerator. Seth couldn't get away from Desiree fast enough.

TWENTY-FOUR

Natalie swiped a tear from her cheek before she greeted her first customer.

Faye's warm, knowing smile eased some of the ache while she patiently perused the menu. "Any suggestions?" she asked.

"What's your usual?"

"Green chai tea with milk alternative. You wouldn't happen to have hemp-milk, would you?"

"You bet."

"And I'll try one of your flax seed apple muffins." Faye leaned into the service window. "I saw Seth leave this morning. I hope he visits. He has such a nice way about him."

"He does." Natalie missed his nice ways already. "We met this summer, while he built my house, but I feel like we've known each other so much longer."

Faye pulled a wad of wrinkled money from a pocket hidden in the folds of her skirt. "Maybe you met in a past life? You never know."

"True. You never know." While Natalie prepped the order, she considered the possibility. Some things were beyond explanation. "One green chai tea with hemp milk and a warm apple flax muffin."

Another resident in the tiny home community wandered to the counter, asked questions about Natalie's home, and ordered. Before long, several people had gathered around while she prepped. Her house/business combo was a curiosity. She promised tours and yearned for the distraction of a little company.

A free moment gave her time to peek at her phone and answer Seth's text.

Seth: *Made it back to Ashwood.*

Natalie: *Glad you're home. Had more customers than I can count. Some want a closer look at what you built.*

Seth: *Or a closer look at the beautiful girl living in it.*

203

Natalie: *I promised a few tours.*

Seth: *Sounds fun. I know everyone will love you.*

She stared at the last two words. Her heart jumped until she read the message again. Natalie typed carefully.

Natalie: *Miss you.*

Seth: *Miss you too.*

***

After dinner, Seth forced himself into his truck and back to Whitewater. The pull of the liquor cabinet was too strong to stay home.

Darkness cloaked the empty shop in elongated shadows from the sodium outdoor lights. Leaves from a nearby maple tree blew across the parking lot and came to rest against his building like a snowdrift. With a heavy boot, he kicked the leaves away and opened the side door.

Settled in his office, Seth turned on his computer. Natalie seemed to be everywhere. She had left her Space Needle coffee mug on his desk, a stash of milk chocolate in his top drawer, and colorful gel pens in a ceramic cup on the shelf.

Seth's phone buzzed.

"Hey, sweetness." After his near miss today, her voice soothed his nerves better than top shelf whiskey.

"Sorry to call so late," she said. "Faye invited me to dinner to meet my neighbors. I just got back."

"No worries. I'm still working on plans for a home."

"Which one?"

"The build for that couple with the dogs."

"With those two big Weimaraners?"

"That's the one. I'll have to get creative with the loft. The dogs sleep with the owners."

"Hmm, sounds cozy. If I had two dogs, I'd need a built-in vacuum system for all that hair."

"Not a bad idea. Mind if I use it?"

Her smile came through on her answer, "I'm happy to be your muse."

"I love the changes you made to the web page," he said, feeling for the first time like this long-distance thing might work.

"I could still help, if Amanda's willing to take the pictures."

"I'd like that, and I know she would too."

"Would you mind if I asked her? I want a reason to stay in touch with your sister."

"Great idea."

"I'll give her a call tomorrow. Don't be surprised if she shows up at the shop."

Seth nodded, though he knew Natalie couldn't see it. He liked this arrangement. The momentary weakness today scared the shit out of him. Amanda might be the best person to keep his mind from wandering toward his ex. His little sister had never been Desiree's biggest fan.

He tipped back in his chair and listened to Natalie's musical voice. As she shared the events of her day, he let go of his earlier anger, choosing instead to be happy for his girl.

When she yawned, he asked "Sweetness, are you tired? Why don't you get some sleep?"

"Trying to sleep without you will be strange." Her long, slow sigh mingled with rustling sheets. She was already in bed, and his arms ached to hold her.

"It'll be hard for me too." Her absence marked everything. Seth didn't want to go home to his empty house, empty kitchen, empty bed.

As he said goodnight, leaving off the *I love you* almost hurt.

Before Seth locked up for the night, he wandered into her darkroom, expecting a tidy vacant place. He smiled when he saw her work in progress. Natalie's personal space seemed lived in and ready for her to come back.

Everything she left behind, at home, in his office, and especially in this dark room shouted one thing—eventually, Natalie would return to him.

***

"Hey, Seth!" His sister's voice echoed through Whitewater's shop.

"You must have talked to Natalie." Seth chuckled as Amanda skipped his direction.

"I did. She brought me up to speed about your website."

"Great. So, are you willing to take over the photography?"

"I'm thrilled to, at least until Natalie realizes she belongs here and comes back."

Seth smiled and nodded. "We can hope."

Amanda gave his arm a reassuring squeeze. "It's only a matter of time. Until then, I'd love to help."

"I have enough work to keep you busy part-time. Is that okay?"

"Okay? It's completely awesome!" Seth fought a grin as Amanda clapped her hands and bubbled, "I'm so excited. I'll get right to work. You'll hardly even notice I'm here."

He choked back a laugh, knowing she wouldn't be easy to ignore. Amanda had come prepared, and brought out her camera, taking a few shots as the team worked.

Seth pulled out his phone and thanked Natalie.

Seth: *Amanda showed up to take some pics.*

Natalie: *How's it going?*

Seth: *Good. She's excited.*

Natalie: *She worships her big brother. You are aware.*

Seth: *So much to worship.*

Natalie: *Especially your humility.*

Seth: *Thanks for making that happen. It was nice having her around.*

Natalie: ☺

Seth: *Anything new at the beach?*

Natalie: *Got in an order of pumpkin muffins and Halloween decorations. I think I'll wear a costume the entire week.*

Seth: *Nice fantasy. You in a sexy Halloween costume.*

Natalie: *Might help sales.*

Seth: *Maybe I'll change my plans.*

Natalie: *I'd like that. Oops gotta go. Customer.*

***

When a lull hit that afternoon, Natalie escaped and climbed the dunes to catch a glimpse of the pounding waves.

A surfer she'd met at Faye's emerged from the water wearing a black wetsuit and carrying his surfboard. Always hungry, Mark had already become a regular.

"Good to see you out on the beach. You work too much." He bent and untethered the Velcro strap from his ankle.

"Business has been almost too good, but thanks for stopping by every morning to grab breakfast."

"Keeps me from surviving on Pop Tarts." Mark's smile was warm, but not tempting.

"I'm more of a Toaster Strudel girl." She laughed. "It's that little packet of frosting."

"Strawberry's my favorite," Mark said with a friendly grin.

"I'll add it to the menu."

"Good. It will give me another reason to stop by."

Steamy furls lifted as the sun hit the dark wet sand. Mark peeled down the top of his wetsuit and revealed his taut athletic body.

"How about a surf lesson sometime?" he asked. "I have an extra board that would work, but you'll need to rent a wetsuit."

Natalie nibbled her lip and considered the churning waves. Her stomach took a dive, but she decided to be brave. "If you have time, I'd like to take up that offer this weekend, while my friend, Kelsey, is visiting.

Mark nodded. "Sure thing. We'll give it a go." Looking past her, he narrowed his gaze and seemed to see something promising in the distant waves. With a quick goodbye, Mark yanked on his wetsuit and ran to meet the gray, pounding surf.

TWENTY-FIVE

Hidden in her loft, Natalie nestled into comfy pillows and clicked through photos. Each one had captured a summertime memory.

Shots landed in separate folders—some taken at the lake with friends, others on the trip to the river. A few starry sky images would be edited later to enhance the Milky Way. From another set, she selected four from the brewing festival, attached them to an email, and sent them to Wade.

She gasped when the screen filled with pictures from that incredible thunderstorm. Clicking backwards in time, she lingered for a moment on the little hummingbird while her fingers toyed with her silver necklace.

A particular shot stuttered her heart, but it wasn't the hummingbird. It was Seth. Slightly out of focus, his warm eyes and tilted smile clearly expressed one thing. His love.

A single frame later, his expression said much more. Mingled with love, Natalie saw fear. "Oh, my God, I hurt him," she said as she enlarged the photo. Her lungs seized, held by Seth's raw, bare emotion on the screen.

All summer long, she'd only worried about her heart, but Seth had also risked his. Her arms ached to hold him and erase the wounds she'd inflicted when she left. Grabbing a pillow, she held it tight, and curled on her comforter. Lonely pain deepened. Tears rolled into her hair. It was too late to apologize, and the damage she'd caused couldn't be undone unless she returned to Ashwood.

***

Natalie flung her door open when Kelsey ground to a stop. She'd never needed her friend so much. Bounding up the stairs, Kels hugged Nate so tight she could scarcely breathe.

"Choking me," she gasped.

"Why did you move so far away?" With her hands planted on her shoulders, Kels scrutinized Natalie's face. "What? No puffy eyes from crying day and night. Seth would be *so* disappointed."

"I'm too busy," Natalie lied, recalling all the tears she'd dried last night.

Over mugs of cocoa, they caught up as the clouds thickened, and the gray day turned into a soggy night. Stuck inside by the endless downpours, the girls itched to escape. The non-stop rain meant one thing—a girls' night out. Both chose snug jeans, heels, and low-cut tops. They tumbled out the door to eat, drink, and dance.

Hungry eyes followed their path as they weaved their way through the packed tavern, settling in a booth near the end of the long wooden bar. A girl leaned in to take their order and yelled over the din. "What can I get you to drink?"

"IPA on tap," Nate shouted over the music. Kelsey held up two fingers, ordering the same.

She nodded. "If you want food, place an order now, the kitchen's slammed."

Kelsey yelled, "Large deluxe-combo pizza, extra cheese."

"Got it, your beer will be right out. The food will take a while."

When Kelsey caught a few men checking her out, she returned one or two smiles before pivoting to Natalie. "I ordered a large so we can have cold-pizza for breakfast."

"Nothing's better," Nate agreed.

Leaning in, Kelsey pointed out how much the bar reminded her of Northside Grill. A sense of loss seeped in. Suddenly, Natalie's spot on the coast felt more like an outpost, and Ashwood seemed like home.

When their beers neared empty, two more arrived. "These drinks are from the guy at the bar." Kels sucked in a breath when Mark stood and moved toward them with athletic grace.

"Hey, Natalie. Are the plans still on for tomorrow?" he asked as Kelsey stared, speechless.

"I hope so, if this rain won't slow us down."

Mark shrugged, his eyes on Kelsey. "We'll be wet anyway."

Natalie reached across the table and nudged Kels from her trance. "This is Mark, he's the surfer I told you about. Mark – Kels will be joining us tomorrow, if that's okay."

An absurd stammer filled in the details. "S-Surfing. Nate asked me to bring wetsuits."

After shooting a quick look, Nate came to her friend's rescue. "Kelsey guides whitewater rafting. She brought up gear so I wouldn't have to rent."

Mark sank into the booth, choosing Kelsey's side. "Good move. Why risk a stale wettie warmer?"

His laugh brought Kelsey from her trance. "Hey, you weren't supposed to tell her that."

Natalie's eyes shot between them "What's a wettie warmer?"

Mark stifled the last of his chuckle and said, "To fight the cold, almost everyone has warmed up with their own . . . liquid heat."

Natalie's mouth gaped. "Really? Even you."

Kelsey grimaced and shrugged. "I guess it's a good thing you love me so much, Nate."

"That's so disgusting. I'd never pee in a wetsuit to get warm."

"It will be cold tomorrow." Mark's eyes danced with infectious laughter. "Just wait, you might change your mind."

When the pizza arrived, Mark scooted to the edge of the booth. Natalie reached across the table, stopping him. "Why don't you join us. We have plenty."

Mark hesitated until Kelsey's smile brough him back to his seat. When she inched a little closer, he slung a muscled arm over the top of the booth. As the conversation shifted to adrenalin driven sports, Natalie began to feel like a third wheel. Kels and Mark were so engrossed, neither noticed when Nate went silent and checked her phone.

The server returned and asked if they wanted another round. Kelsey and Mark ordered beer, while Nate took the role of designated driver and opted for soda. Natalie didn't mind the switch, but she did mind when she became excess baggage.

While Mark ran to the bathroom, Kelsey tipped in and said, "Natalie, why didn't you tell me about *Hot Mark*?"

"Hot Mark?" Natalie rolled her eyes. "I did. I told you we were surfing this weekend."

Kelsey's words flew, "That guy's so much more than a surfing instructor. Do you mind if I go for it? I'd only be crashing on your couch anyway."

On a sigh, Natalie's shoulders curled. "Are you sure?"

"Nate, your summer had way more action than mine. Are you into him?"

"Not at all. I hardly know the guy. Just be careful. You can always visit again in a few weeks and see if there's still something between you."

A glare sharpened Kelsey's eyes. "What's with this judgey thing? I never pitched you shit about Seth."

Hands lifted like a shield, Natalie straightened her spine. "No judgment. Have a great time."

"Sorry, I hope you didn't take that as bitchy." Nothing about what Kelsey said felt like an apology.

"Hope you have fun." Needing space, Natalie got up to grab a box for the leftovers.

Mark jogged back as the last few pieces of pizza landed in the box. "Looks like we're ready to roll. Hey, Natalie, I talked to the manager. He said I could leave my car here if you don't mind me bumming a ride."

"No problem. We're ready to leave if you are." Natalie grabbed the pizza box and couldn't wait to find the exit.

She'd barely stopped at Driftwood Shores before Kelsey grabbed her backpack and ran off with Mark.

As she watched them disappear, she whispered to the breeze and the rain, "At least I'll get a good night's sleep"

***

After brushing her teeth, Natalie nestled into her loft with a book-boyfriend that reminded her of Seth. Midway through a very sexy scene, she grabbed her phone and sent a text, *Are you awake?*

A few seconds later, Seth called. "Hey, sweetness, I didn't expect to hear from you tonight. Did Kelsey crash and burn?"

"No. I'm alone. She hit it off with that surfer."

"Mitch?"

"No, Mark. We'll see if surfing tomorrow works out. I bet they sleep in."

"Shit. I know you missed Kels. Are you okay with this?"

She tugged at a thread on her blanket. "I'm not excited about it."

"I wish I was there."

"Honestly, I'd rather be in Ashwood," she blurted. "At least I'd get a good night's sleep in your bed."

"Trouble sleeping?" His sultry voice heated. "Anything I can do to help?"

Her legs raked across the blankets, heating instantly. She giggled softly and said, "What are you wearing?"

"Damn, woman. Give me a second." Natalie blushed as she heard clothing land somewhere on Seth's floor.

"Listen carefully, sweetness, are you in your loft?"

"Yes."

"Just wearing panties and one of those tiny tank tops?"

"How did you know?"

"Imagine I'm right there with you. I can see you now, all spread out, messy hair, cheeks flushed."

Her eyes raked the ceiling. "Did you install hidden cameras?"

"Damn, no. Wish I would have thought of that. But I can almost taste you . . . all warm for me."

"Mmm, and getting hotter."

"Now, open your bedside table," Seth's voice had taken on that bossy tone she loved. "Take out that sexy toy I know you have hidden."

"Really?" Nerves and arousal mixed in the best possible combination.

"Don't make me wait." Her nipples tightened at the sound of his command.

"Okay, Seth." Her chest rose and fell faster. "Got it."

"Turn it on, low setting. Shit, I'm hard as stone already. Put your phone on speaker. Set it on the pillow next to you. Sweetness—I want you ready to use both hands."

"Oh my . . . m-kay, you're on speaker."

"Shimmy those panties off and tell me how wet you are." He waited. Her breathing hissed as her fingers slid inside.

"I'm so wet," she sighed.

"Dip a second finger in." Seth's sexy growls shook as he gripped himself, stroking harder. "Now babe, take a taste."

She closed her eyes and slipped her arousal-coated fingers into her mouth. "Mm, I'm sweet," she sighed.

"Of course, you're like candy. I could feast on you all night."

When Natalie heard him moan, she begged, "Seth, pull harder for me. Do you have that delicious bit of cum on the tip?"

"Fuck yeah," he growled. "Pick up that toy, babe. Ready?"

"So ready," she moaned.

"Dip the tip, but not too far." A hiss of satisfaction echoed in the loft.

"Now, press that vibrator against that beautiful pearl of pleasure that's begging for my attention."

She followed his instructions and chanted, "Oh God, oh God."

"Dip in deeper this time. Faster, babe. Pump that vibrating cock. Now, I want you to pull on the tip of your beautiful breast. Hard."

Their incoherent moans mingled—the sound of the vibrator and the muscled stroking of his shaft.

"I need . . . to touch . . . my—"

"Not yet. Keep that toy buried," he growled, each word cut short by his need.

"Almost there," she keened, airy and high.

Seth's headboard rattled as he jacked his shaft, his breath catching along with hers.

"Now, sweetness, use your slick fingers to stroke. Ah, this feels so fuckin' good."

"Yes, yes, yes." Her lungs expanded like a tight balloon and held. A moment later, her high-pitched wail sailed over the phone.

"Fuck, fuck, fuck. Babe, you kill me. Shit, I've got cum half-way up my chest."

Seth and Natalie panted together, riding out the duration of their shared release. Her breathing slowed as she settled and relaxed.

Over the connection, Seth listened while she switched off the toy. She sighed, her sheets rustled, then she said, "Mmm, I just had another first with you."

"I like that, babe." He missed her so much it hurt.

"Seth?" Her voice warmed as she snuggled under her blanket.

"Yeah, sweetness?"

"I'm going to hug this pillow and dream of you."

"I'll dream about you, too." Just like he had every night since she'd left. If it were possible Seth would have climbed through the phone to be by her side. "Don't hang up. I'll end the call after you fall asleep."

"Okay," she whispered.

Every cell in his body longed for her warmth. He listened to her sleep and imagined her in his bed. In then out, her breathing slowed, a deeper cadence, then Seth closed his eyes. At some point in the night, his phone died when he didn't end that call.

TWENTY-SIX

Bang! Bang! Bang!

Seth groaned and buried his head under the pillow, hiding from the pounding at the door. Damn it to hell, it was Saturday, and he wanted to sleep in.

Rolling over, Seth closed his eyes and mumbled, "Shit, just go away."

The sound echoed again, this time shaking the entire house.

"Just a minute!" he yelled while rising from bed and pulling on jeans, commando. T-shirt in hand, he staggered downstairs bare-chested and pulled the door open before pulling on his shirt.

He wanted to close the door the moment he saw her face. "Desiree. What are you doing here?"

"Hello to you too, Seth." Her eyes drifted down. "Oh, my. It looks like you're happy to see me."

He shook his head. "It's just morning wood. This has absolutely nothing to do with you."

"You could at least play along and give me credit for good timing." Desiree pushed past him, walked into his kitchen, and helped herself to a tall glass of orange juice.

He followed and pulled his T-shirt over his head as she made herself way too comfortable in his home. "Why are you here?" he asked.

"Man of mine, I heard through the grapevine that your summer fling has flung. About time, don't you think? Finally, we can pick up where we always do. I haven't been tied up and twisted by you in way too long."

As Seth stared, he sent out a secret thank you to the mutt that had pissed on his truck.

Desiree grinned and hopped on the counter, expecting to be served. "Why don't you whip up breakfast first? What I have in mind might require a little stamina."

Seth spun away, unable to recall why he ever wanted this woman. Working slowly, he filled the coffee maker. The rich aroma of roasted beans reminded him of Natalie. As the water dripped into the glass carafe, he turned to deal with his ex. "Not gonna happen. Desiree, just go home."

Shrill laughter echoed from the vaulted ceiling as she slid down and trapped him against the counter. "Have you lost your balls to this girl?" Her eyes dropped to his crotch. "She's long gone. But look, I can still see her talons buried in your dick."

Her fingers crawled up his chest, "Give it up, baby. We both know what kind of kink you need."

Seth cocked an eyebrow. "While your sales pitch is tempting, I will die of blue balls before you get access to them again. Get. Out. Now."

"Fine." Her eyes held as she poked a long, fake fingernail against his chest. "Next time you see me around Ashwood, I'll be staring down my nose at you."

Seth bent his neck and gazed at her finger, leaving his angry stare in place until she took the hint and backed away.

Desiree dumped her orange juice down the drain and dropped the glass into the sink with a clatter. She put a little extra swing in her hips as she stopped across his living room. From the doorway she yelled, "You have needs this bitch will never figure out."

On a grin he called after her, "You couldn't possibly be more wrong."

She narrowed her eyes and hissed, "You were always destined to rot in this shithole of a town."

"Ashwood suits me just fine. Don't let the door smack your bony ass on the way out." Her exit, punctuated by a slam, rattled the windowpanes.

Seth laughed, loud and long, and mentally disposed of the last bad memory of that self-centered bitch. Inhaling deeply, he let it all go on a slow, relieved breath. Finally, they were done.

The coffee maker steamed and sputtered. He grabbed his cup, then traded it for the Pike's Place mug next to it. Even that small gesture made him feel closer to Natalie. Taking out his phone, he scrolled through pictures he'd shot this summer, and good memories immediately brightened his mood. There had to be a way to get Natalie home.

Did you Sleep well, babe? he asked in a quick text.

I would have slept better with you.

Even after last night?

Mmm. It was nice having you in charge.

I aim to please.

Oops, better go. Kels is coming in from the waves and it's my turn on the board.

He laughed and typed, *I hear it now—the theme from Jaws.*

LOL popped onto his screen along with a little heart emoji. His fingers typed I love you, then he deleted those three words just as quickly.

Not yet. He'd save those words for the next time he had Natalie caged in his arms.

***

Mark smiled and his patience held as Natalie struggled, but she knew she wasn't cut out for surfing. Cold, bruised, and battered, she left the waves to Kelsey and Mark, promising to return with a picnic lunch.

Of course, Kels picked up the basics easily. Her toned body popped into position, knees bent, flawlessly balanced on the board.

From her vantage point on the firm sand, Natalie watched the dance of the surfers on the cresting waves. Mark's body communicated with the water, and his fluid motions seemed tethered to Kelsey, too. Stunned by the raw beauty, Natalie stood transfixed until the promise of warmth coaxed her indoors.

Her stomach growled as she laid sliced bread open on her counter with mayo, mustard, and meat on one side, cheese and veggies on the other. As she paired the halves, a motor rumbled, and she peeked outside.

"Ben!" she yelled when he unfolded from his car.

He climbed the stairs and met her with a hug. "Portland was lonely. I took a drive and the miles between us kept shrinking."

"I'm so glad you surprised me." Natalie felt like she'd won the lottery every time she saw his face.

"And don't worry about finding room for me," Ben said. "I'll get a hotel. I know Kelsey's around this weekend."

When the reality of the moment hit, Natalie took a deep breath and tried to soften the blow. "Well, she is, and she isn't. Kels met up with a surfer who lives here at Driftwood Shores. They're on the waves now."

She winced as her brother deflated in front of her. "I'm so sorry, Ben."

"Hey, it's cool. Kelsey and I haven't really gone out. My fault. I guess I should have called." On a huff, he glanced back at his car.

Natalie pulled him inside before he moved an inch. "Please, don't leave. Go out on the beach with me. We'll have lunch with the tailgate down while you tell me all about your new job in Portland."

Ben nodded and forced a smile. "I came here for a perfect day with my sister. Let's do this."

They tossed a big blanket into the bed of her truck, took the access road to the beach, and drove directly over the sand.

When the crashing waves came into view, Ben leaned forward and asked, "Do you remember clam digging with Mom and Dad?"

She shrugged and opened her door. "Barely. I don't think I liked clams very much back then. But I do remember loving s'mores."

Natalie climbed from her truck and paused to watch the action on the waves. The movement on the beach snapped Kelsey's head up, and for a brief moment their eyes locked. Kels wobbled. The surfboard shifted and flew into the air. Blond hair flashed as she tumbled into the churning surf.

"Oh my God!" Natalie covered her mouth and inhaled shock past her trembling fingers.

As Ben sprinted toward the water, his shoes kicked up the dry sand. He called Kelsey's name and splashed in ankle deep. Foam waked up his calves as Kelsey popped to the surface. She waved and gave a thumbs-up and mouthed *I'm okay*.

"It looks like she's fine," Natalie yelled. Her brother took a few steps back, pushed toward shore by a larger swell.

Mark effortlessly rode a wave to within a foot of Kelsey and hopped into the hip-high water. He grasped her around the waist and lowered the zipper down the back of her wetsuit.

Ben froze and watched the intimate interaction. He'd come all this way to witness this. Natalie could almost feel her brother's pain as Mark's fingers explored Kelsey for any signs of injury.

The surf buffeted the couple together until Kels dismissed her tumble with a shrug. She waved off everyone's concern, sloshed a few feet across the waves, and bent to retrieve the bobbing board.

Ben's feet left deep indents as he walked slowly toward Natalie in the sand. She hated this and didn't know how to fix it. Without knowing, Mark fixed it for her when he grabbed his board and jogged to meet the newcomer on the beach.

The crashing waves masked the exchange, but the confusion on Ben's face made it obvious. Mark had assumed the new guy on the beach was Seth.

Natalie waited for Kelsey as the guys talked. "Are you okay?" she asked.

"I'm fine. That was nothing." She dropped her voice and whispered, "When did Ben get here?"

"Just now."

"That's so awkward." Kelsey laughed, clearly nervous, yet she didn't seem to care about anyone but herself.

Natalie clenched her teeth and held back her frustration. It was one thing to ditch all their plans this weekend, but hurting Ben was just cruel.

Kelsey rushed a few steps ahead and hopped into the bed of the truck. "Hey, Ben, nice to see you. What did your sister pack in that basket?"

He stared at her for a long moment and shrugged. "More food than we'll ever need."

Kelsey took a seat on the wheel well of the pickup and waited in silence while Mark dug in.

"Hey, this looks delicious," he said and passed Kels a sandwich. "Here you go, mermaid." His eyes wrinkled at the corners when he smiled.

"This is great, Natalie, thanks for lunch." Mark tore open a bag of chips and glanced from Natalie to Ben. "Before your sister moved to Driftwood Shores, I scraped by on Pop Tarts and hot dogs."

Mark's friendly nature brightened her mood, and Natalie decided to make the best of the crappy situation. "If I take a day off will you starve?" she asked.

"Not with that taco truck in town."

"So, Ben—where are you from?" Mark asked.

"Just moved to Portland from North Carolina."

"Cool. I've surfed the Outer Banks. I had a great time in Carova. Have you ever surfed?"

"No. I've spent most of my time trapped indoors—first school, then an office."

"I hear you." Mark nodded and slung an arm around Kelsey while he ate.

I hear you? Natalie couldn't picture this guy behind a desk or with his nose in a book. Ben's jaw clenched, and he killed the conversation by stuffing a few more chips in his mouth.

Mark finished off his second sandwich before asking Kels if she wanted to head back out.

"Isn't there some rule about waiting thirty minutes before getting back in the water?" she asked.

"Take all the time you need, mermaid, my entire day is yours." Mark slid down into the bed of the truck, leaned his back against the cab, and pulled Kelsey into the V of his thighs, her back to his front.

Kelsey sank against him, took Mark's arm, and pulled it around her waist. The pair closed their eyes and soaked in the sun.

Natalie blinked away from the couple to stare at the ocean. It was clear to her now—Kelsey was definitely not her brother's type.

She just wanted to dispose of the remnants of lunch and hang out with her brother. A few hundred seagulls looked ready to help. Natalie jumped from the truck and tossed sandwich scraps to a flock that had slowly gathered while the four of them ate.

The swarm went from waiting to frenzied the moment the first crumb hit the sand. Natalie ran screaming down the beach but forgot to drop the food. Kelsey and Mark laughed uncontrollably as the screeching flock chased.

Ben yelled, "Drop the bag!" while following Natalie and the airborne mob.

She scrambled and darted, and the birds closed in. When a loud whistle pierced the air, all eyes turned to Mark. He shook a bag of corn chips, and the crinkly sound drew most of the birds his direction. Running backwards, he scattered the bait across the beach.

"Thank you!" Natalie yelled and waved from a safe distance, unwilling to move any closer to the evil swarm.

Mark laughed and waved back. "No problem."

Happy to have her brother by her side, Natalie pulled Ben away. "I'm not going back until all those birds are gone."

He chuckled. "Fine with me."

Natalie picked up shells as they wandered down the beach. Occasionally, Ben found a rock and tossed it far into the surf.

When she glanced back, Natalie saw Mark and Kelsey walking toward the water with their boards slung under their arms.

Mark stopped, dropped his board, and waited for Kelsey to drop hers. He put his arms around her waist, pulled her tight against his chest, and kissed her thoroughly.

Even though she felt like an intruder, Natalie couldn't force her gaze away. The wind whipped, her eyes watered, and she missed Seth so much it hurt. When she finally turned around, Ben was gone. She searched the beach and found him, but he looked small in the distance.

TWENTY-SEVEN

"Do you want anything to drink?" Natalie's question carried from the kitchen to the rooftop deck where Ben waited bundled in a sweatshirt.

"I could go for another beer," he answered.

Natalie emerged, longneck bottles gripped in one hand and a cozy blanket in the other. "I have news," she said as she sat.

"What's that?" He took both bottles, twisted the tops, and handed her back.

"I just got a call, someone made an offer on the condo, and I accepted." She held up her beer and waited for Ben to toast the good news. Glass clinked against glass.

"Damn that was fast."

"It surprised me, too. I'm so glad you took Grandpa's furniture to your place, and I can't wait to see how great it all looks when I visit on Halloween."

She stared toward the dunes and pulled her blanket tighter around her shoulders.

"It's strange, now that the Seattle chapter of my life is over, I feel sort of homeless. And I miss Grandpa today more than I have in months."

Ben reached over and squeezed her hand. "Sis, I've got an extra room in Portland if you decide you're not happy here."

"I'm happy. It's peaceful here at Driftwood Shores. Everyone is fantastic. I've stopped looking for places to move this winter."

Her brother considered her closely. "Wait. I thought you planned to see the country."

She shrugged and admitted with a grin, "Traveling lost its appeal when the person I planned to visit moved to Portland."

***

Kelsey peered through the service window after the Sunday morning rush, her blond hair tossed in a messy bun. "Do you have anything left for two hungry nomads?"

"Sure. Come inside and help yourself." Natalie wished Ben would hurry and finish his shower. She didn't want to deal with Kelsey on her own.

Mark scrubbed his hand over his second day stubble and followed Kels inside. Natalie noticed the pillow creases on his face as he found a spot on the couch. She clenched her teeth. Apparently, the pair had just rolled out of bed and were searching for breakfast.

Kelsey popped a ham and cheese croissant in the microwave and turned it on. The aroma filled the tiny home as she poured two cups of coffee.

"Thanks, Nate. This smells delicious." Kels delivered Mark's coffee and asked, "Do you want anything?"

"How about something with frosting," he said, pulled out his phone, and bent his head toward the screen.

Kelsey hummed as she heated his breakfast then joined him on the couch. "Is the cinnamon roll good?" she asked as he devoured a big bite.

"Better than good," he muttered as he chewed. "Thanks, mermaid."

They seemed so into each other, neither one noticed when Natalie rolled her eyes. She never thought she'd see the day when Kelsey Fisher waited on a guy.

"Is that your surfing app?" Natalie asked as Ben emerged from the bathroom. Steam followed him out, and his t-shirt clung to his damp torso.

Mark tipped his chin toward her brother, a silent hello. "Yeah. I'm keeping an eye on conditions in Tofino. I'll move up the coast before heading to San Diego this winter."

The news surprised Natalie but seemed to have zero impact on Kelsey. She just bit off a big bite of her croissant and hummed, "Mmmm, such salty-cheesy goodness."

After washing everything down with her coffee, Kels tore her attention away from her food. "Hey, Ben, are you hanging around today? Mark and I plan to head down the coast and check out some caves. What do you say, Natalie, are you game?"

Wide eyed, Natalie wondered what the hell Kels was up to. She seemed to be dumping all their plans for a weekend hook-up. Ignoring the sting of rejection, she put on a cheerful front. "Sounds fun, but I think I'll pass. If you have time after you get back, maybe we can hang out for a while."

"Yeah sure. How about you, Ben?"

"No thanks. I've got work waiting for me in Portland."

"Guess it's just us." Kelsey scooted closer to Mark, and he flung an arm over her shoulder. They finished breakfast while laughing over shared images on their phones.

After filling to go cups, they left without giving Natalie any idea when they'd return.

Fueled by anger, Natalie cleared the breakfast dishes and banged the cupboards with a vengeance. To keep from crying, she bit the inside of her cheek when Ben silently stuffed his clothes into his duffle. She knew he needed to work but hated to see him leave.

Out by his car, she finally let her frustrations free. "Kelsey has changed. This isn't like her. She's just so freaking self-absorbed!"

Natalie kicked the ground, taking out her anger on a grassy clump of sand. "Mark seems nice, but I don't understand how Kels could blow off our entire weekend and just disappear. He's not even sticking around this winter."

Her brother caught her shoulder and gave it a squeeze. "Maybe you'll catch up tonight, you know, whenever she makes it back." When he didn't sound too optimistic, she could tell this weekend was hard for him, too.

Ben's goodbye hug gave her a little comfort. "I shouldn't be angry. After you arrived, this weekend actually turned out great." Holding on a little longer, Natalie added, "I love you."

"Love you too, Sis."

***

Just after dark, a knock rattled Nate's door. She opened it and found Kelsey standing on the bottom step. "Hey, can I crash here tonight? It's too late to head back to Ashwood."

Natalie couldn't believe her friend's nerve, showing up here probably expecting dinner and a bed. She flung the door wide open, stepped back, and got out of Kelsey's way. "Sure. Come inside. Where's Mark, anyway?"

"His friends sent a text. I guess they're meeting him in the morning to drive up the coast to Canada. Mark plans to take off at first light. While he packs, I'd only be in his way."

Kelsey flopped on the couch and ignored the anger simmering in the small room. "I'm really glad I met Mark," she said. "Maybe our paths will cross again."

Instead of her usual sunny conversation, Natalie met Kels with a blank stare.

When the silence stretched too long, Kels shrugged, took out her phone, and flipped through pictures she'd apparently taken that day.

"Did he say anything about getting together in the future?" Nate asked, trying to wrap her mind around the situation.

Kels didn't look up. "No. But I have his number and he has mine."

Natalie blinked slowly and trapped her lips between her teeth to keep from screaming.

"What?" Kelsey's tone challenged Nate's tight-lipped judgment.

"I miss you, that's all. Having you here this weekend was really important to me. And you just took off." Natalie's voice trembled, but Kelsey only huffed.

When Natalie rolled her eyes, Kelsey let her unfiltered thoughts fly. "Really? You want to complain about this? Seth consumed all your time this summer, and then you packed your shit and moved out. Did I judge you, Nate? No, I didn't."

"That's different," Natalie snapped. "Seth is important to. . ."

"He's only your summer fling." Kelsey's words stifled Nate. "You left him. Shit, Nate, you're no different than me. Hell, you're not that much different than Desiree. At least Mark and I don't pretend to be something we're not."

Burning with fury and crushed by guilt, Natalie rushed into the kitchen. She couldn't get far from Kelsey before she slumped against the counter, covered her face, and fell apart.

Between bouts of tears she sniffled out. "I know I hurt Seth and I don't know how to fix it. I never thought this tiny house would make my decisions for me, but it has. I just don't want to fail."

Kelsey got up, hesitated for a moment, then approached carefully. She smoothed her hand between Natalie's shaking shoulders. "I'm sorry. This is all on me. Maybe I'm just an envious bitch. I know what you have with Seth is important. It just really hurt everyone when you left Ashwood."

Wiping away her tears, Natalie stepped back and studied Kelsey. "Really?"

"Yes, really. Look around. You're alone out here on the beach. Nate, you don't belong at Driftwood Shores."

All along she'd thought Kels was being selfish, but the way the tables had turned this weekend shifted her perception. Her stomach ached, and she had to make this right. "I'm sorry that I put you second all summer long. Will you forgive me?"

"I already did." Kels smiled softly. "Promise me you'll think about coming home."

Home.

Natalie was still thinking about *home* when Kels suddenly trapped her in a hug. "Do you have any wine in this place?" she asked. "Because damn, I need a drink."

She found a bottle of chardonnay and grabbed a corkscrew while Kels pulled out glasses. They sat with a large bar of chocolate between them on the couch and nibbled, laughed, and drank.

"I'm still jealous," Kelsey admitted once they both had a buzz.

"What is it now?" Natalie laughed, snorted, and took another sip of her wine.

"I envy your courage. When did you get to be so brave?"

"Brave?" Natalie shook her head and laughed. "I wouldn't go that far. I'm still searching just like you."

Silent for a long moment, Kelsey tugged at a tendril of blond hair that had escaped her messy bun. "I'm tired of predictable. It's a dull habit."

"What are you talking about? You take risks every day."

She slumped forward, rested her elbows on her knees, and confessed, "I live for a hit of adrenaline. That doesn't make me daring, addicted to thrills maybe, but not brave."

"What would be a risk for you?" Natalie asked.

Kelsey's eyes searched the room as she thought for a minute. "Commitment. Obligation. A real, long term relationship."

"Pick one and give it a try," Natalie encouraged as she broke off a square of chocolate, popped it in her mouth, and let the bite melt on her tongue.

Kelsey spun her wine glass slowly in her hands. "My boss at Venture, Sig, asked me to join him and expand the business. He wants to offer adventures just for women. I have until November to think it over."

"Wow. That's terrific Kels. Are you interested?"

"Interested? Absolutely. And scared shitless." Kelsey sighed and took another drink. "Another thing terrifies me even more. Risking my heart like you did with Seth. Men like Mark are an easy choice. A little fun and I move on when it's played out."

"Do you know anyone who might be worth the risk?" Natalie knew the answer but needed Kelsey to admit it to herself.

"Ben, but now that he lives in Portland, he terrifies me. If we explore the obvious chemistry between us, and it doesn't work out, what then? I'd hurt you *and* Ben. He deserves someone who's ready."

Kelsey stood and paced the kitchen. She stopped and leaned against the counter, bending her head to hide her emotions behind a curtain of white-blonde hair. "Do you think I hurt your brother this weekend?" she whispered.

"Probably, but you'll have time to fix it. He'll be around, because Ben and I are still trying to figure out this whole family thing." Natalie joined Kels in the kitchen, put the chocolate away, and rinsed her wine glass.

"Nate, I need your help, and you live hours away. As you can tell, I suck at this long-distance thing." Kelsey grinned, but her smile didn't erase the fear in her eyes.

Natalie was tempted to say she was coming back to Ashwood. But she still hadn't decided if that was the future she really wanted. She'd always settled for easy, and she still felt like there was something waiting for her at Driftwood Shores.

***

Early in the morning, Natalie lifted the large window and opened her business to blue skies. She chose orange and brown chalk to write out her specials. After decorating the menu with sketches of fall leaves and pumpkins, she stood back and admired her work.

Kelsey woke to the aroma of pumpkin spice and hot organic apple cider. "I don't know how you handle it. The air alone is loaded with calories."

"You have to try a slice of the apple streusel coffee cake. It was still warm when the bakery delivered it this morning." Natalie waved a slice under Kelsey's nose and enticed her to take a bite.

"Oh. My God. I won't need men if I can have that instead." They ate and talked between customers until Kelsey said she had to go. "I'm swinging by Venture in Hood River to talk with Sig about next year."

"You decided to accept?"

"I think so. It means long-term, but I love the idea of designing trips for women. Sig trusts me, and I've decided to trust myself."

They talked a bit more, had another slice of coffee cake, and clung for a long time to their goodbye hug.

Exhausted by the weekend, Natalie decided to close her coffee shop early. Raw emotion tumbled inside her, searching for an easy target.

She wanted to hear Seth's voice but knew she shouldn't call, not with so many noisy thoughts crowding her mind. If he heard the pain in her voice, Seth would be at her door in a few hours. Tempting, yes, but not what she needed.

Lifting the hatch to the under-floor storage, she pulled the hatbox from its hiding place. Like a lost manuscript, the crisp love letters sent between her grandparents were yellow with age and curled by time. Her grandmother must have tied the red ribbon around them decades ago.

Using her fingernails, Natalie carefully teased the delicate ribbon open and hesitated. These were her grandparents' most intimate words to each other. Was it a violation to read their words?

She decided history outweighed her doubts and spread the letters open. The first dozen were written before they married, when Grandpa first joined the Navy.

The back and forth messages were surprisingly sweet and innocent. He missed her. She worried about his safety. He shared details about life on the ship. She shared gossip from home. All small things, yet each one important when you love someone.

She stretched to ease the sore muscles in her neck, then sank back to pull the stack toward her. A light blue envelope slipped from the pile. It didn't have a postmark or a name.

Why had Grandmother tied this with the rest? The glue sealing the envelope stuck. Natalie used her fingernail to ease the paper apart. Inside was a simple anniversary card. Opening the card, a little envelope slid to her lap, and dirt spilled out.

"Dirt. Why?" Leaving the mess scattered on her clothes, Natalie read the words on the card:

We have already celebrated our silver anniversary, and our gold is coming fast. Year thirty-eight will be our foundation. Sweetheart, this year I'm giving you the spot where we began, the land where I proposed. Tonight, we'll sleep in a tent I pitched by Lake Osprey. Someday soon, I'll build your dream home.

I love you - Happy Anniversary. Forever yours, Peter.

Reading his words again, Natalie laughed first, then cried—Shedding tears for how much her grandpa must have hurt.

Grandma began her fight with cancer a year later. He kept the land but didn't build. He couldn't. Because the dream house was Grandma's . . . and she was gone.

After she dried the last of her tears, she carefully pinched the dirt with her fingers and placed it back inside the envelope.

Nothing would ever entice her to sell the land on Lake Osprey. Only a home, built with love, would ever be right for that land.

TWENTY-EIGHT

Seth's plans to see Natalie derailed when a customer called. A young couple had suffered a kitchen fire in their tiny home. The insurance money was slim, and they were just starting out, so Seth bought tickets for himself and Carlos, hopped on a plane for a trip to New Mexico, and made the emergency repairs himself.

Natalie told him she understood, but Seth heard the disappointment in her voice. He needed to hold her so much it hurt.

With that unforeseen roadblock, Seth regretted the Boise trip. He considered bailing on his cousin, but Wade was stressed about landing investors for his growing brewery.

Seth needed to see Natalie but had to settle for a video chat.

"Our November weekend is blocked on my calendar," he said as he leaned closer to the screen. "Damn, Natalie. You're more beautiful than I remembered."

She giggled and blushed. Her red hair, a bit longer than the last time they were together, fell loose around her shoulders. And her lips, Lord her lips, he wanted them everywhere.

Bending forward, she adjusted the laptop and gave Seth an innocent glimpse of her lace edged bra. He couldn't look away and stifled a groan.

"When you get here, I'll close the coffee shop. We can stay at Driftwood Shores or drive down the coast. I'll be all yours for three whole days."

Mine. Mine. Mine.

"What was that?" Natalie asked.

Had he mumbled his thoughts aloud?

"Nothing sweetness." He cleared his throat. "I love the changes you made to the website."

He told her how much he loved her photos, and how much he loved the way she'd edited her work. But he really wanted to say those three words again — I love you — when he had her in his arms.

***

The sun rose over Wade's Mosquito Creek Brewing truck. Seth put on his sunglasses and followed his cousin toward Boise, down Interstate-84.

When they pulled into a truck stop, Seth sent a quick text to Natalie. *Halfway to Boise. Have a great weekend and tell Ben, hi. I Miss you.*

After this trip, Seth wanted nothing but an entire weekend trapped with Natalie in bed. And with Thanksgiving just around the corner, he wanted her with him and his family for the entire holiday.

Seth's phone buzzed with a return message. *Miss you too. I can't wait to hear about your trip.*

***

Natalie knocked a second time. Some lights were on, but she worried when Ben hadn't busted out his front door to greet her. He was busy, but she couldn't imagine him forgetting their Halloween weekend plans.

After a rattle, her brother opened the door. Yet the person in front of her only vaguely reminded her of Ben.

"Oh, my. You look terrible." Flushed by fever, his eyes were glassy, and his hair stood on end. Weaving back and forth, he looked ready to collapse.

Grasping the doorframe, he swallowed hard. "Oh crap. I'm sorry, sis, I forgot to call. Stay away, I'm sick as a dog."

He turned and staggered upstairs. "Damn, here it comes again." A door slammed and heaving sounds followed.

"Poor, Ben." Natalie stepped inside and closed the door behind her, ready to help.

On a quick inspection, she saw the clues. Closed drapes, a sink piled with dishes, and a sleeping bag wadded on the couch.

"Get in bed," she said when he appeared at the top of the stairs.

"I can't," he groaned. "I missed the puke bucket."

She winced and tried not to laugh. He looked so pitiful.

Ben slowly staggered past her and headed back to the couch. "You need to leave. I don't want you to catch the plague."

Natalie peeled off her coat and hung it on the peg near the door. "Don't be ridiculous. Lie down. I'll get you something to drink."

Ben collapsed on the couch, obediently drank the water she offered, and slept. Three hours later, he opened one eye when she changed the cool cloth on his head.

"Mom?" he mumbled deliriously.

Natalie smiled, recalling how Mom had done that when they were young. And when they were sick, she'd always made them chicken and stars soup.

He was so hot his lips were purple. After begging for another blanket, Ben swallowed some medicine and slept again. Natalie checked on him as she cleaned his kitchen, washed his sheets, and made a grocery list.

When she heard creaking on the stairs, Natalie ducked her head out of his room and watched while he slowly staggered toward the bathroom. She listened for heaving, didn't hear any, and went back to putting his sweats and t-shirts in his dresser.

Ben came out of the bathroom and found her making his bed. "No vomit this time." He held the doorframe and looked around. "You cleaned my room. You didn't have to do that, but thanks."

She nodded. "I'm glad you're feeling better. Why don't you lie down?"

"I think I'll crash in my bed. I owe you big time."

Natalie pulled up his blanket and said, "You don't owe me a thing."

She brought him water and juice. "If you're okay on your own for an hour, I'll run to the store."

"Mm-hum." Ben smiled when she rested her hand on his head. He wasn't nearly as hot.

"I called you Mom, didn't I?"

"You were pretty out of it."

"Thanks for staying and putting up with this."

She smiled and ran her hand over his shoulder, loving that she could help. "I'm glad I'm here."

Natalie came back from the store with Halloween candy for tomorrow and mushy foods. Ben liked the Jell-O, but not the chicken soup, and was able to keep everything down.

By morning, he felt strong enough to take a shower, and by noon, he moved downstairs to the couch. Natalie took care of the trick-or-treating kids while they watched a monster movie marathon together. Ben dozed for a while and crashed for the night early.

After the last trick-or-treater, Natalie finally had time to send Seth more than a two-word text. She told him Ben was improving, but he didn't reply, probably because the crowds at the festival were insane.

***

The next morning Ben felt better, except for his extreme hunger. She wasn't surprised, he hadn't had anything but Jell-O for days. He stabbed another lump of scrambled eggs.

"What was that again?" He stared and couldn't seem to believe what she had just said.

"I'm going back to Ashwood. I'm miserable on the coast. Taking care of you this weekend cemented it. This is the happiest I've felt in weeks."

"Don't say that, Natalie. It's just sad." He shuddered. "Hey, I'm sorry again about that mess in my room."

She swept away his concern with a wave of her hand. "It's not sad. This weekend, I felt like I had a purpose. I've miss sharing my life with the people I love."

"I guess that makes sense. And I love you, too. I might have died this weekend if you hadn't shown up."

Natalie chuckled. "That's a bit of an exaggeration, but you would have had a ton of unhappy trick-or-treaters."

"They might have thought they found the house of the living dead." They laughed, and he admitted that this would be funny someday, but not quite yet.

"I'm just happy I was here to help."

Her sudden decision concerned Ben enough to make him pry. "Before you move, I have to know. Do you love Seth?"

With no hesitation, she answered, "Of course I do."

"And you miss Ashwood?"

"More than I thought I ever could."

"Last thing . . . If you and Seth don't work out long-term, will Ashwood still be home?"

Natalie worried her lip and stared out his kitchen window toward the garden next door. "Yes. I can see myself in Ashwood, building a life there regardless of Seth's desire to be with me or not."

Ben pushed away from his small dining room table. "Well then. When do you want me to help you move back?"

"If you feel well enough to be on your own, I'll pack my home today and leave for Ashwood tomorrow. I already called and talked to Faye. I can't wait to see Osprey Lake from my kitchen window."

"Wow, sis. There's nothing careful about that decision."

"I'm done with careful. It's overrated." Her infectious joy had both laughing.

"Call me tomorrow when you reach the east edge of Portland. I'll follow you into Ashwood and help you set up your place," Ben offered.

"Are you sure you'll feel well enough?"

"Of course. I've had the best nurse in Portland right here caring for me."

After they planned the timing of her move, Natalie shared her discovery of Grandpa's anniversary gift to Grandma. As she dabbed a few tears from the corner of her eyes, she realized her decision to return to Lake Osprey happened the moment she read Grandpa's card.

***

Faye rose from working on the herb beds that surrounded her tiny home. "I'll miss you, Natalie. And I'll miss the compost from your coffee grounds."

"I'm sorry to move so suddenly." She glanced down as Bramble snaked around her legs.

"You lasted longer than I imagined you would. I knew the moment I saw you with Seth that this was not where you were meant to be. Promise me that you and Seth will bring your kids to visit one day."

Natalie blushed. "How can you be so sure about us?"

"Normally I would say I have a sense about these things—because I do. But even a rock could see you two are destined to be together. Keep in touch. I'll be here waiting by the sea."

Natalie left Faye to her gardening to pack her home. Distracted by her move, Natalie missed a text from Seth that afternoon.

She worked into the night and accomplished everything on her own. For her final task, she took down the Little Latte sign, wrapped it in a moving blanket, and stored it in the undercarriage hatch.

An old movie she found online helped to quiet her busy mind. A batch of buttery popcorn rested next to her hip as she curled in her loft with her laptop. Eventually, the patter of rain on her roof lulled her to sleep.

Pulled back to reality by a buzzing sound, her phone vibrated on the mattress. She swept the screen and answered. "Hello, Seth." Her voice was graveled with sleep.

"Sweetness, sorry I woke you."

"That's okay. I fell asleep watching an old movie. How is Boise?"

"Wade's worried, but he's keeping it to himself."

"That's strange. Why hasn't he talked to you?"

"He will, when he's ready. What are your plans for tomorrow?"

Natalie wondered if she should reveal everything but decided to wait. "I think I'm going to take a drive." At least that was partially true. Excitement stretched like a balloon, but she contained it.

"Down the coast?" he asked.

"Maybe inland. I've had enough of the beach."

"I can't wait to see you."

"Soon," she said, smiling. *So much sooner than you think.*

TWENTY-NINE

Light rain fell, keeping the residents of Ashwood indoors. Natalie looped past the full parking lot of Northside Grill, drove fifteen miles, and turned down the narrow road that followed the contours of the lake.

Low branches scraped the roof of her home as she made her way along the twisting road, but the most challenging section lay ahead. Before pulling down the narrow lane onto her property, she tucked her home close to the road's crumbly edge and climbed out to scout her path. She walked the track, searching for hazards that might strike her house before turning back to Ben.

"This looks clear. What do you think?"

"Without leaves it's almost too easy. I don't see any heavy branches that might be a problem. Should we try to park this thing on our own?" Ben asked with a confident grin.

"I had planned to. Nobody knows I'm coming back."

"If anyone spotted you in town, it won't be a secret for long."

"True, but without cell service, I'll never know. Let's give it a go."

Ben walked ahead, glancing back to confirm that the home would clear any low hanging branches. The light drizzle continued, and he pulled a knit hat out of his pocket to cover his short damp hair.

Closer to the water, the sky brightened and so did Natalie's mood. Everything about this seemed right. Trembling with excitement, she stopped and climbed out of her pickup again. "I need to choose a place to park."

"Okay. That will give me time to run back and grab my car while you take a closer look." Ben disappeared down the road, and she inhaled the moist air. Even the drizzle couldn't dampen her happiness.

Pacing a wide circle, she found a gravel layer submerged beneath a mat of weeds and grass. As she tried to find the edges, she discovered hookups for water, sewer, and power behind a wall of tall evergreen huckleberry.

"Yes, yes, yes." Celebrating the moment with a happy dance, she felt Grandpa's presence welcoming her home.

Hooking to power was tempting, but she decided to wait and have Seth inspect the connections. Ben returned, parked his car, and wandered her direction. She pointed out the power and water. "Look what I found."

"Amazing."

"Ben, if you could help me hit this target that would be great." She scraped a stick through the weeds to outline the spot where she wanted her tiny home to land.

"No problem. Roll down your window and I'll guide you in."

Back in the cab and with help from Ben, she inched into the spot. Another checklist led them through the leveling process.

"I wish I could stay here with you tonight, but I need to get back to Portland. Why don't you call Kels and stay at her place?" Ben suggested.

"Don't worry, I'll be okay. I don't need power or water for a few days. My tiny home is set up to be self-contained."

Ben glanced into the dense forest. "Fine. I'll try not to imagine you surrounded by *lions and tigers and bears*."

"*Oh my* . . . Okay, Tin Man. Are you trying to scare me into town?" She giggled and smacked his arm with her open hand.

He grinned. "Is it working?"

Natalie laughed again. "Not at all."

Ben shrugged "Then I guess you'll be on your own."

For a late lunch, they decided on canned soup and bread from the bakery out on the coast. She'd figured that she'd be eating pastries for a week. While washing dishes in a pan of shallow water, Ben saw a boat approaching from across the lake.

"Someone knows we're here."

"I'm sure the neighbors keep an eye out for new arrivals." Natalie pulled on her hiking boots as the boat drew close. She recognized the gray-haired man, from her frequent visits to the farmers' market. He'd sold local organic honey.

He cut the motor and drifted toward the dock as she and Ben made their way to meet him. "Natalie, hello. I wondered when you'd find your way here."

"Ed," she smiled, "nice to see you again. This is my brother, Ben."

He tossed a rope in Ben's direction. "Here, catch the line." Ed jumped out of the boat and onto the dock and grabbed Ben's shoulder. "Little Benjamin, well, didn't you grow up! You look just like Pete did when he joined the Navy. Damn good to see you again, son."

Confused, Ben asked, "When did we meet?"

"Pete brought the two of you up here when you were kids. Your grandpa couldn't make a move without you glued to his side."

Ben gazed over the glassy surface of the lake. "Yeah, I remember a fishing pole, orange I think—it was the same color as that bulky life jacket I had to wear. Where did we stay?"

"He rented a cabin on the west shore. The darn thing burned one spring, and the fire department couldn't get up here fast enough to do anything about the quick blaze."

"Did that cabin have a loft with bunks built in?" Natalie wondered aloud. A pleasant memory flooded her mind, complete with a daisy chain crown in her hair and her brother tossing rocks into the lake.

"You know, I think it did. Pretty rustic as I recall—Pete wasn't picky about things like that."

Tears welled up in Natalie's eyes. Suddenly overwhelmed, she felt her past and present converging and it was just too much to take.

"Ah now, little girl, I didn't mean to make you cry." Ed moved from foot to foot, uncomfortable, until Ben pulled Natalie close, his strong arm wrapped around her shoulder.

She waved her hand in front of her face and laughed a little. "Don't worry, these are happy tears. I'm so thankful to be here and at the same time I miss Grandpa so much."

"We all miss him. Pete was a great friend." Ed climbed back into his boat with a promise to stop by in a few days for coffee.

He had just pulled away when an Osprey plunged beneath the surface of the cold lake and reemerged with a fish dangling from its talons. Resilient wings sprayed water as the bird lifted toward the sky. Flying over the bare treetops, the Osprey disappeared with its catch still flapping beneath it.

Ben and Natalie stared awestruck by the spectacle.

"I've never . . ." he stammered.

"I know," she whispered and reached out to hold his hand, thankful for his presence.

It was nearly dark when Ben turned with an apology, "I'm sorry I can't stay. I missed work last week when I was sick and have a project to finish before Monday. Do you need anything before I take off?"

"I have everything I need, and I'm surrounded by friends on the lake. Don't worry, I'll be fine."

Before pitch dark drove her inside, Natalie put on another layer and grabbed a flashlight to wander the property. Peace settled over her. For the first time in her life, she realized the satisfaction of belonging to one place.

Out in the open and away from the sheltering trees, she slipped on frost that had begun to coat the ground. The grass crunched, and she worried about Seth coming home to Ashwood on the slick roads tonight.

***

Seth counted the communities as the miles ticked by—Baker City, La Grande, The Dalles—each town glittered in the dark like an oasis in front of him then disappeared in his rearview mirror. He sucked down his coffee and didn't know if the caffeine or his full bladder worked better to keep him awake.

By the time they'd pulled up to Wade's home on the banks of Mosquito Creek, the driveway had completely crusted over with a sheet of ice.

Wade kicked the black top in front of his brewery with the toe of his heavy boot. "Damn this is slick."

"We got lucky, considering our speed," Seth said as Wade stretched, working out the kinks in his back. Seth started his rig, giving it time to warm and thaw the ice from the windshield.

"Shit. I'm beat. Let's leave all this gear in the trailers," Wade said past a yawn.

"You'll get no argument from me," Seth agreed, each word a small cloud in front of his face.

Seth was about to leave when Wade asked, "Could we get together tomorrow afternoon? Some things came up in Boise that I'd like to go over with you. Do you mind if I pick your brain?"

"Give me a call after ten, or I may not pick up. I'm going home before I pass out on my feet."

Seth drove the deserted roads, worried. He hadn't heard from Natalie. The fact that she planned to take a drive could put her anywhere in Oregon. He checked his phone hoping to find a text, but nothing was on his screen. He'd try again in the morning.

***

Sunlight streamed through his window, and Seth covered his head with his pillow, wanting more sleep, but his internal clock thought four hours was plenty. Standing in his boxers, he checked his phone. It was completely dead. He couldn't call Natalie.

Damn. He plugged it in and turned to stagger downstairs, desperate for coffee and home-cooked food.

The stunning view from his bedroom window stopped his progress. He gazed over the frost-covered valley, amazed. Every tree sparkled with a thick layer of frost. The lake, a deep sapphire blue, stood out against the silver veneer.

Something reflecting the sun caught his eye. Tucked among the trees, he caught a glimpse of a metal roof beneath the evergreen canopy.

Needing a closer look, Seth pulled on jeans and dashed downstairs to find his binoculars. After slipping on his leather boots, he grabbed a sweatshirt from a peg near the door and ran outside.

Cold chased the air from his lungs and the ice-covered deck nearly took him to his knees. The change in temperature fogged his binoculars. Frustrated, he used his sweatshirt to clear the lens.

After adjusting the focus, he looked again. "Wait. I know that roof. I built that roof. *Natalie.*" Scanning once more, he spotted her red truck parked between the trees.

"Phone!" Stumbling inside, he bolted upstairs and yanked the device from the charger but had to wait for the thing to power back on. "Come on . . . come on." He paced back out on the deck.

He barely had enough battery but placed a call that went straight to voicemail. "Damn, she doesn't have service. That's why I couldn't reach her yesterday. *Natalie came home.*"

A three-minute shower was enough. He found clean clothes and shoved his feet into shoes before hopping in his truck and barreling down the narrow back road. Drops of water from his wet hair dripped down his neck. He ignored the annoying sensation and skidded into turns that looped from his place to the lake. His four-wheel drive slipped on the ice and ground to a stop a few feet from her truck.

Before knocking, he twisted the handle, but her door was locked. *Damn.* He knocked, listened, and knocked again. The place was so small, he didn't know why she wasn't answering. Maybe she'd gone to Kelsey's for the night. Just to make certain, he circled her home, and barely heard the shower hissing inside.

Back at the door, he pounded, frantic to get to her. "Natalie. It's me, Seth. Let me in!"

Faint, he barely picked up her muffled words, "Just a minute, I'm in the shower."

Keys. He had keys. His hands shook as he fumbled with the lock.

Ten steps became four as he leaped from her front door to the compact bathroom. He found her under the spray of the shower, rinsing a cloud of shampoo from her hair.

"Seth, where are you?"

"Babe, I'm right here."

"I can't open my eyes."

"Take your time, sweetness," he said as he stared at the goddess—his own Aphrodite glistened in the shower as he gazed.

As if she was standing under a waterfall, the swell of her generous breasts and hips dripped with the cascade. Droplets hung from the tip of each rosebud peak. The trim hair, barely covering her sex, was nearly the same shade of red as the drenched hair on her head.

"Seth," she said, and his eyes slid to hers. She'd caught him staring with his mouth wide open.

"Don't move." He stripped and tossed his clothes to the floor.

The compact space pushed them together. In one move, his hands pulled her to him, and his lips covered her full wet mouth. With his fingers twisted into her hair, he angled her head to claim a thorough taste.

The shower pulsed and sprayed, beating out a cadence against his shoulders. He didn't care where the water ricocheted—the floor, the ceiling, the walls. Nothing was going to keep him from devouring the woman he had trapped in this tiny shower stall.

As he remapped the delicious contours of her mouth, his hands explored. She moaned when his fingertips skated over the outside edge of her sensitive breasts.

Arching her back, Natalie begged for his touch. As she squirmed, the pinpoint of each sensitive nipple prodded his torso and he had to take a taste.

The water beat on his back as he bent to suck each sparkling peak. Her fingers coiled in his hair, urging Seth to make a more aggressive claim. Pulling her in, he grasped the other breast and she covered his hand with hers, coiling and tightening his already firm grip.

She had never been this frantic for him and he had to meet that need. Yet, if he took her now, he'd miss out on witnessing her epic climb to release. A whimper escaped her throat as Seth pulled his hand and mouth away.

"I need to see you come." He hadn't meant for his words to sound so desperate, but she seemed to be feeding off his craving. Natalie grinned and nodded, more than willing to let him set the pace.

He steadied his breathing and said, "Sit on the bench," while he reached for the shower wand.

Her eyes widened, and she obeyed as she sank to the narrow seat. Natalie blinked away from his face and stared straight at his jutting cock. A slow lick of her lips made his eager shaft jump.

"Not yet," Seth said when she began to lean in.

She swallowed hard and looked up. "Are you sure?"

"God, you're so damned tempting, but yes. I'm sure."

He grinned and adjusted the spray to a gentle pulse, set to tease her sensitive skin. Arching her neck and lifting her breasts, she begged for his attention on each pearled peak. Her chest bloomed pink beneath the warm water spray.

A shift of her hips hinted the spot where she desired that sensation most. Seth nudged her feet apart. He trailed the jets down and she eased her hips forward and opened herself to him.

"You're so beautiful." Every inch of her soft core was on display. Seth dropped to his knees and replaced the water with the heat of his tongue.

Exposed, wet, and dripping, she surrendered. Her head lolled against the wall as he brought her to the edge.

"Please," she begged as her legs began to quake. Leaving the water jetting on her core, Seth tipped his head to claim a final taste. The onslaught of sensation tore an orgasm from her body. She flew apart and incoherent words mingled with his name. Her legs and arms collapsed, and he kissed her stomach, her breasts, and her lips before turning off the water.

Puddles were everywhere, and the pile of clothes he'd left on the floor were soaked. He tossed a towel on the floor, found another for Natalie, and wrapped her in it before taking her to the loft.

***

Sated and boneless, Natalie collapsed to her bed, expecting Seth to follow, but he disappeared.

Cold, Natalie scrambled under her sheets to stop the shivering. Seth came back with a comb, and she smiled sitting up, keeping her legs covered to stay warm.

"I can't believe you're here, sweetness." He climbed behind her on her bed, looking uncomfortably aroused. Natalie tried not to stare, but his size had always been distracting. Seth chuckled when her eyes moved to his. He shook his head and said, "I can wait. Let me comb your hair."

She closed her eyes as Seth carefully smoothed the wet strands, collecting the water from the ends with her towel. No one had ever cared for her like this.

"When did you get here?" he asked from over her shoulder.

Natalie whispered. "After Ben recovered, I went to the coast, packed furiously, said goodbye to Faye, and drove."

"Yesterday?" he asked on a kiss against her damp neck.

"Mm, hmm. . . Yesterday. And today I'm yours." Still damp and chilled from the shower, she shivered.

"Get under the covers."

"I will if you join me." She lifted the sheets, inviting him in.

His fingers traced her jaw, caressed her cheek, and began to twine into her damp red hair.

"I feel like I'm dreaming," he said as he pulled her over his chest and readjusted the covers to trap their collective heat.

Natalie traced his lips with her fingertips. "I intended to surprise you and show up at your door this morning, but you beat me to it."

"I couldn't move fast enough when I spotted your home hidden in the frost covered trees."

After another deep kiss, she had to reveal the truth. "Seth, I've decided to make a change." His hand tightened on her hip. "The coast was an adventure, but my home is here . . . in Ashwood," she said.

"Just Ashwood?"

"More than Ashwood." She hesitated, needing his reassurance.

Seth's gaze intensified. "Ashwood, the coast, hell Natalie, on the moon . . . it doesn't matter where you go, I belong. You're my home. I love you." He kissed her, taking her breath into his body, a small possession of her soul.

Natalie pulled away, and a thankful tear trickled down her face. "I love you, too. I love that you gave me time to pursue my dreams. And while I was searching, you let me borrow your strength."

As he kissed each tear, a vulnerable gift, he settled between her hips. Each slow plunge magnified his love, as he trusted Natalie with his entire soul.

Welcoming him intimately, she committed herself to a man who cherished her heart, appreciated her gifts, and set her desires free. Branded by the heat of their bodies, they spent the day recalling the moments that built their love.

She admitted how much she'd stalked him before they met. Seth confessed how jealous he was when Kent beat him to the picnic basket in the Stop-n-Shop parking lot.

Both confirmed that fate played a part, bringing Natalie to Ashwood when she needed Seth most.

"It was scary," Natalie admitted. But I first knew I loved you when you rushed to Seattle, kissed me right in front of Elsa, and said you were sorry."

"If apologies do it for you, then I'm your man. I promise to make at least one mistake every day." Laughter brought her forehead to his, and he kissed the end of her nose, playfully.

He toyed with her hair and confessed, "I knew I loved you the moment you peeled off your clothes and walked into the river."

On a giggle, she pushed him away. "Because I was willing to get naked outside?"

"Not at all." Seth pulled her on top, chest to chest, her soft to his hard. "You fit me so naturally and became the best part of my world. I love you, sweetness. Forever."

"I love you, too. Please, Seth. Show me how much you love me again." She claimed his lips as he shifted their bodies, moved over her, and took her to that perfect place once more.

***

Hours later, the couple emerged from their seclusion. Seth took a moment to inspect her home.

She laced their fingers together and led him to the dock.

"I found letters and a card from Grandpa to Grandma. I know why he kept the property." She explained her discovery, and her promise to Ben and herself to hold onto the land.

"I can imagine Grandma's cabin right here," she said.

"And I can almost see your grandfather fishing from this dock."

She tipped her head to his chest as his arms wrapped around her. They stood in silence and watched the fog drift over the glassy surface of the calm water.

He hoped Natalie would plan her dream cabin someday. And he'd build it for her, on the shore of Osprey Lake.

THIRTY

On a small, breathy sigh, Natalie eased from Seth's embrace. "I'd better let you get back to work," she said.

She passed Wade on the way to her darkroom and waved him into Whitewater's office. Still mesmerized, Seth stared at her hips gentle sway, wanting to follow.

After welcoming his cousin with a nod, Seth settled behind his desk. He gave his full attention to the meeting they'd put off for three days.

Huddled together, they went over the Boise trip, and the opportunity Wade had been offered. Seth hoped Wade would consider an idea he had in mind. "I know growth is important, but what are the negatives if you don't expand Mosquito Creek Brewing?"

"Creativity and satisfaction more than money. Yes, if everything works as planned, it will be extremely profitable, but you know that's not my primary concern."

Wade leaned forward, elbows to knees. "If I stay where I'm at, I'll only have enough space to produce the most profitable lines. The demand for Double Deet has grown beyond my current capacity. As I expand into new markets this problem will only magnify."

Seth nodded. "I'm assuming you want to stay in the area. Do you have a space in mind?"

"Yes. I need to find the owners of those vacant buildings." He glanced out the window, in the general direction of the original lumber operation. "Do the Fraser's still own it? I haven't been able to track them down."

Hesitation slowed Seth's answer before he revealed something only Natalie knew. "The Fraser's aren't the owners anymore. They sold the entire mill property to me."

"No shit?" Wade fell back in his chair. "Impressive. How did you manage to pull that off?"

Seth tapped the surface of his desk with his fingertips. He figured it was about time someone in his family knew how invested he was in this community.

"At first, I rented this space and worked with the mill for the custom wood products I needed. When the economy tanked, tiny homes took off. At the same time, so did the food-truck market."

"I get that." Wade nodded. "Everyone was downsizing."

"Exactly. When the need for lumber in the housing market decreased, the Fraser's got in a bind and planned to close permanently. I purchased the mill for a great price and kept the lumberyard running. I took a loss at first, but after a year it offset the growth on the tiny home side."

"Damn. Congratulations, not only for your success but for keeping this under wraps."

"Thanks, I guess. It was necessity and luck." Seth said with a shrug. "It appears you're in a similar spot. You need to expand, and as luck would have it, I own a huge empty building that needs an occupant."

Seth paused and chose his words carefully. This wasn't a handout—it was an investment. "During the Boise trip, I had time to think while I drove. I admit Natalie was on my mind most of the time."

"No kidding," Wade said on a chuckle.

"But I also thought about your need to expand. Mosquito Creek Brewing needs more room. Let me offer you the space rent-free."

Wade lifted his hand. "That's not gonna happen."

"Just hear me out," Seth said, nearly pleading. "Don't waste your capital on a lease. Invest in the expansion and let me help Mosquito by providing space and improvements."

Wade nodded slowly. "That does sound tempting."

"My crew can handle the hammer and nails part of the project. I know this old mill's quirks and can get the job done quicker than anyone else."

Wade sunk back in the leather couch and ran his fingers through his hair. "Seth, have you really thought about this?"

"Only for the past couple years. Not many businesses need this much square footage. If you don't take my offer the buildings might sit vacant for years, maybe forever. Once you're settled, you can slowly buy the building. You'll be helping me and helping Ashwood at the same time."

After a slow, deep breath, Wade moved suddenly and slapped his thighs. "Okay, let's do this. I don't trust anyone more than I trust you." He stood and held out his hand. Unfolding from his chair, Seth rounded his desk, grabbed Wade's hand, then hauled his cousin in for a backslapping hug.

"Let's get over there and take a look," Wade said on a step back.

Seth fished for the keys in his desk and said, "I do have one condition."

"What's that?"

"Free beer for life."

"Of course, that's one of the many perks of co-owning a brewery."

Wade grabbed Seth's shoulder as they crossed the wide gravel lot and said, "Thanks for taking a risk on me. It means a lot."

As they neared the first massive structure, wood blackened by decades of exposure, Seth shared one concern. "Investing in your brewery doesn't scare me, but where I'm headed with Natalie does. I don't want to fail again."

Seth sorted through his keys and unhitched the heavy padlock hanging from a chain. He pushed the massive door open, and Wade stood for a moment, examining the space.

"I'm guessing you plan to pop the question?"

"Yes, I'll do my best to convince her."

"Congratulations," Wade said with a grin.

"I don't even have a ring."

"Don't worry, she's the one."

THIRTY-ONE

Amanda and Natalie added decorative touches to the Thanksgiving table, little pumpkins, and a sprinkling of autumn leaves. A flurry of activity overwhelmed the kitchen—mashing potatoes, turkey carved, and casseroles coming hot from the oven.

Everyone joined hands and thanked God for a year filled with family, friends, and good health. Seth laced his fingers with Natalie's as the pair listened to his father's reverent words. She smiled, peeping up from downturned lashes.

After the meal, Seth pulled Ben aside, stealing him away while Amanda and Natalie cleared the remains of the feast. Outside, they wandered away from the lights of the house, taking a path toward the now dormant garden, where a few stray pumpkins had collapsed and frozen to the ground.

"Ben, I wanted to know . . . well, I thought I should ask . . . I want to marry Natalie. Would you give us your blessing?"

"Wow, Seth, I'm honored. Of course, nothing would make Natalie happier. Have you asked her?"

"No, I wanted to talk to you first. Can you keep this between us? I have a few things to take care of before I ask the big question."

"Congratulations, Seth, I can't wait to celebrate your engagement."

"She hasn't said yes . . . yet."

***

Two weeks before Christmas, Natalie and Seth pulled on boots, gloves, and scarves. At barely twenty-five degrees and with seven inches of snow on the ground, they set out to find the perfect tree.

Dreading the cold, Natalie shivered as soon as she walked out the door. "Are you sure you don't want to go to the hardware store? I saw quite a few beautiful Noble Firs already cut and set up in their lot."

"Are you kidding?" Seth shook his head. "This is the best part of Christmas!"

She gestured ahead. "Then lead the way, lumberjack."

He stomped a path through the snow ahead of her, clearing a trail with his boots. Natalie stepped into his large tracks, nearly falling until they reached the packed snow on the road.

Holding hands through winter gloves, they wandered in the direction of her property.

Seth turned down a well-concealed path. It meandered until it met a tall, perfect tree. Natalie gasped when she spotted an evergreen looped by a red velvet ribbon.

"Seth, you've had your eye on this tree, haven't you? I love it, but it looks so happy here. Are you sure you want to cut it down?"

"I think it wants to come home with us." He lay his jacket on the ground and kneeled on his coat, ready to go to work with the bowsaw.

"Natalie, would you step over here and hold up this branch? I need to get a better look at the trunk."

She held the branch out of his way, watching Seth as he sighted the best spot to make the cut. Instead of picking up the saw, Seth drew a crimson box from beneath the evergreen. The small box gleamed with the same rich color as the velvety red ribbon encircling the branches.

Natalie held her breath and trembled.

Seth stared up at her from his perch on one knee and said, "Natalie Journey, I've loved you from the first moment you drove into Ashwood. My love grew as you discovered where you wanted to build your life. Sweetness, I can't imagine a future without you. Please, be mine. I promise to love you forever. Will you marry me?"

"Oh, Seth." Tears brimmed her eyes. The cold didn't matter as she knelt on the snow next to him. "Of course, I'll marry you. I'm already yours."

Carefully, he released the solitaire from the velvet box, removed her glove, and slipped the gorgeous ring on her finger.

Natalie gasped and admired the diamond. "It's so perfect. So beautiful, I love you."

"Sweetness, I love you, too. More than I ever thought was possible."

On their knees in the snow, beside their first Christmas tree, Natalie accepted Seth's timeless promise and his tender kiss.

*****

Did you love *Inheriting Trouble*? Then you should read *Trouble Brewing*[1] by Kinney Scott!

She owns the local dive bar. He brews terrific beer. Kegs collide in Ashwood when Iris and Wade cater a surprise party together.

They both know one hot night doesn't come with long-term guarantees.

A brewing convention in Las Vegas has the potential to fulfill Wade's dreams. When he meets with investors who promise to expand his popular brewery, no one reveals that the money comes with an enticing string attached—Ravenna Silvestre. She's smart, sexy as hell, and stunning.

---

1. https://books2read.com/u/47zBo7

2. https://books2read.com/u/47zBo7

Even though Wade's obsessed by the instant connection, he would never betray Iris. They've been friends too long, and he wonders if there could be something more.

Ravenna might have all the right connections, but there's something about her that he can't quite trust.

Will this petite executive use her position of power to control Wade's future in the high-stakes brewing world? Or will she warn the brewer about a plot that could bring him down?

Read more at https://kinneyscott.com.

Also by Kinney Scott

Watch for more at https://kinneyscott.com.

About the Author

Kinney Scott writes contemporary romance from her home near Puget Sound on the rainy side of Washington State. Her steamy heroes and complex heroines feel most at home in the rugged and uniquely romantic environments of the Pacific Northwest. When she has a moment away from her computer, Kinney escapes to her garden or spends a few hours hiking trails near her home.

Want to know more? Visit Kinney at https://kinneyscott.com

Read more at https://kinneyscott.com.